Sally—

phoebe
UNFIRED

Germaphobes unite!
We've got this!
XO Charlie

also by amalie jahn

The Clay Lion Series
The Clay Lion
Tin Men
A Straw Man
Under the Rainbow – A Prequel Companion
Brooke's Time Travel Notebook

The Next to Last Mistake
Before Checkmate – A Prequel Companion

The Sevens Prophecy Series
Among the Shrouded
Gather the Sentient
Beyond the Sanctified

Let Them Burn Cake!
(A Storied Cookbook)

phoebe UNFIRED

amalie jahn

BERMLORD PUBLICATIONS

PHOEBE UNFIRED. Copyright © 2021 by Amalie Jahn

www.bermlord.weebly.com

BERMLORD, Charlotte, North Carolina

ISBN-13: 978-0-9910713-8-8 (BERMLORD)

First Edition, June 2021

Typeset in Garamond
Cover art by Natalia Lavrinenko and Iryna Spodarenko
Author photograph courtesy of Bitmoji

for grandpa

Our family's eternal worrier.
I may have inherited your anxiety,
but I wouldn't change a thing.
For it came with your passion for life and
penchant for singing silly songs.
I'm grateful for every bit of me that was first part of you.

CHAPTER 1
week one

Approaching the subway entrance, I work to steady my breathing. Oxygen in—one, two. Carbon dioxide out—one, two. My heartbeat quickens taking the first tentative step down the stairs, and I resist the urge to grab the handrail for support, focusing instead on the mosaic tile of the wall ahead. Anything to distract myself from an impending panic attack as I make my way underground. The wad of gum on the stair tread and the rotten stench of greasy food wrappers in a nearby trashcan beg for my attention, but the germs don't need me to acknowledge them into existence. They live on every surface and coalesce in every enclosed space with or without my approval, which is why there is literally no place worse for me than the subway.

Except maybe a hospital.

Or a Port-a-pot.

But I digress.

Subways are gross.

Still, I can't dawdle at the base of the stairs. There's no time to wax nostalgic over my old N-95 mask or prepare my lungs for a deep enough breath to make it past the turnstiles.

Not when I have less than half-an-hour to make it all the way to Midtown.

As I edge along the corridor, I silently chastise myself for not leaving pottery class sooner. There might've been a few moments for proper germ preparation if I hadn't wasted the last twenty minutes of studio time on a raw lump of clay. Now, in the interest of time, I forgo my typical sanitation rituals, choosing instead to take shallow, inconspicuous breaths while giving wide berth to anyone who looks remotely unwell.

Or even in need of a nap.

And, of course, I keep my hands safely tucked in my pockets because when it comes to touching anything, the answer is always no.

No. No. No.

Passing the closest metro card dispensary, a man sneezes into his hand, and without giving a second thought to the spread of infectious pathogens, smears his germ-covered fingers all over the screen. His complete disregard for proper sanitation is a good reminder of why I avoid touching other people. Not to mention all handrails, doorknobs, turnstiles, and of course vending machines. Now, as I fish through my cargo pockets for my metro card, I also retrieve my trusty bottle of hand sanitizer. You never can be too prepared where subways are concerned.

The terminal begins to fill with early commuters, and I sidestep two businessmen with their noses buried in their cell phones. Dodging people is an artform I've perfected. I can spot a distracted walker from fifty paces and adjust accordingly. No one has so much as brushed into me in over a year, and that's really saying something when you live in a city of over eight million people.

Navigating the station now, there's commotion ahead—a large group of passengers bunching up on the far side of the turnstiles. It's not unusual to see a bottleneck on this side, but things typically open up once people pass through ticketing.

"Oh, man, that's disgusting," someone cries out.

"Just walk around," another calls.

Uncertain of what's ahead, I plan my trajectory, sanitizer at the ready. Two steps later the acidic smell of vomit overtakes me.

And then I see it. The bile. The mucus. The chunks. All of it bathed in germs like some infectious primordial ooze.

The elderly man who has recently been sick all over the floor is now sitting on a nearby bench where a young woman appears to be assessing his condition. Although I hope he's going to be okay, I won't be sticking around to find out. Instead, I swallow back my own regurgitative urges, and with willful disregard to what anyone else will think, tuck my nose into the crook of my elbow and make a run for it. In the presence of such obvious viral contamination, there is no other option but to turn back in the direction I've just come. I slip into the queue of other passengers leaving the platform, mentally calculating a circumspect route across town.

Most people in my time-constrained situation would make the logical decision to use the most expeditious means of getting to work. They'd hail a cab or request an Uber. Quick and efficient. But logic is wasted on people like me.

Back on the surface, a yellow taxi slows to the curb, and my stomach knots as a woman reaches for the door. How many thousands of people have touched that handle? How many viral and bacterial organisms are now transferring themselves onto her hand? Maybe she can risk being sick by morning, but I'll never be able to talk myself into a stranger's car. Instead, my only viable option is to take the Q as far south as 72nd Street where I can cut back over to the 6, resuming my usual course to Dust Jackets, the used bookstore where I work part-time.

Mom calls me her Master of Mass Transit.

More like Master of Microorganism Manipulation.

A glance at my phone confirms what I already know to be true—this circuitous route is going to make me seriously late.

After a two-block trek down 96th Street, I descend back into the tunnels. This new station is crowded and unfamiliar so I move more deliberately, splitting my attention between platform management and people monitoring. There are reasons my life is scheduled to the minute and much of it has to do with avoiding rush hour. Unfortunately, in the time it's taken me to race from one station to the other, the afternoon commute has gotten underway and people are now bustling shoulder to shoulder.

I silently curse the public puker, but then feel guilty about being angry as I sidestep a group of boisterous middle schoolers racing off the platform. It's not his fault I can't handle myself around other people's bodily fluids.

There's a break in the crowd ahead and I jockey for position, slipping past one person after another, gunning for freedom. When you operate solely on the principle of universal precautions, treating everyone as if they are known to be infectious for pathogens, it's easy to stop seeing people as individuals. Instead, as my eyes dart from passenger to passenger, from businesswoman to fast food employee to construction worker, I see only potential contaminants blocking my way to work. Obstacles to be avoided.

My germ-centric view of the world once led a therapist to suggest I might enjoy a job at the Occupational Safety and

Health Administration.

Turned out to be our last session together.

Dad said he was paying her to fix me, not for career advice.

Despite all the dodging and weaving, my train is pulling away as I reach the platform. It'll be at least ten minutes before the next one arrives so to help calm my nerves, I use the extra time concentrating on something positive—the smoothness of the clay against my skin back in pottery class. I'm still mentally finishing this week's project when two teenage girls appear beside me, grumbling together over a text. Their heads and shoulders rest against one another as they pass a phone between them.

"I can't even believe he said that about you," says the taller of the two girls, cracking her gum against the back of her teeth. "He's trash."

The shorter girl, sporting pink pixie haircut, takes a Chapstick from her pocket and swipes a layer of gloss across her lips. "It's a good thing your brother told us what an ass he is. You know I'm a sucker for guys with abs, and if Jake hadn't warned us, I probably woulda slept with that jerk."

They laugh together about Pink Pixie's lucky break, and I try to imagine how incredible it would be to have a girl friend to confide in. Probably better than any therapist. Their easy back-and-forth leaves me longing for a bestie to help thwart the advances of any trashy, albeit chiseled, would-be boyfriends.

Not that any guy has ever been interested in me. Nobody wants to date a girl who refuses to touch.

Communal by design, most humans seek out physical touch—as evidenced by nearly everyone around me. The northbound train screams into the station, metal brakes

5

against metal rails echoing from wall to wall and back again, and passengers spill onto the platform in a rush of humanity. A husband brushes a smudge of dirt from his wife's face. A teenage guy licks Dorito cheese from his boyfriend's finger. A grandmother takes her granddaughter by the hand.

Scientific research correlates touch with decreased violence, increased emotional intimacy, stronger immune systems, and even economic gain. I know all of this because Dust Jackets has an extensive psychology section. I also know all of this because I've spent the last couple of years systematically working to suppress this biological urge. Avoiding touch is the only way I'm able to quiet my anxiety.

But the relief comes at a cost.

The Dorito guys are kissing as they head past me up the stairs. Their connection makes me ache. My heart burns with jealousy.

"Take a picture, freak," a middle-aged guy says as he shuffles past, and I avert my gaze, embarrassed by my voyeurism. It's not the first time I've been called out, and it probably won't be the last. Especially since watching other people connect is the only safe alternative to chancing physical contact of my own.

The northbound train fills, the platform empties, and in the quiet following its departure, the melancholy vibrato of a lone violin echoes from somewhere further down the hall. It's as if all the desperation of this journey—from the ill-fated vomit and foot race across town to the teenage besties and lip-locked lovers—was given a tune and now it's reaching out to me, calling me in.

If it had words it would say—*Phoebe Benson, I understand your loneliness.*

Without stopping to overthink it, my feet move in the

direction of the sound to the neighboring platform. I swerve around an elderly couple and a group of rowdy construction workers still wearing their tool belts. The music grows louder as the din of the laborers quiets behind me.

And then I see him.

Pressing against the strings with focused intensity, his fingers tremble as they move across the fingerboard of the violin. His eyes are closed as if the music is welling up from inside him before seeping through his hands into the instrument. A bead of sweat lines his brow and as the song intensifies, he shakes his head, damp hair clinging to his forehead. The anguish of the minor key is a shocking contrast to the euphoria on his face. I probably wear the same expression when I work clay between my hands at the wheel.

The song reaches a fevered crescendo, and it's as if he's playing just for me. In the notes, I hear all the apprehension and disappointment associated with my solitary life. All the longing to be carefree instead of anxious all the time.

As the piece comes to an end, the bow pulls across the strings, whispering the last poignant note across the station. The violinist bows his head, completely spent, and once the music has faded, I allow myself to look past the instrument to the man, who, upon closer inspection, is most certainly still in high school. Although his cheeks are covered in two-day stubble, the skin on the rest of his face is as smooth and earthen as clay, save for the tiny crinkles at the corners of his eyes, indicative of a childhood spent playing in the sun.

What might it feel like to run my fingers against those cheeks?

Without looking up, he begins his next piece just as my train arrives, drowning out the tune. The doors hiss open. Passengers emerge and hurry out of sight. I linger on the platform a beat longer, listening, but now all I can hear are voices. Without bothering to look back, I slip onboard, strangely disappointed at the notion that I may never cross paths with the violinist again. Collapsing into a corner seat, the melody lingers in my head, a veritable soundtrack for my years of regret.

CHAPTER 2

week one

The little bell over the door chimes merrily as I skid into Dust Jackets, drawing Walter's attention from the book he's reading behind the register.

"Oh, thank God!" he cries, tossing his well-worn copy of *Mindfulness Matters* across the counter with his usual dramatic flair. It slides onto the floor with a thud, and after putting on one of my trusty latex gloves, I gather it up.

"I know, I know. I should've let you know I was running late." I reply, still panting from the final hundred-yard dash down the block. He takes the book from my hand as I continue. "But I can explain. There was vomit."

He looks suspiciously at his paperback as if there's a chance it's been contaminated, before setting it to the side. "You have no idea how worried I've been. You could've been dragged into a ditch. Beaten by muggers. Abducted by a traveling circus. Why in God's name didn't you call?"

I fling my backpack behind the counter and slide down the historical fiction shelf to the floor, hugging my knees to my chest. "I would've texted, but I had to take the Q and double back to the 6 because of the puke, and you know I have rules about texting and walking at the same time, especially after the stress of an exposure." I allow myself to take a few deep breaths, burying my head between my legs. "I'm sorry for worrying you, but I was in survival mode out there."

He humphs, but I know he won't stay mad for long. By the time the air conditioning has cooled my core temperature back to pre-aerobic levels, he's shuffled out from behind the counter to stand in front of me in his maroon jogging suit and matching Puma sneakers. "You wanna talk about it?"

Now it's my turn to grunt at him. "No." I slide over so he can sit beside me—close, but not too close. "Maybe." I sigh, reconsidering. "It was gross."

He pulls at his salt and pepper mustache and nods introspectively. "Did you have a full-on panic attack?"

I shake my head. "No."

"Heart palpitations?"

"Not too bad."

He smacks his lips. "Well, then I'd say this experience should get tallied under the win column."

I sigh, remembering the terror I felt facing the sickness. Running halfway across Manhattan to avoid it sure didn't feel like a win.

Walter continues when I don't respond. "Think about it. Last year when that kid sneezed beside you in algebra, you didn't even come to work. As I recall, you left school early and went straight home."

I throw him a half-smile. "It was a huge sneeze. Like, there was no way I wasn't inundated with particulates. It required an immediate shower."

"I think today was worse," he counters. "It was vomit. V-O-M-I-T. And you didn't race home. You figured out a solution and made it to work. A little late and without regard to your boss's anxiety, but you made it."

I consider him, peering over his bifocals, daring me to disagree. "I ran away from it, though. I didn't push past it. I didn't *sit in my anxiety*." I use some of the buzzwords therapists threw at me for months.

He scoffs. "Screw 'em. So, it wasn't textbook. You did what you had to do to cope with the situation, and I for one am proud of you."

I *had* been quick on my feet, coming up with a solution to avoid the vomit while still meeting my responsibilities. Maybe Walter's right. Maybe today is a win. I smile over at him and notice the skin on the edge of his thumb is raw and bloody. Any satisfaction I felt a moment ago disappears. I motion toward his finger.

"Is that because of me?"

His eyes shift from my face to his thumb and he tucks it into his palm. "Uh, no. Not you. Something unrelated."

Everyone suffering from anxiety has an involuntary tell. Some are visible, like Walter's. When he's struggling, he picks the skin on the side of his thumb with the nail of his index finger. He's had surgery to repair the damage. Twice. Still, he picks.

Other people, like me, don't necessarily have a physical tell. Mine's more psychological. I get moody and despondent. I have trouble focusing and have been known to lash out, especially at the people I love the most. Walter has definitely been on the receiving end of my tell on several occasions. Lucky for me, he's both understanding and forgiving. An incredible boss. An even better friend.

My only friend, these days.

Now, as a flush of embarrassment rises to his cheeks, it's

my turn to inquire into his well-being using a line from his playbook. "Wanna talk about it? Did Beverly stop by again? I swear you need to take her on a proper date. You don't need to go far—just the deli at the corner for sandwiches…"

Walter struggles to his feet, bracing himself against the bookshelf as his knees creak under his weight. "Not today, Phoebe," he says, silencing me with a wave of his hand. "You've already wasted half-an-hour of your shift this afternoon, and I left a huge box of donations in the back room for you to sort. Better get to it."

I know not to push him into conversation—he never pushes me—so I let it drop without another word. Beverly, a slight grey-haired widow with a seemingly insatiable thirst for literature has become something of a fixture around here in recent months, finding excuses to visit with Walter at least twice a week. I know Walter would like something more serious to develop between them but his anxiety keeps them apart.

His anxiety keeps him from leaving the building.

Like me, Walter is something of a work-in-progress.

I weave between the shelves, breathing in the sweet mustiness of aging paper while sidestepping a stack of hardbacks perilously close to toppling over on my way to the storage closet. Cataloging the contents of a donation box is one of my favorite tasks at the store. It's like being a detective, sifting through the subjects of someone's discarded library. What are their interests? What do they love? What are their lives missing? A person's choice of literature says a lot about them. I once shelved a box full of nothing but dog-eared Harlequin romances and imagined the previous owner was something of an American Bridgette Jones. Sometimes we get deliveries of children's picture books, and as I flip through classics like *Curious George* and *Hop On Pop*, it reminds me of years ago when I would read to my little brother, Toby. My favorite boxes, though, are the ones chock full of nonfiction—cookbooks, travel books, and self-help.

You can tell a lot about a person by what they eat, where they vacation, or what they want to improve about themselves which is why I'm thrilled to discover a vast array of reference books in today's delivery. I close my eyes, reaching my gloved hand into the box to pull out three random books. It's a little game I play with myself to help ward off the monotony—Guess The Gifter. I make my selections and set them on the table. I've chosen *101 Vegan Crockpot Recipes*, *Ancient Balinese Art*, and *Crossfit for Dummies*.

This one is way too easy—single guy just out of a relationship looking to unload baggage and memories after the breakup. I check the consignment slip attached to the side of the box to confirm. Sure enough, one of our regulars. Nailed it.

I make stacks of similar titles from the remaining books, weeding out the fiction from the nonfiction and the hardbacks from the paperbacks. I'm almost to the bottom of the box when I pull out *Coping for Couples: Dealing with Your Spouse's Anxiety in Five Simple Steps*.

I know exactly where this book belongs.

I'll place it on the shelf I perused the first time I wandered into Dust Jackets looking for answers of my own a year ago; when I convinced my parents I didn't need the stress of finding a new therapist after my third and favorite, Roz, moved away. Her wife landed some new position at a Chicago hospital, forcing her to relocate out of my life, but I'd promised my parents if I was going to give up formal treatment I would remain committed to 'getting better' on my own. Although Roz and I continued our therapy sessions via Zoom for a little while, it wasn't the same as sitting beside her on the couch every week, so in my quest for an anxiety-free existence I tracked down the only local copy of *Worries Be Gone* to Dust Jackets, hoping it would help me create an action plan for myself.

I didn't get the therapy I was expecting from the book. Instead, I got Walter.

CHAPTER 3

week one

Back in pottery class the next day, the stress of the vomit exposure is nearly forgotten as the clay turns beneath my fingers at the wheel. The coolness of the mud's damp texture eases the tension of my anxiety, and for a few blissful hours, I'm able to forget my loneliness and concentrate instead on my creation.

I'm passionate about creating something elegant from something hideous was the first line of my application essay for the class I'm taking here at the Keechad Pottery Studio this summer. Ceramics isn't offered at my high school during the academic year, so I had to convince my parents to let me use my earnings from Dust Jackets to pay for the six-week class. The instructor must have liked the imagery because he accepted me during the first round of selections. What he doesn't know is what I wrote is a load of crap. I mean, yeah, it's nice to have something pretty to look at once I'm finished, but I never keep anything I make.

If I still had friends, I would give my pottery to them. But since I don't, most of my pieces end up at Goodwill.

Either way, the finished product isn't what draws me to

ceramics. Nor is the satisfaction of a job well done. Instead, what keeps me at the wheel is the clay itself. I could sit for hours and never get tired of feeling it—the lumps, the cracks, the smoothness, the ridges—reminiscent of my skin in so many ways. If the rest of my class wouldn't think I was possessed, I'd happily turn the raw ball of mud on my wheel all day without creating anything. But I'm spending 'good money' and my parents expect me to have something on display at the final showcase in August. Six creations all entitled *Sphere* will not cut it.

As I sit at the wheel today, putting the finishing touches on this first week's project, I have to admit I'm pretty proud of my creation. It's a fluted vase, wide at the bottom and pinched at the top, with an intricate swirling pattern at the base reminiscent of the ocean. I've already decided to paint it blue once it's fired. Now, though, in a motion that feels something like a surgical removal, I slip the thin cord between the vase and the wheel to release one from the other. Free from the constraints of the wheel, the vase is now its own entity.

I have to fight the urge to throw it against the wall so I can start over.

Aarush, my instructor, slips his glasses off the top of his head to get a better look. "That turned out really nice, Phoebe. Good symmetry, nice linework, interesting shape." He peers over the rims at me. "You have a real gift."

Heat springs to my cheeks. "Thanks," I mutter, handing him the vase to be fired. Beside me, my neighbor Eleanor looks up from her bowl, brow furrowing in dismay as she checks the clock on the wall. Along with the rest of our classmates of various ages and abilities, she's still working frantically to complete the week's assignment before our three o'clock dismissal. It's a relief knowing I'm already finished with almost an hour to spare. If I leave now, I won't need to sprint across Manhattan the way I did yesterday to make it to work on time.

"Would you like to get started on next week's project?" Aarush asks, nodding toward the large plastic bin on the far side of the room where the raw clay is kept.

A surge of adrenaline floods my system, and I wonder momentarily if the euphoria I feel for clay is the same others experience before a band recital or a soccer match. The pads of my fingers rub together in anticipation of the fresh ball of mud.

I walk with him across the room, work forgotten. "Sure. What's the focus again?"

"Joining two pieces together with smooth seams and edges using the score and slip method." He sets down my vase on the counter and opens the clay bin on the floor beneath. "Take as much or as little as you need, but don't be wasteful."

I thank him and help myself to a grapefruit-sized lump, then hurry back to my workspace where I immediately throw the clay onto the wheel. There's a moment of raft anticipation as I pull water into the sponge before wringing it over the clay. Tiny rivulets cascade down the sides like rain on a windowpane. I set down the sponge, and as my hands hover over the mound a small sigh escapes my lips. From the corner of my eye, Eleanor gives me a look like she's accidentally walked in on her parent's making out, and I work to suppress my obvious urgency, rearranging my face into a less euphoric expression.

My eyes close as I connect with the clay. Applying gentle pressure to the pedal, the wheel begins to spin, turning the clay in my hands. This is the part I love the most.

This is the part I can make-believe I'm not alone in the world. When I can pretend I still have friends and the clay isn't actually clay but my mom's arm or my brother Toby's hand. When I can close out the rest of the world and imagine I'm not petrified of making an actual physical connection with another human being.

The first time I was allowed to touch Toby was nearly a decade ago during special sibling admission day at the neonatal intensive care unit. I stared in wonder at the tiny, premature baby who seemed more cyborg than human, wires and tubes sticking out of his face, chest, and arms in every direction. The nurse explained how the beeping and whooshing machines were keeping him alive, but that eventually he wouldn't need them anymore and he would be healthy just like me.

Sporting the same head of straight dark hair and fair skin as Mom and me, Toby and I already looked like siblings, despite the breathing tubes. It wasn't hard to imagine how wonderful our life together would once he was finally able to come home. I'd been allowed to slip my hand into his incubator and brush the tips of my fingers against his petal-soft cheek. His skin felt as fragile as tissue paper, and I thought maybe it was since I could see the blue of his veins just beneath the surface.

I don't know what I was expecting when Mom and Dad brought Toby home after two months in the hospital, but I remember feeling relieved I couldn't see the blood pulsing beneath his skin anymore. As Mom placed him into my willing arms for the first time, I felt not only the weight of his tiny frame but the massive responsibility of big-sisterhood.

Drawing on that responsibility now, I know exactly what I'm going to make to demonstrate my mastery of the score and slip method—a four-part storage caddy for Toby to house his drone parts. These days he, capital L, loves flying drones in the park with Dad and has recently started constructing his own designs by cannibalizing used parts from other people's crashed drones off eBay. Mom's always fussing at him for leaving nuts and bolts and screws lying around the apartment, so it might be a good idea to give him a designated place to store them.

The tricky part will be making sure each of the four vessels is exactly the same shape and size—my brother deserves perfection. After creating the first container, I'm struggling to get the second one to match in both height and width, and in a moment of rare frustration, crumple the pot beneath my hands. The clay oozes between my fingers, and I relish the cool sensation against my fingertips. Is this what it feels like to hold someone else's hand? It's been so long, I've nearly forgotten.

Taking note of my destructive tendencies, Eleanor casts a wary gaze in my direction with obvious concern for her own creation. She shifts slightly on her stool, putting more space between us, and I can't help but laugh to myself.

What the heck, girl? I'm not gonna wreck your project.

Class is over before I have a chance to restart the second container, so I wrap the first with a wet towel and place it in a plastic bag to keep it from drying out over the weekend. Once it's safely stowed, I throw a quick wave to Aarush as I head out the door.

CHAPTER 4
week one

Walking down 96th Street from class to the subway, it's hard not to see all the germs. They're clambering across benches, multiplying along railings, and lying in wait on every door handle along the way. With my hands stuffed safely in my pockets, it's nearly impossible to remember a time before Covid when I didn't see them. I do, however, remember the exact moment Mom explained to me how dangerous they could be to kids like Toby. Kids who were born with damaged lungs.

"I know you've heard people talking on the news and around the neighborhood about this new virus," she'd said one afternoon back in early 2020, sitting beside me on our family-room sectional, Toby out of earshot in his bedroom reading comics. "No one knows much about it, but if it gets here to the U.S., it might be really bad for your brother."

"The doctor on TV said we need to wash our hands and cover our coughs," I interrupted, desperate to impress her with how much I already knew. "But that's only for adults. Kids don't even get it."

"If it's true, that would be wonderful," she said. "But just in case kids *can* get it, knowing how to keep germs from spreading is especially important now. Toby was born before his lungs were fully developed, which is why some germs make him very sick even if they don't make the rest of us very sick at all. It's up to us to keep him safe by protecting him as best we can." She'd paused then, looking deep into my eyes for some confirmation I understood the seriousness of the situation. "Will you help Dad and I keep Toby safe?"

Of course, I told her I would, but I never imagined keeping that promise would lead me to where I am now.

Lost in thoughts of Toby, I'm cruising on autopilot, halfway down the steps to the 6 before remembering yesterday's vomit. All at once, the terror overtakes me as my palms begin to sweat.

It's gone, of course, removed by some mass-transit sanitation employee with a broom and pressure washer overnight. Still, picturing the vomit where it was on the other side of the turnstile cements my feet to the ground. I can practically see the germs skittering across the floor in my direction.

Worse still, the germs could be lingering in the air surrounding ground zero.

It's a stupid thought, and Roz's voice in my head reminds me that although it is *possible* for some rogue infectious microbes to remain, it is not *probable*. And if an event is improbable, it's not worth worrying about.

Pedestrians rush past on either side while I attempt to talk myself through the turnstile.

The vomit is gone.

The germs are *probably* gone.

The chances of being infected by day-old pathogens are infinitesimally small.

And yet, I can't force myself to move.

I'm stuck in the same way I've been stuck since the day I was sent home from school with a fever just days after Mom's warning about some weird new virus spreading through the city. After a painful nose swab and a seemingly endless five-day quarantine cloistered in our tiny Jersey City apartment, the pediatrician finally called to confirm that although my headache and cough were nearly gone, I had the 'rona. Mom's voice was frantic but quiet as she padded down the hall past my room to convey my diagnosis to Dad. I couldn't make out much of their conversation from my side of the door, but I did happen to hear them mention 'co-morbidities' and 'viral loads' and 'incubation periods.' It was still early in the pandemic, but I knew enough about how the disease spread and who was most at risk to realize they weren't worried about me.

They were worried about Toby.

The ramifications of my pathogenic negligence spread like glass-laced ripples through my family. Somehow, despite wearing a mask and eating meals in my room, I managed to infected Toby anyway, and while I fully recovered from Covid in a little over a week, he developed MIS-C and battled the virus with his weak, damaged lungs in the ICU for nearly a month. I'd never seen Dad cry before so I didn't believe him when he assured me everything was going to be okay, and that none of it was my fault.

Because when you almost kill your little brother with your germs, how can it not be your fault?

"Get out of the way," someone calls, finally forcing me into action. Behind me, an impatient looking woman with a stroller barrels in my direction. I need to make my decision now—push past my fears and risk potential contamination getting to the 6 or do an about-face and hustle over to the Q for the second day in a row.

Sigh.

The entire walk down 96th Street consists of one long self-castigation. This is the part the anxiety manuals don't tell you about. Sure, avoidance therapy is a great coping mechanism for relieving the anxiety associated with a stressor. Want to avoid vomit-induced anxiety? No problem. Just take another route. The tradeoff is you're left feeling like a complete failure.

A weak, pathetic loser.

Entering the station for the Q, the conversation in my head goes something like this:

Me: You could've just gone through the turnstile furthest from the puke. At least that would've been something.

Other Me: Yeah, but germs travel. None of the flooring is safe, especially if no disinfectant was used during the cleaning process.

Me: Are you kidding me right now? The puke is long gone, Phoebe. You could've marched right over the spot where it was, and absolutely nothing would've happened.

Other Me: Nothing? You can't be certain of that. And I definitely would've had to wash my shoes. Think of the time I won't be wasting scrubbing soles tonight.

Me: Walter's gonna be worried if you're late again.

Other Me: He'll understand. I'll let him know.

Me: You're impossible.

Other Me: Don't I know it.

I send Walter a quick text before descending the stairs into the station so he doesn't worry.

More puke issues. Everything's fine. On my way. See you soon.

My train is heading out as I pass through the gate, and a quick glance at the overhead schedule confirms the next train isn't due to arrive for another nine minutes. Instead of hunkering down beside the line of men waiting against the wall, shoulder to shoulder in polos and khakis, thumbing mindlessly through feeds on their phones, I explore the new station, hoping to find a less populated area to wait. Although most of the men look harmless, you can never be sure where illness is concerned.

I scan both directions for an indication as to which way looks less crowded when I hear the music—the same haunting melody from the day before—and my heartbeat quickens involuntarily in a not completely awful sort of way. Professional buskers aside, most street performers change locations a lot, so it seems unlikely that the violinist from yesterday would return to the same spot again today. Still, there's no mistaking the angsty tone of the rendition or the butterflies taking up residence just below my ribcage.

I follow the music down the platform without quite knowing the reason why. It's not like I carry change for tipping or know the first thing about interacting with strangers. Despite my insecurities, however, something nascent compels me along, and my breath catches as the violinist comes into view.

He's angled away from me, his shoulders hunched, his face bent against the instrument. The tempo slows as the piece comes to an end, and I force air into my lungs. A nearby commuter places a five in his case, and he thanks her with a nod of his head before returning his bow to the strings.

The first echoes of the inbound train momentarily draw my attention, but instead of racing toward the cars, something compels me to stay. I want him to see me. To know I've been listening. I need him to know he's not alone. The train's brakes screech against the metal wheels eradicating all other sounds, and he chooses that moment to turn around.

Our eyes meet.

And he smiles.

Behind me, the car doors open and commuters flood onto the platform in a massive wave. Their heat is oppressive and despite my desire to stay, it propels me into motion. I slip through the doors just as the distinct two-tone beep signals the train's imminent departure. A perfunctory glance over my shoulder as we pull out of the station leaves me with the disturbing pang of disappointment—the violinist has moved on to his next piece, and I'm no longer there to hear it.

From my seat in the most isolated corner of the car, I silently curse myself for not having the courage to say something—anything—to him instead of standing there like an idiot, dumbfounded by the entire situation. Any sensible human being would have had the decency to at least smile back, but not me. Nope. I can't even handle the simplest of human interactions.

Screw you, Anxiety Disorder.

Screw you.

CHAPTER 5

week one

"More vomit out there again today?" Walter asks as I push through the antique wooden door and stumble into the bookstore. "Is there an epidemic out there or something?"

I let out a huge sigh and join him behind the counter where he's cataloging new books into the computer's inventory. "No, actually. It was just the same vomit from yesterday."

He looks up from the screen, horrified. "It was still there? New York isn't known for its pristine sanitation, but that's ridiculous."

I throw him a wary smile. "It wasn't still there. It had been cleaned up, but I couldn't get past *the spot*. Lingering contaminants and all."

His eyes are sympathetic. "Tough situation. Wanna talk about it?"

This is the beauty of Walter and one of the many ways he's different from actual therapy. Because when your parents are shelling out their hard-earned dollars for you to sit in a room for an hour with a professional to talk about what's bothering you, you better damn well talk. But with Walter, I can talk. Or not. And he always gives me the option.

I shrug. "I guess I'm just disappointed in myself for not pushing past it. I mean, I could've at least forced myself to get a little closer to the scene of the crime, but I totally bailed. So much for all those months of CBT."

Walter scans another barcode into the system and throws me a sideways glance. "Cognitive behavioral therapy only works when the patient works with it."

I can't help but laugh at this. "Says the man whose self-mandated meditation therapy involves watching old *Taxi* reruns on TV."

"It's a good show. Helps me relax more than any of that new age 'ohm' crap. But touché. Point taken."

I scan the written list of tasks he's left for me to accomplish this afternoon. More inventory. Pulling discards. Vacuuming. Nothing out of the ordinary.

Unlike the violist's smile, which was completely *extra*ordinary.

I can't believe I'm still thinking about him, but if Walter's curious gaze is any indication, preoccupation's written all over my face.

"Something more on your mind?" he asks.

I really, really don't want to tell him about the violinist. Too bad there's no one else to tell.

"It's just that the worst part of my trip wasn't the disappointment over my avoidance behavior."

"No?" I have his undivided attention now as he sets his book down on the counter, assuming his therapist role.

"No. The worst part was seeing this busker at the other station and not having the courage to approach him. His music was surreal, like, fueled by this passion that resonated from his bones, you know what I mean? I could actually *feel* his angst inside the notes. And, if I'm being honest, he was super cute. But did I go up and say anything? Drop a dollar in his case? Of course not. Because besides being a complete loser, I don't even carry cash." I roll my shoulders to work out a kink, the result of being hunched over a potter's wheel all day. "I'm just sick of being so isolated from the rest of the world. I'm a total life failure."

Walter pulls at his mustache and considers me over his glasses. "How can you count yourself out as a failure when your life has just begun?" I roll my eyes, but he continues. "Think of it this way, if you were one of your clay pots, you'd still be greenware. Pliable. Moldable. Able to change. You have lots of time before getting thrown in the kiln, huh? Plenty of time to figure things out. In the meantime, you're not completely isolated. You have your family. And your pottery instructor." He pauses to emphasize the seriousness of his commentary. "And of course, you'll always have me."

"I know."

"But maybe having an old man as your only friend isn't enough anymore."

This statement comes out of nowhere, taking me aback.

"You're a wonderful friend. Of course, you're enough," I counter, although it's not entirely true.

He waves a hand at me. "Feh! You're a vibrant young lady. I'm a boring old fuddy-duddy. You should be spending your time with people your own age not wasting it here with a curmudgeon like me." He raises a bushy eyebrow, scrutinizing my face. "We made a promise to each other the first day you wandered in here looking for that book, remember? That we'd be there for each other."

Wondering where all this is going, I narrow my eyes as he

slips past me, careful to avoid making contact before disappearing into the shelves.

"Come on," he beckons. "There's a new book I want to show you."

The first time I came to Dust Jackets, I'd been looking for a self-help book much like the one Walter's flipping through now. In the weeks following Roz's departure, my quest for the best way to cope with my anxiety was going nowhere until a desperate online search uncovered the book, *Worries Be Gone*. It was touted as the holy grail of cognitive behavior therapy, but of course, it was out-of-print.

Dust Jackets was the only store in the city with one copy in stock.

Located less than three blocks from school, I decided to walk over and pick up the book before heading home one afternoon. I expected to find the book on the shelf and the cure to my anxiety between its pages. What I found instead was a man who carried over three-hundred books about anxiety in his store, and after reading them all, knew enough about psychoeducation, self-monitoring, stimulus control techniques, relaxation, exposure strategies, self-control desensitization, cognitive restructuring, worry exposure, worry behavior modification, and problem-solving to start his own practice.

When I inquired about *Worries Be Gone* and disclosed my intent for it, Walter insisted on gifting me the book and offered me a job on the spot.

With one minor caveat.

In addition to earning a paycheck, I had to promise I would 'work to improve the quality of my life.'

And I had to promise to help him do the same.

"You know my wife's death triggered my anxiety," he

tells me now, holding an unfamiliar book open across his forearm. "Losing the most important person in the world after forty-one years together will do that to a person. Especially losing Rita out of the blue the way I did. I couldn't eat. I couldn't sleep. I couldn't get out of bed. And it wasn't because I was depressed. It was because I felt certain I had used up all the good parts of my life leaving only the bad. I became the king of worst-case scenarios." He shrugs. "And then you walked into my store."

He's told me this story a dozen times, about how I showed up at just the right moment, something of an answered prayer.

"Talking to you has made things easier. Sharing must be the reason therapy helps so many people, but after Rita's hospitalization, I couldn't afford doctor's appointments for myself. Discussing strategies with you—how to breathe correctly, relaxation techniques, keeping the worry journal— I'm coping better every day. But you…"

He reaches out as if to touch me, and instinctively, I back away.

"I don't know if I'll ever be able to help you feel comfortable touching things or people again, but there are some techniques in this book which might help you overcome your isolation. Maybe this new method will help you let other people back into your life and allow you to finally make some friends. And I'm talking about friends your own age, not just old folks like me." He flips the book over and places it in my hands. It's opened to Chapter Ten: Facing Your Fears—Exposure. I close the book and hand it back.

"Thanks anyway, but you and I both know I've done plenty of exposure therapy already. Unsuccessfully, I might add."

He pushes the book into my ribs. "This book came in a few weeks back, and I read it cover to cover. It was just published this year and there are some interesting new strategies I think you should try. Starting with establishing a goal and a creating a fear ladder."

Begrudgingly, I take back the book, scoffing at the title. "*Anxiety's Awful, But You're Not?* Are you for real with this thing?" I stop just short of laughing out loud. "If it's so great, why'd somebody get rid of it already?"

He glares at me. "Perhaps it worked so well, whoever it was doesn't need it anymore."

This is highly improbable. But not impossible. His buoyant expression forces my concession. "Okay. Let's say I buy in. What kind of goal are we talking about? And don't say licking a toilet seat because I won't do it. I'll die first."

He pinches the bridge of his nose in frustration. No one said being an ad hoc therapist was easy. "I'm not going to ask you to lick a toilet seat. That's disgusting. But there are some innovative ideas presented in this book about coping with phobias. Instead of addressing the phobia directly, one suggestion is to address the resulting social isolation. When you came in here today less concerned with the vomit than you were not knowing how to interact with the busker, I immediately thought of this book. Maybe you're ready to try something new?"

I reopen the book to chapter ten and skim the first paragraph.

"You want me to stop focusing on a cure for my germaphobia and start focusing on letting other people back into my life. My phobia pushed them away, and now you want me to learn to let them back in."

He nods.

"Because increasing social interaction might lessen the anxiety perpetuated by my phobia."

He nods again. Now he's smiling.

"You want my goal to be making a new friend."

"Or maybe even a boyfriend," he says, waggling his salt and pepper eyebrows at me, fancying himself a matchmaker. I can't believe I'm considering this. If I do it'll be because he needs the help as much as I do.

I scan the second paragraph. "If I agree to this, you need to do something in return."

"Figured as much. Name it."

I tuck the book under my arm and lift my chin, imparting an air of authority to my request. "You need to give in to poor Beverly and leave this building. You need to take her out on a proper date. She comes in here all the time to visit, and you never reciprocate. It's time, Walter."

He nods introspectively, then raises his hand above his head for one of our silly 'air high fives' which I happily return, our fingers stopping just inches from one another. "You've got a deal."

CHAPTER 6
week one

The new therapy book from Walter sits heavily on my lap during the train ride home from work. A less anxious person would use the free time to read through another chapter or two but constant vigilance is required when riding public transportation. During this final leg of the journey out of Manhattan into New Jersey, I've secured a corner seat on the PATH which is always slightly less stressful than having people on both sides. The man sitting next to me smells as if he hasn't showered in a month, though, so I'm not taking any chances.

Thankfully, the stinky man is the most exciting part of my trip home, and Toby calls out from the kitchen as I come through the door.

"Hi, Phoebe!" he says, his voice labored, a persistent reminder of the damage I caused.

"Hey, T."

I hang my bag on the wall hook before venturing into the kitchen. The smell of marinade from Mom's famous beef barbeque bulgogi wafts down the hall and I'm glad, like always, they've waited dinner for me.

"I'm starving," I tell Mom as I set my new book on the table and slide past her on the way to wash my hands at the sink. "It smells so good."

"I stir-fried the beef in grandma's homemade sauce, just the way you like it." She hands me a roll of paper towels. "How were class and work?"

I take my seat across the table from Toby where he's got two dozen mechanical drone parts spread between us. "Class was great. Making a little something for you next week, Toby."

He looks up from the contraption he's screwing together. "Tell me."

I wag my finger. "Not until it's done. But I'll give you a hint. It might help keep all your loose screws from getting lost in the carpet."

"Dad and I will be happy about that." Mom sets a bowl of rice and a plate of iceberg lettuce leaves on the table. "Speaking of Dad, will one of you go grab him from his office?"

Before I can offer, Toby pops out of his seat and runs down the hall to the walk-in closet Dad uses as his in-home tax attorney office. Although our apartment is small, I can't keep from worrying every time I see him dashing about. Maybe he can pretend his Covid-related lung damage isn't severe enough to land him in the ER, but his most recent hospitalization is still plenty fresh in my mind. It's almost as if he enjoys tempting fate.

Or maybe he just likes trying my nerves.

Beside me, Mom sets our plates on the table and notices my new book. "Anxiety's Awful, But You're Not?" She raises an eyebrow. "Is this another Dust Jackets special?"

"Walter pulled it for me. Says there are a few new

techniques he thinks might be worth trying."

After scooping Toby's project to the side, she takes her seat beside me and wipes a non-existent smudge from the table with her napkin. "I thought you've been doing okay?"

Okay is a relative term, and Mom often sees what she wants to see. It's easier for her that way, and I'm not interested in bursting her bubble.

"I'm fine," I tell her.

The timer on the oven dings, and she gets back up to dish out the beef. "You do remember Walter's not a licensed therapist. He's just an old man with a laundry list of his own problems."

Dad and Toby race down the hallway, skidding into the kitchen like they're in the medal heat of the hundred-yard-dash. I hold my breath in anticipation of an impending attack. Asthma for him. Panic for me.

"Who's just 'an old man with a laundry list of his own problems?' Me again?" Dad settles himself into his seat while Toby pulls a nebulizer from his pocket and sucks in a puff of medicine. Luckily, it immediately quiets the rattling in his lungs and the pounding of my heart.

"No, although it's an apt description," Mom teases. She nods at the book. "Walter's found another treatment suggestion for Phoebe."

Dad picks up his fork and gives me a wink. "Maybe this one will be the silver bullet."

I shrug and take my first bite of barbeque so I don't have to respond. Dad has been on the quest for the elusive cure to my anxiety since my first virus-related panic attack, eternally hopeful the right combination of treatment and circumstance are waiting just around the corner so we can finally put all this germ nonsense behind us once and for all. How I wish I shared his optimism.

Mom scoops rice into the lettuce leaf on her plate. "Well, I was just going to say I think it's a waste of time. I mean, honestly, you're taking extra classes, working part-time... Perfectly normal teenage stuff."

I take another bite of dinner, chewing through the beef and Mom's assessment of my current situation. Using the word 'normal' in the same sentence to describe me seems disingenuous. I've obviously gotten better at concealing my coping mechanisms. But concealment and elimination are two entirely different things.

"Right, honey?" Mom prods.

I nod dutifully.

"Phoebe's making me something at her class," Toby says to Dad, redirecting the conversation. "She says it'll help with my lost screw problem."

"If it keeps me from finding them embedded in the bottom of my feet, I'll be happy. You think you're gonna be ready for the big race next Saturday?"

Toby's been working on his latest drone since the end of the school year in the hopes of entering it into the kids' round of the Liberty Cup First-Person-View Racing Event. He was supposed to compete in a different race back in the spring, but when a simple cold developed into pneumonia and a partially collapsed lung, he was forced to withdraw from the competition. Now, he's resolved to fly a drone of his own creation instead of a stock model in next week's race as a way to prove himself to the community. His determination is more than admirable.

"Yeah," he says through a mouthful of rice. "I think I've got the kinks worked out after the crash the other night. The left side was a little out of balance. Now it's adjusted."

Excitement over Toby's upcoming competition quickly takes over the discussion, and my latest self-help book and proposed therapy fall off the radar. Toby and Dad remain so deep in conversation that after loading my plate into the dishwasher, I'm able to retreat unnoticed to my bedroom where I settle in to reread chapter ten for the third time.

Walter was right about the method of treatment being unique. The idea of working toward an attainable goal that just happens to be in direct competition with my phobia is something I've never tried before. And the thought of actually finding the courage to make a new friend?

I can hardly imagine what it would look like.

The book's author suggests making a list of ten increasingly difficult goals leading to the desired outcome. Achievable goals within the confines of my comfort, at least initially. If I want to start letting people into my life again, what's the best way to start?

I pull one of my many journals out of my desk drawer, turn to a clean page and write:

'Operation 'Phoebe Makes a New Friend'

1   Believe in myself. Believe I'm capable of meeting someone new. Repeat 'I deserve to have friends in my life' at least five times each day. I can do this.

2   Try not to look as afraid as I actually feel. Keep my hands in my pockets if necessary but be casual, not creepy.

3   Smile.

4   Say hello.

5   Introduce myself. 'Hi, my name's Phoebe.'

6   Ask for the person's name (But pray to God they offer first.)

7   Assume the person might be shy, too. Maybe they're just as nervous as I am. (Fingers crossed.)

I tap my pencil against my thigh, unsure of where to go from here. I still have three more goals to identify for this fear ladder but have run out of ideas. Remembering the appendix, I flip to the back of the book and find exactly what I'm looking for—fear ladder examples.

There are a couple of suggestions that might work for my situation so I copy them directly from the book, adding my own additional notes.

8. Find mutual interests. Do we have anything in common? Focus on those things and ask more about them.

9. Chat matter-of-factly. Fake it til I make it. Pretend I know what I'm doing.

10. Be fully present and listen. Stop thinking about the germs. Stop thinking about the germs. Stop thinking about the germs.

I read the list over several times before ripping it out of the journal and slipping it into my folder labeled Important Lists. An inventory of germ rules I made right after Toby's bout with Covid sits on top where it's resided for the past two years—the steady beacon directing me to where ultimate peace resides. My fluid script, with its angled lines and flowing loops stares back at me, familiar and comforting. 'Just follow me,' it beseeches, 'and everything will be okay.'

Except everything isn't okay. I'm not okay. The stupid germ list hasn't made things better. It's stifled my relationship with my brother and destroyed all my friendships.

And yet…

Hesitantly, I take the new list I've just created and bring it to the front of the pile, setting it on top. Maybe it's time to let a new list be my guide.

CHAPTER 7
week two

After completing my fear ladder, I decide making friends with someone in pottery class is out of the question. If it doesn't go well I'll have to face them every day for the next five weeks, and I definitely don't have the strength. Instead, I psyche myself up to chat with a stranger waiting for the subway after class on Monday afternoon. My only goal is to say hello because—baby steps. By the time I make it into the tunnels, though, part of me (a rather large part if I'm being honest) is desperately hoping to be greeted by the sound of a violin. But when the only person I'm interested in meeting isn't there, I have trouble forcing myself to approach anyone else.

The violinist is a no-show after pottery again on Tuesday, so I scope out a teenage girl with an Aeropostale bag, a three-year-old racing his Matchbox car across a nearby bench, and an elderly woman stooped over her walker. For ten minutes I mill around the platform, unable to say hello or even smile at any of them. When my train arrives and I still haven't mustered the courage to interact with anyone, I feel myself deflate as the adrenalin flushes out of me for a second time.

At class on Wednesday, I accidentally ruin the third section of Toby's parts container, but even the allure of the clay's skin-like texture is lost on me. Usually, it's no big deal when I make a mistake at the wheel. There's no better excuse than an unintended slip-up to warrant starting over, resulting in more time for my hands to enjoy the clay. But how can I concentrate on the task at hand when my mind is already an hour ahead on the train platform?

As I lift the toppled mess of clay off the wheel in an attempt to begin again, I repeat the mantra I've been listening to on repeat inside my head since Monday.

I deserve to have friends in my life.
I deserve to have friends in my life.
I deserve to have friends in my life.

I don't realize I've been speaking the words aloud until I feel Eleanor staring a hole in the side of my head. She indiscreetly slides her entire wheel a good six inches away from me, the scraping of the metal feet against the linoleum echoing around the room.

Within seconds, Aarush is at my side. "Everything okay over here?" For a moment, I think he's going to reach out to touch my shoulder in some well-meaning show of solidarity. I hold my breath, leaning my torso just out of his reach. Fortunately, he slips his hands into his pockets before going on. "Do you need some more space, Eleanor? Some better lighting perhaps?"

"I'm fine," she says curtly. It's obvious she thinks I'm bonkers.

"Phoebe?" Aarush asks.

"All good," I tell him, ignoring Eleanor's glare.

Between fixating on the possibility of meeting (or not meeting) the violinist and Eleanor's dirty looks, I'm no closer to finishing Toby's container by the end of class. Instead of staying behind to prepare my workspace for the following day, I hightail it outta there, moving as quickly and safely as possible to the Q. At the subway entrance, I pause to do my breathing exercises but cut them short, the anticipation of what could be waiting below being far too great.

I'm going to say hello to someone today if it kills me.

Although the smell of baked garbage greets me at the entrance, the allure of abandoned turnstiles compels me further into the station—an indication I've arrived between departures. A lone couple meanders past me up the stairs, and I race through ticketing, fumbling with my hand sanitizer and metro card as I tumble through the gate. A train is just disembarking and passengers spill out of the cars, their conversations echoing off the low ceilings. Hugging the wall, I continue down the platform, my ears piqued. At first, people's voices are too loud. Babies cry. A woman laughs enthusiastically at her boyfriend. Some guy screams at another to get the hell out of his way. Eventually, though, once the train pulls out of the station and the people have finally dispersed up and away, all that remains is the pounding in my chest and the mournful vibrato of a distant violin.

He's here. Just around the corner.

The rising panic terminating my forward progress isn't new to me—the way my lungs are suddenly averse to converting oxygen. The way every sweat gland on my body suddenly goes into full-production mode. There's nothing shocking about these familiar sensations. Toby had barely been out of the ICU a month the first time I experienced them, the day I found him gasping face down on the bathroom floor, inciting my very first panic attack.

We'd been playing one of our many games of quarantine

hide-and-go-seek, and he'd finally outsmarted me, sneaking around one corner of the kitchen island while I waited for him to come around the other side. When I discovered him in the hall bath, instead of racing into action or even calling Mom to help, I just stood there, mouth agape. All the worst-case scenarios played out in my mind—he'd caught Covid again, he was going back to the hospital, and this time he was going to die.

At the time, I didn't know there was a diagnosis for the way my heart beat uncontrollably inside my chest, threatening to burst through my ribcage. I didn't know there was a clinical name for how my head felt as if it was no longer attached to my body and my lungs felt like they were full of sand. I didn't know the cold sweat breaking out all over my body was indicative of a full-blown panic attack.

Or that it would be the first of many.

In the months that followed, I learned to give my body exactly what it wanted in the early throws of an attack—a way out. Avoidance behavior is a little coping mechanism I developed with the help of a few of my therapists. Not a path I chose as much as a path that chose me. Because when I run away, the symptoms disappear.

Simple cause and effect.

My symptoms are triggered by adrenaline—an innocuous hormone we all have coursing through our bloodstreams. For most people, the fear reaction produced by adrenaline is a good thing. If your house is on fire, the adrenaline signals for you to get the heck out. This instinctual response kept our cavemen ancestors from being exterminated by saber-toothed tigers. It's our body's way of keeping us safe. Propagation of the species and all that.

Unfortunately, those of us with anxiety disorders have

bodies that overcompensate in response to real (and imagined) stimuli. Instead of getting a healthy dose of 'you might want to get out of the way of that bus careening in your direction' we get a mega-dose of 'this seemingly harmless act of saying hello to another human being might result in a death-inducing case of typhus so don't even think about it if you know what's good for you.'

And therein lies the difference.

My body's just an overachiever. At least that's what I like to tell myself.

Leaning against the pillar of the deserted platform for support, I know better than to reason with myself now. Reason has no functioning place in my life. I could stand here until my legs stiffen with exhaustion listing all the reasons why saying hello to the violinist probably won't make me sick. Because at the end of it all the only thing that matters is the infinitesimally small possibility he could.

I force air into my lungs.

Repeat my mantra.

I deserve to have friends in my life.

Take one hesitant step forward.

This isn't so bad.

I'm lying to myself now, skipping all the way to number nine on the list—'fake it til you make it.'

Like I said, I'm an overachiever.

It occurs to me as I'm standing here that the music has changed, from slow and somber to something more upbeat. It's not hard to imagine the melody taking me by the hands, coaxing me along, and I let this image guide my second tentative step. And my third. And my fourth. By the fifth step, I've rounded the corner to where I can see him fully. The motion of my approach attracts his attention, and he lifts his face off the chin rest ever so slightly, giving a nod in my direction.

Every cell inside my body screams for me to turn around, leave the station, run back to the 6, and never ever come this way again.

Then, he smiles.

The music changes a third time, and unlike the other, more classical pieces, I recognize this song immediately.

Carly Rae Jepsen. *Call Me Maybe.*

Is this guy for real?

My feet are poised, ready to make a hasty retreat when, in an unexpected turn of events, he starts walking toward me. He's still playing the song, moving into the chorus, the part about being crazy, and I'm starting to wonder if he actually is. Maybe I've got it all wrong, and he's some sort of sociopath. Walter would know, but of course, Walter isn't here.

In the time it takes me to debate the merits of a guy who unabashedly rocks out to muzak inspired pop songs on his violin, he's closed in on me and is now within arm's reach. Finishing the last stanza, he drops his bow and peers at me over the neck of his instrument.

"Are you stalking me?" he asks with a soft Spanish accent.

My mouth is dry. I suck my cheeks, trying to produce enough saliva to answer. The conversation I'd prepared in my head didn't begin with him leveling an unprovoked accusation, and I'm not sure how to respond. Unfortunately, my mouth answers honestly before my brain can object.

"Yes?"

His eyes widen beneath dark lashes and he laughs, robust and soulful. But something in the way he's looking at me confirms it's not at my expense. "Was not expecting that response." He tucks his violin under his arm. "Should I be worried about you? Like, are you an undercover cop or something, because I don't need a permit to play here."

Of course, this is as close as I've ever stood to him. He's taller than me, but only slightly. What he lacks in height he makes up for in bulk. This guy is solid. A little too solid for a violinist. More like a rugby player. I consider his question, wondering if concern over arrest is an actual thing for him. If it is, the upward curl of his lips proves he's only playing now.

"I left my badge and cuffs at home so you're off the hook."

He makes the sign of the cross. "Gracias a Dios! You had me worried for a minute, Officer...?"

I'm fidgeting with the bottle of sanitizer inside my pocket, and it accidentally opens, trickling liquid into my palm. The comforting smell of rubbing alcohol distracts me momentarily before it occurs to me we're already on step five—introductions.

"Phoebe?" I say.

"You sound uncertain."

"No. It's definitely Phoebe."

He switches the bow to his left hand before extending his right hand in greeting. "Please to meet you, Officer Phoebe. I'm JP."

There are calluses on the pads of his fingers, and I try to imagine what they must feel like. His nails are trimmed short but neat—he's not a biter. There's a cut on his knuckle which probably requires some Neosporin and a Band-Aid, and while I consider mentioning this, it finally occurs to me he's waiting to shake my hand.

After a quick mental review of my list of rules for this conversation, I'm reminded there are none specific to physical contact. And number ten about ignoring his germs is a stretch. Regardless of how long I stand here pretending to ignore the millions of microbes covering his palms, there's no way I'm letting him touch me.

I take a step back, just out of his reach. "I don't touch," I tell him.

He raises an eyebrow. "Don't touch strangers?"

"Don't touch anyone."

A beat passes, both of us digesting what I've said. I can't believe the truth fell out so easily, especially when it took a dozen sessions with my first therapist, Dr. Bostitch, to admit my post-Covid PTSD manifests itself as germaphobia. How'd this random guy disarm me with nothing more than a perfunctory introduction?

Was it the music?

His sultry Spanish accent?

The weightless sensation brought on by his smile?

More pressing than the reason *why* is the looming consequence of my confession. Dr. Bostitch didn't have the option to walk away; my parents were paying her to stay. But this guy? I expect nothing less than for him to take the nearest stairwell out of this Upside Down of a conversation.

So much for getting to number eight—finding mutual interests.

So much for learning to let people into my life.

Instead of making a hasty retreat, however, he lets his hand fall to his side, disheartened but not defeated. He looks at me the way Toby does when I slide away from him on the couch watching reruns of *The Flash*.

"You don't touch *anyone*? What's that about?" he asks with genuine concern.

I shrug, wondering how long it will take for JP to give up

on this ridiculous exchange. I honestly can't believe he's hasn't given up on it already.

"I've got some issues," I tell him.

At this point, I assume he will do and say what others have done and said when confronted by my challenges in the past. To do what my best friend Kara did when we finally returned to in-person school after lockdown, and I no longer wanted to hang out with her, or anyone else for that matter.

I expect him to walk away and never look back.

Instead, he laughs. He laughs so hard his shoulders shake, and he nearly drops his violin from under his arm.

"You kiddin' me? Girl, we've all got issues."

He says this so matter-of-factly, I'm tempted to take his assessment of my situation at face value. Is it possible I'm making more of my anxiety than I should?

Behind me, my train speeds into the station, its screeching brakes effectively ending our conversation. I take another step back, mentally preparing to board when the lines between his brows deepen, and the smile fades from his lips.

"Comin' through this way again tomorrow?" he asks over the rumble of wheel against track.

I nod. Words elude me.

His smile returns. "Oh, good. Then I will, too. See you later, Officer Phoebe."

Passengers have taken all the seats by the time I stumble into the nearest car. I throw a wave over my shoulder at JP as the doors close behind me and brace myself for the impending lurch as the train leaves the station.

CHAPTER 8
week two

"You spoke with the violinist?" Walter asks, coming around the counter to greet me as I enter the store. I'm trying to play it coy but the gigantic smile on my face must give me away.

"He actually spoke to me first," I admit, tossing my bag to the side.

"And?"

It isn't lost on me that, in the absence of an actual best friend, this sixty-four-year-old Jewish widower is the best surrogate around.

"And he wanted to shake my hand."

Walter grimaces empathetically. "I assume physical contact is not on your fear ladder."

"Definitely not," I confirm. Touching is not within the scope.

Walter returns to his wooden stool behind the counter. "So, you didn't shake his hand. What'd you do instead, and how'd he react?"

I remember the way a dimple formed in JP's cheek when he'd laughed about everyone having issues. The way he didn't run away. The way he stayed.

I tell Walter.

"And then you just got on the train when it came instead of staying to talk?" He wags a finger at me. "You do have issues."

I grab my to-do list off the counter and throw him a mildly offended glare. "I have a job, remember? Didn't want to be late. Especially since my boss will go off the rails if I'm not on time."

The little bell over the door chimes, signaling a familiar customer's arrival—dear, sweet Beverly. When he sees her, Walter brushes me off with a wave of his hand. "Tomorrow," he whispers, "just be late."

Beverly asks about purchasing a copy of Bridge to Terabithia for her granddaughter as I make my way between the shelves to the back of the store. It's a ruse, I'm sure, but I know we have a bunch of copies. It's one of my favorites.

"I'll grab one," I call to Walter, pulling a latex glove out of my back pocket while I try to remember where he had me shelve them during his last whirlwind reorganization. He's always coming up with better ways to classify the books—alphabetically by author, alphabetically by topic, chronologically, and by genre. Melvil Dewey's system doesn't stand a chance against Walter's anxiety-induced insomnia. The most recent arrangement came as the result of an all-night infomercial binge in which he decided all the books ought to be organized by year of publication.

A quick Google search on my phone confirms Bridge to Terabithia was published in 1977. On my way to the shelf containing books published at the end of the twentieth century, I overhear Beverly laughing at something Walter's said. There's a sincerity to it, but also a longing that cautions me to keep my distance for a while longer. Book in hand, I peek between the stacks at them. He's leaning casually against the counter while she grasps her purse expectantly. Her smile is radiant. She's beaming at him.

She laughs again, and I look at the book in my hands. It's an old library edition with hand-drawn renderings of Jess and Leslie, not the newer movie tie in one with the actors. I read the book long before seeing the movie, but my original visions of them are marred by the film depictions now. Still, just looking at them reminds me of the heartache associated with Leslie's tragic end. Jess and Leslie's story was the first book to ever make me cry. If simply reading about death can evoke such powerful emotions, I can't imagine how hard losing the love of your life would be.

Some days Walter says he doesn't know how he survives without Rita.

Some days he tells me it's all he can do to exist.

Watching him through the shelves chatting with Beverly, it's obvious he's having one of his better days. Like anyone who suffers from anxiety, he has his ups and downs. One of his lowest was the afternoon I arrived to work and discovered the store's entrance bolted shut. After calling, texting, and disturbing more than a few of his neighbors, I tracked him to his upstairs apartment, still dressed in his plaid flannel pajamas, sitting in the center of his 'safe zone' on a cushion surrounded by a blanket fort. It was the day he confided to me about his wife Rita.

Rita's death had been his trigger. Of course, like many of us, he was a 'worrier' long before his official diagnosis, but her untimely demise, the result of being hit on the head by a random piece of construction scaffolding on the way to the market for eggs, was what ultimately sent Walter over the edge. When death arises from something so arbitrary as a loose piece of metal hitting the exact wrong spot on a skull, it's understandable that a person might move on from that experience assuming everything in life has the potential to kill. Now Walter spends his days agonizing over what indiscriminate nonentity is going to be the one to take his life.

Or mine.

The murmur of conversation at the front of the store lures me to them. They're standing beside one another now, their heads bowed conspiratorially over a behemoth volume of text I recognize as one of Walter's favorites, The Complete Works of William Shakespeare. I didn't know it was possible for a sixteen-year-old to be jealous of the chemistry oozing from two elderly people, but I find myself eyeing their intimacy with a great deal of envy. How I would love to share space with another person the way they are now—breathing the same air, aware of the other's heat.

To be so close.

Beverly places her hand on his wrist. "I was considering getting tickets to A Mid-Summer Night's Dream at The Public Theater in Central Park. Perhaps you'd like to join me?"

Without a beat of consideration, he replies to her in a most theatrical voice, "I'll met by moonlight, proud Titania."

She giggles, birdlike, which strikes me as odd, as it never occurred to me that an aged woman should have reason to giggle. But Walter has apparently charmed her in much the same way he charmed me.

In much the same way he probably charmed Rita forty-some years ago.

I let out a cough to warn them of my intrusion as I approach. "Found the book you're looking for," I say to

Beverly, holding it out. "This copy's in great shape. Not a single dog-eared page."

"Thanks, Phoebe." Walter takes the book from my hand and passes it to her. "This book is for her granddaughter."

"That's what I heard. And it also sounds like you've found someone who shares your enthusiasm for Shakespeare."

Beverly regards me with a bemused expression. "I've never thought to ask, but is Phoebe your granddaughter, Walter?"

He grins at me. "She wouldn't have me," he teases. "But no, my two grandsons live in Pittsburg. I'm just lucky this stand-in grandchild stumbled in here one day looking for a job."

"Looking for a book," I correct him.

"Like me," Beverly adds.

"Yeah. Exactly. And once you check in to Dust Jackets, you can't check out. You should post a warning on the door," I scold.

Their laughs harmonize with one another, and I see myself out of their conversation as they return to their arrangements for Shakespeare in the Park. From the supply closet, I listen to them setting a date for the proposed engagement, knowing all too well how easy it is for Walter to make plans from the protective confines of the store. It's encouraging that he's attempting to keep his end of our bargain by arranging this date with Beverly, but venturing into Central Park will be a huge undertaking for him. From now until the day arrives, I'll be the one convincing him it's safe to go into the world.

After Beverly leaves, I make my way to the front counter where Walter's already picking the side of his thumb raw.

"Shakespeare in the Park, huh?"

"I didn't know what to say." There's an unmistakable edge to his voice. "You heard her. She has her heart set on going with me, but if I tell her the truth about my... situation, she might stop coming by altogether."

"So, don't bail on her. Let's figure out a way to help you feel more comfortable about going out."

He closes the enormous volume of Shakespeare with a thud and stashes it beneath the register. "Fine. Why don't you tell me what's been going on out there? At least then I'll know what I'm up against."

I sigh, considering just how much information to give. Too much and he'll shut down on me. Not enough and he'll know I'm sugarcoating reality. It is New York City after all. "There was a Legionnaires' outbreak in Astoria last month. Nine people affected. Seven hospitalized. No deaths."

"Legionnaires' won't kill me. I can take some antibiotics. What else?"

"Uh, there were a bunch of fires set by an arsonist in Washington Heights, but I think they caught the guy a couple days ago."

"Okay. One less thing to worry about."

"Right. One less thing." I'm tempted to scroll through the Twitter feed on my phone for another nonissue when I remember last week's explosion. "You know about the steam pipe that burst in the East Village a few days ago, right?"

"No. Tell me."

Oh crap. Crap. Crap. Crap.

"It was really nothing. Not a big deal." My voice trails off. I know better than to go on.

But Walter's not buying what I'm selling. "Phoebe?"

"No one died."

He glares at me.

"Police shut down First Avenue. Cordoned off a few blocks." I tuck my chin. There's no way I can maintain eye contact with him. "There was some asbestos," I whisper.

"Asbestos?!"

"They cleaned it up."

"They cleaned it up? That's supposed to make me feel better? What about the hundreds of other steam pipes running under the streets? What happens when they start exploding, too? What happens when there's asbestos all over the city?"

"That's not gonna happen. It'll be fine. I'm sure people are monitoring the situation. And there probably aren't any pipes under Central Park anyway."

As this comes from my mouth, I'm struck by how sensible I sound. How easy it is for me to be rational about other people's phobias. When it comes to my own issues, however, I'm never able to take my own advice.

Walter takes off his glasses and rests his head in his hands. He's quiet for a long moment. "It's never easy, is it?"

"No. It's not."

"I'm gonna do it, though. I'm gonna leave this building."

What he needs right now, more than anything, is a reassuring pat on the back. I wish I could give him one, but of course, I can't. Instead, I give him my most supportive smile and tell him I believe.

CHAPTER 9

week two

I hear JP before I see him Thursday. Or more accurately, I hear his violin. Today's song is an aggressive contemporary, and I'm to the corner before I realize it's 2 Chainz *We Own It*. Hesitating at the bend, just out of sight, I consider both the anger he's channeling to play the piece with such conviction and the advantage I hold over him in this exact space and time. I know where he is, but he has absolutely no idea I'm standing only fifteen feet away eavesdropping on his soul. I could easily turn around, climb on the train, and go to work without him ever knowing I was there. If I wanted, I could simply avoid him for the rest of my life. It would be ridiculously easy.

But I told him I can't touch him, and he didn't walk away.

So, perhaps I shouldn't either.

I perform a quick scan for contaminants, noting what appears to be the remains of a homeless person's nest on the far side of the tracks. Although the hand sanitizer in my pocket is of little comfort where airborne germs are concerned—(if only Mom hadn't gotten rid of all my masks)—I take a step forward anyway, shoving down the heat rising from the pit of my stomach.

Once I turn the corner, he'll see me, and there'll be no turning back. Avoiding him isn't an option, though, as I clearly have some explaining to do.

Without permission from my nervous system, my feet take off on their own—dashing, instead of edging cautiously, around the turn. Luckily, I don't crash into anyone on the other side. Luckily, I don't crash into him.

I do attract his attention, however, and at the sight of me, he drops his bow and his composure.

"Officer Phoebe. You've returned."

"I have."

"Here to issue a citation?"

"Not today."

He's only standing about ten feet away, but we're practically yelling to one another over the thrum of the commute. Beyond him, several dozen passengers mill about the platform, some with noses buried in their phones, others deep in conversation. There are a pile of coins and a few bills in his case on the ground. Not for the first time, I wish I carried change.

"I actually owe you an explanation. From yesterday. It was rude of me not to shake your hand."

He takes three steps, closing the space between us. I could reach out and touch him if I wanted.

Do I want to?

"You don't owe me anything. It's fine. No big deal."

He's right, of course. I don't owe him a thing. He's a stranger, nothing more. The only person I'm truly accountable to is myself, and as such, I need to see this ridiculous experiment of Walter's through to the end so I can prove once and for all whether I'm still capable of letting people into my life.

It's not looking good. But, perseverance.

"No. It's just… I didn't mean be to be offensive or…"

I'm still fumbling over my words when he turns from me and walks over to his case. For a moment I think he's going to raise his bow and begin playing again, effectively ending our conversation. But he doesn't. Instead, he pockets the cash, packs his bow and violin into the case, and returns to me, a goofy grin plastered on his face.

"I've made just over thirty-six dollars today. More than enough for two coffees. You want one?"

His invitation takes me by surprise and while considering his offer, I can't help but notice the way his shoulders slump when I don't immediately respond. The idea of sitting across from a stranger drinking coffee in a crowded Starbucks makes my skin crawl. Everything about the request is petrifying. The potential for contamination is astronomical, what with the sheer number of people who patronize coffee shops on a daily basis, coughing and sneezing onto the sugar packs and cream dispensers. There's a reason I only eat food prepared at home and now this guy wants me to consume something made by a stranger?

In addition to the logistics of public ingestion, there's also Walter to consider. I can't not show up for work. He'll think I've fallen to my death into an open sewer grate.

"I want to it's just that I have work and…"

His face falls. He's not even trying to hide his disappointment. What's that about? Aren't guys supposed to be super chill about this stuff?

He says, "Yeah, I hear ya. Maybe another time," at the exact same moment I say, "I'll need to call my boss and let him know not to worry."

For a split second, I don't know why I've agreed to go with him, but then he smiles at me.

"Oh. Okay. He won't mind you being late?"

Not if I'm late because I'm letting someone into my life.

"Uh, no, he's cool. I just need to check in."

He heads toward the closest stairway, and I send Walter a quick text as I follow JP into the daylight. On the sidewalk, he slides in next to me so we're walking side by side. Every muscle in my body tenses beneath my skin. Together, we're taking up too much space, exponentially increasing my chances of bumping into someone as we head through the city.

"There's a place a couple blocks away I like," he says, oblivious to the war raging on inside of me. "It's super low-key. My band and I play there sometimes during open mic night."

Knowing the place we're headed isn't a Starbucks brings a modicum of relief. Still, germs know no boundaries. They don't care how low-key the joint is.

"What kind of band do you play in?"

His dimple returns at the mention of his group. I resist the urge to press my finger into it.

"It's like a folk-rock ensemble. Just a few of us from school. Percussion, bass, vocalist, and me on the violin."

A strange longing stirs inside of me—a desire to see him perform.

"Where do you go to school?" I ask.

"Talent Unlimited on 67th. It's a performing arts high school. What about you?"

This information propels us forward to number eight on my list—finding mutual interests. Maybe there's hope for this floundering exercise-in-futility after all.

"I go to the High School of Art and Design on 56th."

He turns to face me, intrigued. "No kidding. Do you play an instrument?"

I shake my head, mindful of his growing proximity. "No. I don't do the performance thing. I'm not big on crowds so I make pots."

He chuckles at this and suddenly his dimple isn't quite so endearing, especially if he's mocking my craft. But he goes on before I can express my indignation.

"For a second I thought you meant you were a dealer. Like a pot dealer. Because honestly, a lot of the kids at my school are. None of them would come right out and admit it to a stranger, though." He's cracking himself up now. "But you aren't talking about weed. You're talking about ceramics. Pot-ter-ry." He stops walking and doubles over to catch his breath. "I thought Officer Phoebe was turning out to be some sorta herbal shaman."

I don't want to laugh, but I can't help myself. I'm a lot of things but herbal shaman isn't one of them.

"Definitely not a dealer," I say, once he's composed himself enough to return to an upright position. "At school, they expose us to most of the artistic mediums. Except throwing clay on the wheel, of course, which just happens to be my favorite. I'm taking a pottery class at the Keechad Studio not far from here. I'm coming from there now." I show him my hands, palms up. "The clay never comes completely out of the cracks."

He glances at my hands and throws me another smirk. "So, it's not pot. It's crack. I knew it."

I laugh at him despite myself. He's charismatic and funny, and talking to him almost makes me forget who I am.

But then I notice a family heading toward us from the

opposite direction wearing NYC paraphernalia and overwhelmed expressions. Tourists always make me nervous, but encountering them so far from Midtown triggers a heightened sense of caution. I want to move out of their way, but JP has me boxed in. My only option is to come to a full stop and fall into step behind him while they pass.

Maybe he won't notice.

But of course, he does, and I don't realize he's paused to wait for me until it's too late.

I crash right into him.

My bare arm against his bare arm.

Skin against skin.

Our eyes meet. His brows furrow in confusion. He doesn't understand why I'm screaming. He doesn't understand why I pull out my hand sanitizer, douse my arm, and without a word of explanation hurry in the opposite direction back toward the station.

CHAPTER 10

week two

"You're home early," Mom says from the couch in the family room as I close the apartment door behind me. She's watching Dr. Phil, the man with all the answers. "Did Walter give you the afternoon off?"

"Not exactly." I have no intention of talking to her about what I know will go down in history as one of the most embarrassing days of my life.

Unfortunately, she hears the anguish in my voice and pounces like a hungry lioness. "Everything okay? Something you want to talk about?"

Nothing is okay. Nothing will ever be okay. I'm a disaster.

"No. I'm fine. Just had a rough trip home. I'm gonna take a quick shower before dinner if that's okay."

I duck into the bathroom before she has a chance to question me further, and after tossing my dirty t-shirt and shorts into the hamper, I step into the tub. The water hits the top of my head, raining down over my face, my neck, my torso and legs before flowing down the drain, carrying away the filth of the day, if not my humiliation.

I allow my tears to flow freely. In the whole world, the

shower is my one safe haven. The place where everything is clean and germ-free. Where, with soap in hand, it's safe to touch my own skin. I scrub the part of my arm where I brushed JP until it's angry and pink beneath the lather, a painful reminder of my lapse in judgment. I know better than to forget myself again.

When I'm finished and dressed in my robe, I pad across the hall to my bedroom, only to find Toby sitting at my desk. He looks up at me expectantly, knowing how I feel about him being in my room.

There was a time he was as welcome in my room as I was in his, like in the weeks following his return from the hospital after I infected him with Covid. As part of his continued post-discharge therapy, a nebulizer treatment was established as part of his bedtime routine. Dressed in his Avengers jammies, he'd rest flat on his stomach in bed as Mom attached a face mask over his nose and mouth, securing it around the back of his head with an elastic band. Every night he'd lay there, staring at the machine on the nightstand beside him, seemingly mesmerized by the pump's churning motor delivering life-saving medication directly into his bronchial tubes.

I couldn't stand the thought of him enduring the nightly treatments alone, so once Mom finished, I dragged the desk chair from my room beside his bed and read to him from his favorite series, Diary of a Wimpy Kid. Once he fell asleep, I'd watch his shoulders rise and fall, matching the rhythm of our breaths. Sometimes, when the tension in his fists released, I slipped my hand into his waiting palm, marveling at the strength of his reflexive grasp even as he slept. But mostly during the time we spent together in those uneasy first months, I just apologized. Over and over and over.

"I'm sorry I almost killed you," I'd whisper. "I didn't mean to, and I love you. From now on, I'm going to be more careful with my germs."

Every night I would ask for his forgiveness, and every day he would get a little better. Whatever I was doing was working, so I kept it up like his life depended on it.

Because it did.

"Mom said you were sad." Toby sounds sheepish like he already knows I won't buy his explanation for being in my room. "I'm here to help you feel better."

I want to be mad at him for invading my personal space without asking. I want to explain how I don't take precautionary measures against the spread of germs in my room so it's not nearly as safe for him to be here as it is in the rest of the house. But I know how stupid my rationalization will sound to him. Like the rantings of a lunatic.

Instead, I say, "I'm almost finished with your surprise. The project I've been working on in pottery class. You can't have it until the end of the summer, though, after the art show."

He rocks back on my chair, balancing on two legs. "Okay," he says. "I'll wait." He pauses then, studying my face from across the room. "Are you coming to my race this weekend? I mean, I totally get if you don't wanna, but I built in a turbo throttle for the straightaways, and it's gonna be epic."

The annual drone race is held in the massive open space behind the Liberty Science Center here in Jersey City. Thousands of spectators, flock to the event every year, and although most won't admit it, I think the main draw is the possibility of glimpsing a crash as the drones speed around the course. Like Nascar and hockey, people are captivated by carnage.

Toby and I went as spectators last year. I only agreed to go because Dad promised there would be plenty of room to spread out, away from the crowds.

But he was super wrong.

Instead, we were corralled into viewing areas like cattle off to the slaughter. Bodies pressed against one another, slick with bacteria-harboring sweat. I ended up having a full-blown panic attack and spent the better part of two hours in the medic tent before Mom finally took me home. Before my run-in today, I'd considered going as far as the parking lot to support him, but now…

"I heard the science center is doing a live feed on their website. Thought maybe I'd stay here and record your race for you on my computer. That way it'll be archived, and you can use it to make improvements for your next race. I'll still be watching, and you can call me before and after."

His face is inscrutable. Is he offended? Pissed? Apathetic? "You're assuming I'm gonna need to make improvements." He deadpans, leveling a glare at me before releasing a disappointed sigh. "I didn't figure you'd come after that freak out last year." He shrugs. "Just promise you'll record all my heats."

"I will. I won't let you down."

As I say them, the words feel hollow in my mouth. I'm already letting him down by not going along in person to cheer him on. I'm letting him down by allowing my anxiety to control my life.

"You wanna hear something even more embarrassing than when I hyperventilated at the race?" I ask laying across my bed. He nods, so I continue. "I met this guy yesterday, and I was walking with him to get some coffee this afternoon. I accidentally bumped into him and started screaming like a baby right in the middle of the sidewalk."

Accustomed to by outlandish behavior, Toby merely raises an eyebrow, unfazed by the ridiculousness of my admission. "What'd the guy do?"

"Just stood there looking at me like I'd lost my mind. I think he said something. Maybe tried to calm me down, but I just ran."

He lowers my chair to the floor and turns to face me with an expression far too serious for any nine-year-old. "You should try again."

"Getting bumped into?"

"No. Go out for coffee with the guy." His childhood naivety is enviable.

"Toby, he's never going to want to talk to me again. It had to have been incredibly embarrassing for him to be next to me while I was having the attack. You know how humiliating I can be."

He grins. "I still like hanging out with you, even if you are a weirdo."

I cast off his deflection with a roll of my eyes. "Only because you don't have a choice. Mom and Dad force you to put up with me."

In one swift motion, he stands from my desk and heads toward the door. At the threshold, he turns to me. "I don't like you because Mom and Dad make me. I like you because you're nice to me and don't get annoyed like everyone else when I can't keep up because of my lungs. And also, it's funny when you do stupid stuff. You make me laugh, and I'm actually really glad you're my sister, Phoebe."

CHAPTER 11
week three

After briefly reconsidering, I don't go to the drone race. Instead, I stay home where it's safe. From the sheltered confines of my bedroom, I watch virtually from my laptop as the kid whose brush with death triggered my anxiety has a blast racing his drone like a boss—far more concerned about a tournament-ending crash than contracting any contagious diseases.

Happily, Toby's plane survives all six heats, placing him third overall for the under-eighteen-category. Ranking in the top three earns him an invitation to a regional tournament in the fall, and the joy of this announcement is written all over his face. Tears pool at the corners of my eyes as I watch him climb the podium on the live feed, and I have to admit seeing him on the screen isn't nearly as fulfilling as being there would've been. I rub at my eyes, pretending the tears are solely brought on by the pride of his accomplishment. Secretly, I know my own melancholy has something to do with them as well.

Life with an anxiety disorder is a daily choice between being beaten by a dirty rock or a rusty hammer. Every decision I make forces me to choose between fear of the unknown and abject disappointment. Too bad, regardless of the situation, both options always suck. Because when you're a germy kid with a chronically sick brother, you have no choice but to isolate yourself from the person you love the most for the sake of his health.

I came to realize this not long after Toby's nebulizer treatments began. In addition to the familiar whooshing of the machine and Toby's shallow breathing, there was no mistaking the sound of my parents lingering just outside the door every night. Dad began enticing me out of Toby's room, saying my brother needed his rest and shouldn't be disturbed, but nothing could lure me away from my self-imposed penance. It was my fault he was tethered to the machine every night. It was my fault he was broken.

The nebulizer and I were the only ones who could make him better.

"Breathe in. Breathe out. Breathe in. Breathe out," I told him. "And everything will be just fine."

And everything was fine… until it wasn't.

"You shouldn't go in with him tonight, Phoebe," Dad said one evening, blocking me at Toby's bedroom door. "You've had a runny nose all day and…"

"And it's probably just allergies," Mom interrupted, stepping out of the bathroom behind Toby, still wrapped in his Superman towel. "She hasn't left the apartment in a month."

The passing look between them made me worried someone was going to cry.

Dad's lips pursed into a tight line. "Or," he said, "she might be contagious with something, in which case I think it would be prudent of us to keep them apart." He cut his eyes down the hall, a nonverbal request for me to move along. "Especially since the CDC just announced it's possible to contract the virus a second time."

Over my shoulder, I saw Mom and Toby watching after me wearing identical frowns.

That was the moment I realized just because I wanted to hang out with Toby didn't mean I should, and my life of no-win decisions began.

After pottery class on Monday, I'm faced with one of those lose-lose situations. My two options for getting to work via subway are the Vomit Line or the JP Line. Choosing between possible contamination and probable humiliation is tough, but in the end, I force myself past the long-since-removed puke area onto the 6.

In the absence of any resulting stomach pain or nausea, I make the same decision and choose the 6 again Tuesday afternoon.

By Wednesday, however, I can't keep Toby's encouraging words from replaying over and over again in my head. Is it possible JP might actually be interested in getting to know me, even after my 96th Street meltdown?

In a rare burst of self-confidence, I decide I owe it to myself to find out, so instead of descending into the Lexington Avenue station for the third day in a row, I huff the two blocks down to Second Avenue.

Unexpectedly, JP isn't playing in his usual spot out of sight beyond the bend. He's standing directly at the base of the steps like he's waiting on something. Today's musical selection is heavy and foreboding, probably penned by some Russian composer obsessed with minor keys. Linking these two unrelated pieces of information together, a more optimistic person might deduce JP's upset I haven't been by.

But I am less-than-optimistic and recognize this interpretation as nothing more than wishful thinking.

I take a deep breath of above-ground air before descending the steps into the station. On the way down, I remember Toby's words about liking me because I'm funny, so I decide to diffuse this potentially awkward situation with JP by making him laugh. Retreating into my comfort zone and hiding behind humor feels like a bit of a cop-out, but I've already made a fool of myself in front of him so whatever I do now can't possibly make his opinion of me worse.

At least that's what I'm hoping.

On the third step from the bottom, I cry out, "Freeze, JP. You're under arrest for playing depressing music without a license."

I'm acutely aware of the way the air's burning my lungs while I wait for him to acknowledge me standing above him. He's either going to be happy to see me or he isn't.

Please God let him not call me out for being a psycho.

He turns toward me, adjusting his cheek against the violin's chinrest and meets my gaze. The lines of his face soften as relief spreads across it. "Phoebe?"

"Hey," I reply.

Instantly, he's by my side. "I'm so sorry about the other day. I felt awful. I don't know what happened. I didn't realize I hurt you. But I've been worried sick, wondering if you're okay."

I stare at him.

He's.

Apologizing.

To.

Me.

"You were just there, and then you weren't, and I didn't know whether to come after you, so I didn't. But then once you were gone, I realized I didn't have any way to find you. When you didn't come by Monday, I started freaking out. And yesterday... I'm just..." He pauses then to catch his breath and to look at me with his rich, soulful eyes. "I'm just so sorry I upset you."

In the five days since I last saw him it never once occurred to me that he might be worried. It didn't dawn on me he'd feel anything but embarrassment at my behavior.

"It's... okay," I stammer. "I didn't realize you'd be concerned, and so I'm sorry, too." I notice a distinct lack of funds in his case. I guess Russian composers don't bring in the cash like 2 Chainz. "You have time for that coffee? On me this time?"

CHAPTER 12
week three

On the way to the coffeehouse, I send a quick text to Walter, letting him know I'll probably be late and not to worry. Then, as an explanation for my rude behavior, I confess to JP about my anxiety.

"The reason I don't touch people or objects is that I'm wildly germophobic. I've been in therapy for a couple years, but I'm still…" My voice drops off as I consider a suitable adjective to describe myself. Broken? Sick? Struggling? "Anyway, when we bumped into each other the other day, the physical contact set me off. I reacted poorly, and I'm sorry for running off like that. Believe it or not, I'm actually a lot better than I used to be even though I'm no longer seeing a therapist," I add. "At least not a licensed one."

He raises an eyebrow. "You think it's safe to trust your mental health to someone who's not a professional? I mean, you've seen those shows, right? The ones where people go to Tijuana or somewhere to get lip injections, and they end up getting shot full of concrete."

This makes me laugh aloud, and I wonder if his sense of humor is what's putting me at ease, allowing me to feel safe enough to open up. "My shrink stand-in is right here in the city. He's my boss, actually. The guy who owns the bookstore where I work."

"And he's qualified to give you medical advice because...?"

I throw some side-eye in JP's direction. Of course, I'm defensive of my best friend but also curious about why JP would even care about Walter's credentials. This curiosity is probably what compels me to continue explaining. "Because he suffers from anxiety, too. His is more generalized than mine. Where my anxiety centers around germs and the fear of contamination, Walter's afraid of lots of stuff."

We come to a red light, and he adjusts his violin case strap across his chest. I'm still staring at the space below his collarbone, wishing it was made of clay when he asks, "What kind of stuff?"

The tone of his voice suggests genuine interest, and I continue prattling on as the walk sign illuminates. "Pretty much anything he thinks could take his life. His wife was killed by a rogue piece of scaffolding, so in Walter's head, everything's a possible threat."

"That's horrible."

I nod in agreement. "He misses her a lot. But recently, this woman named Beverly has been coming into the store a lot. She and Walter really hit it off."

"Nice."

"Yeah, except now she's invited him to go to Shakespeare in the Park with her this weekend. He agreed like it was no big deal, but I'm the one left trying to convince him he's not going to die if he leaves the building."

JP intentionally blocks someone coming out of a building, allowing me to pass by unobstructed. "Wow. That's intense."

It occurs to me as I'm divulging all of Walter's personal heartache like I'm some sort of Lifetime television special, I might be doing it on purpose to avoid having to talk about myself. Because if I don't tell him any of my dirty little secrets, maybe he won't run away. Maybe he might stick around.

I keep going anyway. "Yeah. Well. His technical DSM-5 diagnosis is 300.21—Panic Disorder with Agoraphobia. And it's definitely difficult for him."

"So, what's your diagnosis? Officially?" he asks.

My stomach lurches as the panic of full-disclosure sets in. It's almost surreal, talking to someone besides my family or a physician about all of this. Discussing my anxiety is not on my fear ladder, but no one besides Walter has ever cared enough to ask about my diagnosis, and JP's curiosity seems sincere.

Am I actually doing this?

"300.29—Specific Phobia under the Anxiety Disorder heading."

"That's it?" His voice sounds disappointed.

"Pretty much. My whole life centers around relieving my anxiety. Focusing on the easiest way to avoid putting myself into germy situations. It's the reason I haven't touched anyone in almost two years. Anyway, that's why my freak out in the street on Friday wasn't your fault. Freak out is my default setting," I tell him as he opens the café door for me.

"You're telling me you haven't touched anyone since the pandemic?"

I'm relieved to see only a handful of customers scattered about and fall into line beside him. "Not on purpose. Bumping into you last week was the first time in well over a year."

He grins at me, full lips and dimples. "So, I'm part of an elite club."

"You're not getting a membership card," I tell him, inching forward toward the register, unconsciously flipping the lid of my hand sanitizer open and close in my hand. "I'd honestly prefer if there weren't any members at all."

His eyes narrow, as if squinting will somehow help him make sense of me. "How do you feel about what we're doing now—eating in a public place with germy people all around?"

"I dunno. I haven't eaten in a restaurant since before the first Covid lockdown."

His mouth drops open like a Warner Brothers cartoon character. "No McDonald's?"

I shake my head.

"No Slurpees from 7-Eleven?"

"Oh God, no."

"But you're here having coffee with me." He looks more than a little smug. "Why?"

The person in front of us approaches the register, and although JP steps forward, I stay right where I am, relishing the extra space between us. Part of me wants to lie to him. The other part wants to tell him the truth. "I'm hoping maybe you'll be willing to help with my latest therapy?"

He swallows, clearly searching for a suitable response. "If I can't have a membership card for bumping into you, will I at least get a therapy assistant certificate if I choose to participate?"

Without waiting for me to respond, he steps up to the counter and orders a medium black coffee. Then he shifts to the left for the barista to take my order. Too bad I've never purchased a cup of coffee in my life. There are three dozen choices on the wall in front of me. Cappuccino. Iced sugar-free vanilla latte. Chai tea. Caramel macchiato. I have no idea what to pick.

Sensing my discomfort, JP speaks up on my behalf. "She'll take a medium iced mocha Frappuccino. And if we could get two extra cups to go with it please, that'd be great." To me, he says, "Don't worry. My mom loves these things. You will, too." Before I can react, he pulls a wad of cash from his front pocket and plops it on the counter, counting aloud as he goes. "Ten dollars and thirty-seven cents." He hands the change to the cashier.

"I was supposed to be taking you for coffee, remember?"

"No way. When I invited you last week we never made it. This first one's on me."

I roll all the implications of the word first over in my head. Of course, the first of anything infers there'll be a second, and the idea of going out for coffee with JP a second time is not completely horrifying.

Unfortunately, before I have a chance to split the bill with him, a horde of stroller-wielding moms and cranky toddlers tumble into the café. Serenity eradicated, the coffeehouse erupts into chaos as I glance at JP, who has taken the receipt and is causally pulling napkins out of a nearby dispenser, none the wiser to my sudden spike of adrenalin.

"I can't stay here," I tell him over the children's laughter.

He looks up from his stack of napkins to survey the scene. Over a dozen women have already set about rearranging tables while their progeny run manically around the café, spewing germs in every direction. A look of understanding crosses his face. "What do you want to do?"

I scan the room. What I want to do and what I need to do are two entirely different things. "I need to leave. Can you come with me?"

Something crosses his face. It's not quite annoyance. More like resignation. "I'll get the drinks, and you can wait for me outside. Then we'll figure something out."

Months of avoidance training allow me to deftly maneuver my way between tables, around children, and past the stroller brigade, making it to the exit in record time despite the trembling in my arms and legs. I kick the door open with my foot and rush onto the sidewalk. Instead of stopping, however, adrenalin takes over, and I'm halfway down the block, almost to the next traffic light when I hear JP calling from behind.

"Phoebe! Wait!"

I slow my pace, forcing my muscles to relax. As the fear of contamination subsides, embarrassment takes its place. The last thing I wanted was to cause another scene, but there was no way I could handle being around so many children in such a confined space. If nothing else, I know my limits.

Doubled over, tears pricking my eyes, I can't imagine why JP is wasting his time coming after me. Clearly, I'm a lost cause, incapable of a simple outing. Seemingly undeterred, however, JP's sneakers pound the pavement behind me, and a moment later, I hear his ragged breathing by my side.

"For Christ's sake, Phoebe." He pants. "Why didn't you just wait outside by the door? Are you running away?"

Am I running away?

I keep my chin lowered knowing my eyes will betray me. I don't want him to see how scared I am. I don't want him to see how much I hate myself.

But I also don't want him to leave which is why, eventually, I'm forced to meet his gaze.

Beside me, sweat trickles down his face and is pooling unattractively under his armpits. His violin case is slung over his shoulder, and he's balancing a paper tray of coffees in his right hand and a pile of napkins and straws in his left. I open my mouth to speak, but nothing comes out. No apology seems adequate enough.

"This obviously isn't easy for you, and I wanna get this right, Phoebe, but you gotta at least meet me halfway. I want to help. To understand. But you can't keep running away." His brow furrows. Is he being sincere? "I know a secluded place we can sit to drink these not far from here, back toward the subway station. No people. No germs. I promise. But you gotta try to pull yourself together, okay?"

The light changes and bodies swarm around us. A moment later it's just the two of us left standing on the corner. I've steadied my breathing but worry the lingering tremor in my voice will give me away so I remain silent. I really am trying to dial it down.

He shakes his head in an attempt to cover his frustration. "Look, I got extra cups so we can slip this cup with your coffee inside into another cup no one has touched. Plus, I grabbed a handful of straws and they're all in wrappers—perfectly sterile." There's a hint of dimple playing at the corner of his mouth. "And if it makes you feel better, I'll even douse myself in your Purell, okay?"

I don't know why he's trying so hard, but the way he's making me feel inside—like I'm someone worth trying for—makes me suddenly glad that he is. "Okay. Take us to your park."

CHAPTER 13
week three

JP leads us to a tree-shaded park on the corner of Third and 99th, and after slathering himself in copious amounts of sanitizer, instructs me to pull one of the extra cups from inside the other to use as a protective sleeve over the Frappuccino cup the barista touched. Then he selects a straw and tears off the bottom half of the wrapper before slipping it into my drink. Once in place, he pulls the top half off to reveal the germ-free straw.

"See. There you go. Perfectly sterile. No one touched the cup or the coffee. And there's no one else here at the park, so we've eliminated every possible threat of contamination from the situation. Now we can get down to business."

"Which is what?" I ask, taking a tentative sip thru the straw.

"Your therapy, of course. And we better get started because I'm charging by the minute." I laugh, wondering just what I've gotten myself into as he continues. "So, tell me about this new treatment plan prescribed by your therapist/not-therapist Walter. Does it have you confronting your fears?"

"Not exactly," I tell him. "I've done plenty of exposure therapy in the past. The actual goal now is to allow people into my life again. Because when you're afraid of getting too close physically…"

"It's hard to get close emotionally," he finishes for me. "That makes a lot of sense." He pauses, considering me. "How am I doing so far?"

There's a playfulness to his voice implying the question is rhetorical. I take another sip of coffee, which is good—way better than the stuff Mom makes at home, even with the vanilla creamer. I close my eyes, 'sitting in the moment,' forcing myself to be present and to acknowledge how I feel about JP and the experience—both in and out of my anxiety.

How I feel is surprisingly okay. So okay, in fact, I'm almost temped to opening up to him about everything. But something holds me back.

"Why are you here?" I ask.

He looks taken aback. "My parents immigrated from Ecuador before I was born."

I almost choke on my coffee, coughing and sputtering as I laugh down a sip. "No, not here in the country. Here in the park. Hanging out with me. It doesn't make any sense. I'm a total mess. There's no reason you haven't bolted already."

JP leans back on the bench, settling in like a three-year-old at story time. He's sitting far enough away as to not be threatening, but the intensity of his gaze still has me feeling slightly unnerved—in a surprisingly good way. "The first time I saw you in the tunnels, you reminded me of my brother."

Now I'm the one who's taken aback. "Your brother is a teenage girl?"

He smiles sadly, setting his cup on the ground. "No. My brother was lonely, too."

A mouthful of Frappuccino nearly lodges itself in my throat. "Was?"

"My little brother, Andre, was born with a heart condition. He spent his childhood in and out of hospitals. Had seventeen surgeries before his fifth birthday. Kindergarten came and went. First grade. Second grade. He never got to go to school. Never got to go outside and play on the playground the way I did. He was pretty much housebound until his heart finally gave out for good when he was eight."

Memories of Toby's premature birth and Covid battle come rushing back, including the times he nearly died. I think of him now, unable to run and play with the other kids because of his damaged lungs. The damage he sustained because of me.

"I'm so sorry," I say, searching for the words to make it better. "Were you close?"

JP coughs, composing himself. "He played the viola. I played the violin. Mom wanted to make sure we had something we could do together." He picks at a callus on his finger before going on. "There's also my name. JP is actually short for Juan Pablo. Living in the states, my mom wanted to make sure I retained something of her Ecuadorian heritage, but when my brother Andre was born, Juan Pablo was too hard for him to say. He's the one who started calling me JP." He looks up from his hands to a bird flying overhead and watches it until it disappears over a nearby rooftop. "Anyway, that's why I haven't given up on you. You're lonely like Andre was. I knew the moment I saw you I needed to help."

There's an awkward silence, both of us ruminating on his confession. A group of elementary schoolers has descended on the nearby play equipment, and it occurs to me I hadn't even noticed. I search for the nervous urge to get away, but it's small and buried beneath an unusual sense of peace.

"So, now that you know why I'm here, you need to tell me why you picked a stranger instead of someone you already know for this assignment," JP says, breaking me from my introspection. "Wouldn't that have been easier?"

It's a valid question—one I hadn't even considered. There'd been no need.

"Both the neighborhood kids and my school friends wrote me off pretty quickly once life finally got back to normal after the pandemic. My aversion to them made me a pariah, and to be honest, I didn't care. They were gross and germy, and if they avoided me it meant I didn't have to work so hard to avoid them."

"Harsh."

I shrug. "Truth."

He nods in agreement. "So, if Covid caused your anxiety, but now there's a vaccine, why are you still germaphobic? Is your mom one of those anti-vaxxers or something?"

My mom is a lot of things, but anti-science isn't one of them. "No. She took me to get my vaccine the day I was eligible, and I was so excited I couldn't sleep the night before. I figured one shot in the arm and my anxiety was just going to—poof!—go away. And it did. For like a minute. But then, I realized there could be some new Covid mutation no one knew about or even worse, another more deadly virus lurking on the horizon. So, I kept maintaining the three Ws…"

"Wear. Watch. Wash," we say in unison.

I laugh. "Yeah. Exactly. And the weirdest thing is, since Covid's airborne, I never thought touching would be my biggest hang-up. It doesn't even make sense." I shrug, realizing how ridiculous I sound. "But I guess that's the thing about phobias… you don't control them. They control you."

"Okay. I get that. But you can't seriously be telling me you have no friends." Concern pulls at the corner of his eyes. It almost makes me want to lie to avoid having to witness his disappointment as well. But I don't.

I shift uncomfortably on the bench. He should know what he's getting into. "When I started at HSAD freshman year, I didn't try to hide my anxiety from people. But I didn't try to explain it either which was probably my first mistake. In ninth grade, I overheard this kid telling a bunch of other kids in English class I was a snob. After that, most people probably just assumed I kept to myself because I was stuck up. When someone eventually did invite me to sit with them at lunch, they acted like I was this cool pet they could show off to their friends. Like 'Oh, have you met Phoebe? She doesn't touch anyone cuz she's scared of catching germs. Isn't she so interesting?' Once the novelty wore off, though, and they realized how boring it was to have a person around who couldn't go anywhere or do anything, they moved on pretty quickly."

"That's awful." JP's voice is thick with sympathy.

"Is it? I mean, can you blame them? Would you be here if I'd refused to go out for coffee?"

He flinches so slightly, it's almost imperceptible, but I notice and so does he. His nose scrunches, trying to find the right words to say. The perfect explanation for why he's different from everyone else.

Even if he's not.

Letting him off the hook I say, "It's okay. I understand now that if I want to get off the isolation train, I'm gonna need to meet people halfway. I'm gonna have to do better."

He leans toward me. I can smell the coffee on his breath

and the musky scent of perspiration. My gut tells me to slide away. He's far too close for comfort, but it's almost as if he's somehow able to see past my anxiety, so I stay right where I am. The way he's looking at me now, it feels almost as if I'm the only thing he can see.

"So out of all the strangers in Manhattan, why'd you choose me?" A nervous smile plays at his lips.

A lock of hair falls across his forehead and if I was someone else, I'd be inclined to reach out and touch it. It appears soft but could be coarse. It's been so long since my fingers brushed through anyone's hair but my own, my judgment on such things can no longer be trusted. He's watching me now with such intensity, waiting for his answer. I tell him the only reason I'm prepared to give.

"It was your playing. Your music. The first time I heard you it was as if the melody was speaking to me, calling for me to find myself inside the notes. It sounded sad and hopeful at the same time."

"Kinda like you."

Am I that transparent? "Sorta," I say.

He turns from me, plucks his case off the ground, and takes out his violin. His head falls, his chin resting upon the instrument as if it was born to lie there. As if his neck prefers being crooked instead of straight. Without a word, he wets his lips, raises the bow to the strings, and begins playing the song from the first day. Although he's not looking directly at me, I'm relieved when his eyes close and I'm no longer bound to the invisible line tethering us to one another. My mind wanders as the melody rises and falls, the melancholy giving way to a less somber tone. How strange it is to be sitting here beside this amazingly talented musician.

The piece ends, and JP regards me in obvious anticipation

of my reaction.

"That was the song. The one from the first day."

"The one that spoke to you."

It's embarrassing to hear him repeat my own words back to me. I sound ridiculous.

"Yeah. It's really pretty. What's it called?"

He tucks his bow and violin back into the case. "Believe it or not it's from an anime series, Final Fantasy. It's called Sad Romance. I played it with my band for our performance final exam last year. Earned me an 'A' and a spot in the senior showcase for this year."

"I bet it was amazing," I say, considering how it would sound accompanied by the harmonies of other instruments.

"It was." He's looking at me again, the weight of a thousand questions behind his stare. "I was thinking, you should come hear us play sometime, as long as you're looking to let people into your life and all. Everyone in the band is awesome. I know they'd love to meet you."

An invitation is the last thing I was expecting from this tentative spark of friendship between us. A chat now and then in the subway terminal? Sure. Grabbing another cup of coffee? Perhaps. But a request to attend a performance and to meet other people?

Definitely not on my radar.

The tightly wound ball of anxiety buried beneath the familiarity of our conversation awakens from its slumber, igniting a painful fire in the pit of my stomach. I don't go out. I don't meet other people's friends. Those things aren't safe.

I'm still trying to figure out how to say no when my phone jingles on my lap. The screen illuminates to reveal a text from Walter. It's getting late. When am I coming in?

"Your boss?" JP asks.

I fumble to unlock the home screen as I stand. "Yeah. I'm super late. Probably should be heading out." Beside me, I can feel his heat. And also, his anticipation.

"You'll come, though, right? To see us play?" He keeps going, not waiting for me to respond as I make a break for the sidewalk. "Our next gig is this weekend, Saturday night, nine o'clock at Club 73. It's a super small place, and I bet the owner would let you sit offstage so you wouldn't need to be near anyone. I could meet you before. Maybe at the 72nd Street station around eight?"

My head is already conjuring up visions of a seedy dive bar a la Law & Order: Special Victims Unit. Dank and dark with bodily fluids everywhere.

I wrack my brain for an excuse. Homework is out, and I already told him I have no other friends. Maybe a family obligation?

"Come on, Phoebes, just say yes."

The last person to call me Phoebes was my friend, Kara, circa middle school. My heart pounds through my chest. I cannot commit to this, regardless of what he calls me. "Eight o'clock at the 72nd Street station?"

He nods. "I'll help you steer clear of any germs, okay?"

In my pocket, my phone vibrates again. Another text from Walter, I assume. I have to make a decision now. "I'll be there."

CHAPTER 14
week three

Mom lays the pizza box in the center of the table, and I take the first two slices before anyone else can move. There's nothing I hate more than communal food. Toby grabs a slice for himself while Dad takes drink orders.

"And don't forget, you two are on your own Saturday night. Dad and I have dinner reservations for our anniversary."

I stare at her, dumbfounded. Could she not have mentioned this earlier? Say, before I needed the excuse of a family obligation this afternoon. I suppress a groan, wondering if this is the universe's way of telling me I shouldn't venture into the world with JP. It would be easy to let him know about the change of plans if I see him tomorrow.

Or I could go to the club anyway.

"I can't stay with Toby," I blurt out, knife and fork in hand, poised to take a bite.

Mom looks like she's been struck. "Why not?"

"I have plans."

"Plans?" Even Dad's interest is piqued now.

"Yeah. Plans," I say through a mouthful of pizza in an attempt to sound as nonchalant as possible.

Mom continues her interrogation without missing a beat. "What kind of plans? Seems unusual for Walter to have you working late on a weekend."

Blaming Walter and work for my evening tryst would be one option. But who am I kidding? They're not stupid enough to believe Dust Jackets attracts a hip late-night crowd.

"I'm not working. I've been invited to go out with some friends."

Around me, my family falls silent. They stop chewing. They stop breathing.

"What friends?" Mom eventually asks.

If any other mother asked any other daughter this question in any other family it would retain a flippant connotation. But in my family, it's a perfectly reasonable question.

"It's actually only one friend, but he invited me to watch his band play, and I said yes."

Mom is incredulous. "Saturday night?" I nod, and she continues. "Okay, so out of nowhere you've been invited by some musician to hear his band play Saturday night at a yet undisclosed location, and I'm supposed to be okay with this? Where'd you even meet this guy? School or pottery class or the bookstore?"

My night on the town is meeting with far more resistance than I anticipated. They've been begging me to make friends and go out for months. Spent thousands on therapy in the hopes that someday I'd be fixed and could live the life of an ordinary girl. I thought they'd be thrilled by the prospect of me dipping my toes into the pool of normal teenage life.

"I met him in the subway."

Mom winces. "The subway? As in *the subway*?"

"Yeah. He's a street musician. Plays the violin and goes to Talent Unlimited," I tell her matter-of-factly as if just thinking him doesn't make me feel all gooey inside. As if I'm not already thinking about the next time we'll be together. Assuming I'm not going to be put under some sort of arbitrary house arrest, and there'll be a next time.

Dad sets his slice of pizza on his plate and regards me with narrowed eyes and a curious expression. "Wait a minute. Does this recent desire to go out on a Saturday night with your peers have something to do with the new treatment Walter prescribed last week?"

The tone of his voice suggests his line of questioning may lure me into a trap, but after seeing the resolve on Mom's face, I take the bait. "Yes?"

He shrugs as if the matter is officially settled. "Then you should go. This is a big deal, Phoebe. Finally, a treatment that might actually work."

The strange part of being human is the capacity to feel a dozen conflicting emotions all at the same time. Dad's permission jostles several to the surface, not the least of which is fear over having to go through with my decision to meet JP Saturday night. Now that I've put it out there, he'll expect me to go. I'm balancing the stress of this endeavor with latent-longings of my heart.

Because for the first time in years, someone wants to be my friend, and I'm ready to accept the challenge.

"Okay, so then it's settled. I'm meeting the violinist, JP, at the 72nd Street station, and he's walking me to the venue, a small club about a block away. He said he's gonna get me a seat offstage so I don't need to be in the crowd. He's an amazing musician, and I'm excited to hear him perform." I say all of this as unemotionally as possible, hoping some additional details will help put my mom at ease. What I don't expect is to set off Toby instead.

With a most uncharacteristic burst of anger, he shoves his chair away from the table, almost knocking it backwards onto the floor. After throwing a venomous glare in my direction, he takes off for his room, slamming the door behind him.

I turn wide-eyed to my parents, looking for an explanation. I don't know what in the world I've done.

Mom takes a sip of water, washing down a bite of pizza with a shrug. "You'll go out with a stranger but not your own family. How's that supposed to make him feel, Phoebe?" Her spot-on assessment of the situation slaps me across the face, causing me to wince, but if she sees my pained expression, she chooses to ignore it and continues. "I mean, he's gotta be asking himself why now? Why this guy instead of him?"

In response to the question, I'm overtaken by memories of JP's music and the way it made me feel connected to something outside myself. About his smile and how he looks at me as if I'm whole. The way I forget to be afraid when I'm around him.

But I cannot say any of this aloud.

Instead, I excuse myself from the table and head down the hall to Toby's room, giving a gentle knock on the door.

"Go away," says the muffled voice of someone whose head is buried beneath a pillow.

"Toby, let me in. We need to talk."

"No."

"Please, Toby. Just open the door."

There's a long, contemplative pause. "Open it yourself if you want to come in."

This is not the response I'm expecting. Everyone knows I

don't touch doorknobs. Ever.

"Tobyyyyyy," I whine, pathetically.

"Come in or don't. It's up to you."

I let out a heavy sigh. Who knew the chaos of letting someone into my life was going to extend so far? JP and his friends were expected. But my family? Not so much. Still, my brother's doorknob likely harbors far fewer contaminants than anything I'll come in contact with at the club Saturday night. Probably best to get it over with now. Just pull off the Band-aid with one swift tug.

Beneath my hand, the knob is cool and smooth as I turn it, and I push the door open to reveal Toby's darkening room. I can almost feel the microorganisms transferring themselves onto my skin. But the damage is done now. I'll deal with them later.

As expected, he's sprawled across his bed with his head tucked angrily beneath his pillow. At the sound of the door hinges creaking, however, he pops straight up. "You touched the knob."

"I touched the knob." I demonstrate with a few twists of my wrist.

I have his full attention now, and he's gaping at me. "I can't believe you did it."

Although I'm mindful, as I release the handle, of keeping my hand from touching other parts of my body until I'm able to wash, I allow myself to bask in the warmth of Toby's approval. Unlike the burden of shame, which is exhausting to lug around day in and day out, pride feels virtually weightless. How has this been lost on me?

I cross the room to sit beside him at the foot of his bed. "I'm sorry I hurt your feelings," I begin, not knowing exactly what to say to help him understand. "The thing is, even though I'm the only one in our family with anxiety, I'm not the only one affected and I'm tired of having such a negative influence on your life." I hesitate, remembering the first time I nearly killed him. "Did you know before Mom got the Prius she used to drive a Mini Cooper?"

"No." He shakes his head. "What happened to it?"

"I crashed it. Well, Mom crashed it. But it was my fault."

He leans forward. "Was I there?"

"Yeah. But you were a baby. And you were tired. Overdue for a nap. You were super fussy, and I tried to calm you down by playing peek-a-boo and singing songs but nothing worked. You were inconsolable."

"What did Mom do?"

"She wanted me to find your pacifier…"

Years before stupid Covid was even a thing, Toby's premature birth left me acutely aware of germs and their potentially fatal consequences. I knew the flu could kill him. RSV could kill him. Even a simple fungal infection could be the thing to end his life.

On this particular day, I'd located his blue pacifier with the teddy bear handle on the floor beneath the driver's seat before Mom even asked. If I unbuckled I could reach it. But I didn't.

"Phoebe?" My eyes met Mom's in the rearview mirror. Hers were pleading. "Look around, and see if you can find his binky," she instructed from the front seat as she merged into traffic. "I can't concentrate with all the screaming, and it might help him fall asleep."

Toby wailed, overcome by exhaustion and frustration. If babies could glare, he was glaring at me. I picked out a board book from the box of toys between us and began to read.

"Once upon a time, there was a turtle who didn't have a shell…"

Toby bawled even harder, lip quivering, tears streaming down his face.

"Phoebe, I'm not kidding. Traffic's terrible. There's no place to pull over. And I can't concentrate with the noise. Please just find his stupid pacifier."

A quick glance at the floor revealed it had rolled toward the center of the car. All I had to do was reach down and grab it. It was right there.

Ignoring the pounding in my chest, I folded myself in half, straining against my seatbelt. Toby let out a howl, and for an instant, I almost forgot about the germs. Except I didn't. I couldn't. There was no way I could touch something he put in his mouth with my dirty hands.

"Oh, for the love of God, Phoebe!" Mom cried, her hand crooked into an unnatural position as she struggled to reach the pacifier on the floor behind her. She was so close, her fingers less than an inch away when she turned around for a split second to see what she was doing.

And that's when we rear-ended the pickup truck in front of us.

In the aftermath of the accident, no one said it was my fault—at least not out loud. Mom never actually uttered the words 'if you had just given Toby his pacifier like I asked, none of this would've happened.' There would've been no ambulance. No police. No tow truck.

No smashed Mini Cooper.

She didn't need to, of course. I was perceptive enough to read between the tears and disappointed glances. And it didn't matter how virtuous my motives were. Trying to protect Toby from the germs had put us all in another sort of danger. For most kids, this realization would've been enough to shock them back into reality. To make them appreciate the real threat of crashing one motor vehicle into another over the perceived risk of potential pathogens.

But I'd never been a typical kid.

In every way that matters, I'm still not.

"I can't believe Mom crashed a car," Toby says as I finish my story. "But the accident wasn't your fault. I was the one crying."

I roll my eyes. "You were a baby. Babies are supposed to cry. I, on the other hand, could've prevented the whole thing if I hadn't allowed my anxiety to control me." I catch his gaze. The story worked. His demeanor's softened. "You and I both know my anxiety is still controlling me which is why I need to give my best effort to this new treatment. And while I work through it, I need to give myself a little space from you guys. There's just something about having a fresh start with someone new while I try this hard thing. And hey, if I screw it up, at least I'll only be disappointing a stranger instead of you."

He gives me a crooked smile and takes a hit off his inhaler. "You touched my doorknob, though. You never touch doorknobs. Maybe you're starting to get fixed already."

He says the word 'fixed' the same way Dad does as if all that's needed is a bit more determination on my part. As if the Promised Land is just over the next ridgeline—a place where there'll be no need for the vat of hand sanitizer I keep stashed beneath my bed. Where perseverance is rewarded with ambivalence to all forms of contamination.

If he only knew how desperate I am to wash my hand right now.

"I'm doing the best I can," I tell him diplomatically. "So,

are you gonna be okay with my new therapy? You won't be upset if I hang out with another person while I'm figuring things out?"

"No. I'm good," he says, although his expression begs to differ.

I slide over, leaning a bit closer so we're face to face, and all the nights spent gazing at him during his nebulizer treatments come rushing back. He needed me then. He needs me now. "If you have something you want to say, say it. You can tell me anything, you know that, right?"

"I know. It's just…" He hesitates, turning his inhaler in his hands.

"Yeah?"

"When do *I* get to be part of your new therapy?"

His question squeezes everything inside of me like a vice to my heart. It's been a long time since I wanted to hug another person as bad as I want to hug Toby now. "Soon," I tell him. "Hopefully real soon."

CHAPTER 15
week three

Since my outing with JP caused me to miss all but an hour of work on Wednesday, I promise Walter I'll get to Dust Jackets on time the rest of the week. This means taking the least circuitous route—the 6 instead of the Q.

This means not seeing JP.

When I arrive at the store Friday afternoon Walter is nowhere to be found. I know he can't be far since the store is wide open, and his reading glasses are beside the register. He never goes anywhere without them.

"Walter?" I call into the back. "You here?"

There's a loud crash of something falling.

"Walter!" I race in the direction of the storage closet. At the threshold, I discover him inside, perched on the top rung of a WWII-era ladder reaching for a box on top of a shelf. On the floor below him are the remains of a long-dead potted plant.

"Oh, Phoebe." He's breathless, the ladder wobbling beneath him. "I'm so glad you're here. Help an old man down, will you?"

I step over the broken pottery and wriggle between two

stacks of boxes, bracing my body against the wall and ladder in an attempt to stabilize the situation. "Why the heck are you up there?"

He takes a tentative step down, cursing in Yiddish under his breath. "I've been looking for this old hat of mine all afternoon. Can't seem to find it anywhere and thought maybe it got thrown in here somehow."

He reaches the floor and shudders involuntarily, letting out a heavy sigh.

"You want me to keep looking?" I ask, eyeing the rickety ladder.

He shrugs, moving past me. "No. It doesn't matter anyway. Finding the hat was just a stupid thing to distract myself."

I follow him into the stacks. "Distract yourself from what?"

He shakes his head, shuffling to the front of the store, back hunched, chin tucked. "It's nothing, Phoebe. I'm not really in the mood to discuss it further."

I stop, midstride, and it occurs to me what this is all about. We have an unspoken arrangement in which we don't push the other unnecessarily. It might be necessary to push him now, though. "Tell me about the hat, Walter," I say in my best 'therapist' voice.

He ignores me and settles in behind the counter. It's like he doesn't even know me. Like the silent treatment will effectively end the conversation.

"Walter. The hat."

At the computer now, he types frantically into some search engine, pretending to be busy. If I touched people, I'd smack him over the head.

"Walter!"

He looks up, eyes narrowed into slits. "There's a hat I wore back in my thespian days. One of those Tutor-style Renaissance caps. Anyway, I thought it might be fun to wear to the play with Beverly tomorrow night."

A huge but hangs in the air between us.

He shoves his keyboard across the counter. "I thought if I could just focus on something other than going out I could trick myself into not getting all worked up about it."

Redirection is a coping mechanism I'm overly familiar with.

"But you've spent all day looking for a missing hat, and you're more worked up about it than ever."

He nods in the affirmative.

"Having second thoughts about going to the park?"

"And third. And fourth."

I lean back against the counter and cross my arms. Walter needs to get out of the building. Walter needs to go see Shakespeare. Walter needs to spend time with Beverly.

And this is my last chance to figure out a way to make him go.

"I'll make you a deal. If you don't go with Beverly to the play, I'm not going with JP to the club."

He raises an eyebrow. "You already told me you've committed to going with him. There's no way I'm letting you use your outing as a bargaining chip now."

"Ha," I scoff. "I'm no more committed to him than you are to Beverly. You and I both know we're chronic backer-outers."

He considers this. "My play is at six, and your concert isn't until nine. I could go, and you could still back out. How's that a fair deal?"

I throw him my most sympathetic smile. "Life's not

always fair. Sometimes you just need to have faith."

The weight of his commitment to Beverly rests miserably upon his shoulders, growing heavier with each passing hour. If I could open his head and look inside, I know it would look a lot like mine—all what-ifs and catastrophic endings. In our world, the scales always tip toward mayhem. The possibilities always loom larger than the probabilities.

And yet, I see the need for him to push past the doubt. He sees the same for me.

"What if something happens?" He closes his eyes and pinches the bridge of his nose.

Here we go. Time to play the Worst-Case-Scenario game for the hundredth time. I'll take Anxiety for a thousand, Alex.

"What if it does?" I reply.

"We could get stabbed in the subway."

"Not likely."

"Hit by a taxi."

"Just… no."

"To avenge a love triangle gone awry, a rogue stagehand from the performance could attempt to murder his lover, accidentally firing into the crowd and hitting us instead."

"None of that is going to happen," I tell him. "You know what is going to happen, though? You and Beverly are going to watch an amazing performance together and have a wonderful time. That's it." He's staring past me out the window to the street. I'm not getting through him, so I try again. "Walter, what if you'd never risked going on your first date with Rita? Think of all the life you would've missed out on."

He cuts his eyes to me, glassy with tears. "It's so hard."

"The hardest."

With apparent resolve, he straightens his back and

shuffles a mess of invoices into a stack. After a moment, he glances at me again. "You better go to that club and bring back photographic evidence or don't bother coming back here Monday. Your job will not be waiting."

"You're a liar." I smile at him. "But I promise I won't let you down."

CHAPTER 16
week three

I watch Netflix. And Instagram videos. And have a Tumblr account. Social media has taught me most girls worry about what to wear and how to act and what to say when they go out with other people.

But, of course, I'm not most girls.

Instead of stressing over normal stuff, I'm contemplating the possibility of stashing yet another bottle of Purell and an extra latex glove in my back pocket as Mom and Dad leave to take Toby to Grandma's so they can enjoy a child-free anniversary dinner.

"Be home a reasonable hour," Dad calls over his shoulder as they head out the door.

"What's reasonable?" I mumble in reply, realizing I might be the only teenager in the history of forever without a curfew. Before tonight, I'd never needed one.

The PATH train from Jersey City into Manhattan is almost as full tonight as it is during the weekday morning commute. I'm surrounded by young couples with dinner reservations dressed in skirts and sport coats, boist-

groups of scantily-clad men and women already several drinks into their evening's binge on the way to the bars, and even a few families here and there, probably taking in the Big Apple on their summer vacations. The middle-aged man in the Star Wars t-shirt beside me is alone, and I can hear the pulse of a backbeat thumping from his headphones while he plays solitaire on his phone. I wonder where he's going. If he's meeting anyone. If someone's expecting him at the end of the line.

JP waits for me right where he said he would, leaning against the tiled wall of the 72nd Street station, violin case slung across his chest as the train screeches to a halt. The doors slide open. People scurry off. People scurry on. And I remain woefully attached to my seat.

I try forcing myself to move but fear shackles me in place. Leaving the car will mean risking exposure. Exposure to everything.

A flash of a woman racing for the door catches my attention, and when I turn my head, JP notices me still sitting inside the train. Our eyes lock and there's no mistaking the disappointment in the downturned corners of his mouth.

The door tone sounds, signaling the train's imminent departure, and I scramble to my feet, barely slipping through the exit onto the platform before it does.

The dimple appears in the corner of JP's cheek. "Thought you were gonna bale on me." He saunters over to where I'm still standing just beyond the gap.

"I almost did," I confess, forcing my feet into motion.

He's next to me now in an almost familiar way. "But you didn't. That's something, right?"

We fall into step, climbing the steps into the humid night air. "Yeah, definitely something," I say, surprising myself with how strangely calm I am now that he's beside me.

On the walk to the club, he enlightens me about the other members of his band. Nevaeh, whom he's known since second grade, plays the drums and aspires to be the next Cindy Blackman.

"Cindy is this amazing drummer who toured with Lenny Kravitz back in the day," JP explains noticing my bewildered expression. "It's probably a good idea if you don't bring her up with Nevaeh, though, because once she starts talking about the great Cindy Blackman, we won't be able to shut her up." He shakes his head and rolls his eyes. "Girl is big on stats."

I laugh as he continues explaining about their bass guitarist, Zaq. "His parents lived in Seattle during the whole grunge era so he grew up on stuff like Nirvana, Pearl Jam, Sound Garden—mosh pit bands. He still wears his dad's old Doc Martins and won't let us play anything where the bass line isn't 'critical to the piece.' He's a total diva but in a good way."

I'm still trying to remember the difference between a bass and a rhythm guitar from my Fundamentals of Music class freshman year, but JP's already moved on to his exposé of the final member of their quartet.

"That leaves Luke, our singer, who has a messed up home life and has also been known to play the tambourine on occasion." For some reason, this strikes me as funny, and I bust out laughing. JP immediately joins in. "You think it's funny now, wait 'til you meet him."

Listening to him recapping his bandmate's shared history as if it's the plotline of some teen show on the CW almost makes me forget we're nearing our destination. But as the illuminated Club 73 sign comes into view, my stomach turns itself inside out, knowing in a few short steps, I'll be expected to walk inside.

"When they kicked out their lead guitarist for being a douche and couldn't find anyone else, they took a chance on replacing him with a violinist instead. I guess I've been a good addition because we've been scoring a bunch of gigs thanks to our 'unique' sound, whatever that means." He pauses at the entrance to the club. "You good?"

I am definitely not good.

The double doors of Club 73 are propped open, and the cacophony from the patrons inside spills into the night, enveloping me like the unwanted embrace of a stodgy great aunt. Canned music plays from the speakers, ice clinks against glasses, and friends laugh and call to each other over the din.

If I look closely, I can almost see the germs ricocheting around from one person to another—hands to lips, lips to drinks, drinks to hands.

"Listen, there's a direct line from the door straight back to the stage in the rear. I'll go in first and clear a path. Just stay close and walk directly behind me." While he searches my face for something to indicate I'm down with the plan, I turn back to the horde of people milling around just beyond the threshold. "It's okay, Phoebe," he says, his voice calm. "You can do this."

Although I lack his confidence, I dutifully follow him into the club, concentrating on shallow breaths and tiny steps. It's a bit like walking through the hallways at school, but I've managed to navigate them effectively through trial and error and plenty of adequate lighting. This place is so dark I can barely make out anything ten feet in any direction so I focus my attention on the small of JP's back where his shirt has ridden up slightly to reveal the waistband of his boxers.

The American Eagle logo serves as a successful distraction, guiding me to the back of the club without incident. JP motions for me to step onto the pseudo stage which is little more than a raised platform in the corner of the room illuminated by a single bank of track lighting. On the far side, a black girl with dreads and a nose ring makes adjustments to the club's drum set while an enormous lumberjack of a guy fiddles with an amp up front.

"Hey, guys. Any word from Luke?" JP calls to them over the buzz.

Nevaeh and Zaq look up from their respective projects and cast JP concerned looks. Upon seeing me, however, Nevaeh's furrowed brows relax, and a smile spreads across her face. She practically trips over her cymbals getting to me.

"I'm Neveah," she says brightly, arms outstretched as if she's coming in for a hug. I take a step back at the same moment JP throws out his arm, a reminder of some previously discussed directive.

"Oh, right." She drops her hands to her sides as if suddenly remembering herself. "No touching. You'll have to forgive me if I forget. I come from an affectionate family. Squeezers, the lot of us."

Her entire demeanor is wide open making me grateful I'm not saddled with a similarly affectionate family. How would I survive? But her laugh is infectious, and for a second it almost makes me wish I was.

Paul Bunyan has lumbered up beside me and nods in my direction. "I'm Zaq." He keeps his hands busy, pulling at his sandy beard instead of reaching out to shake.

"Phoebe," I tell them. "Thanks for letting me hang out."

"Any friend of Juan Pablo's is a friend of ours." He throws an elbow into JP's rib and continues before he can respond. "And Luke texted me ten minutes ago. He says he's on his way."

"At least he doesn't have equipment to deal with," Neveah says, returning to the drum set. "Just a mic he can soundcheck last minute."

JP grabs an unoccupied chair from the bar and places it on the edge of the stage for me as the banter between the bandmates continues. I give the stool a once over with a handy-wipe from my bag before taking a seat, settling in for what's to come. Around me, hundreds of twenty-somethings dressed in cleavage and bicep-revealing clothing mingle with one another, drinks in hand. Their proximity to one another is alarming—strangers pressing their bodies against one another comfortably, as if sharing space and air is the most natural thing in the world.

On stage, JP and Zaq tune their instruments, razzing each other over some inside joke. Between snickers, JP keeps giving me little nods over his shoulder, checking in to make sure I'm not on the verge of embarrassing him with another panic attack. It's sweet but unnecessary. Everyone in my general vicinity seems healthy enough. There are no children, of course, and no one's coughing or sneezing which is a relief. What I notice instead is that everyone in the club seems to belong.

Everyone, of course, but me.

At quarter to nine, a guy who I can only assume is Luke comes bounding onto the stage like a gazelle in Levis and a slouchy hipster hat before dropping dramatically to the floor. He stares at the ceiling from his sprawled position. "You guys, I can't even with my parents. I'm so sick of being their pawn. I need to move forward with the whole emancipated minor thing."

Nevaeh sets her drumsticks on her seat and kneels beside Luke, brushing a lock of hair from his eyes. "More fighting?"

"More everything," he says, sitting up. "They put me on house arrest, but I slipped out the back fire escape. It won't take them long to figure out I'm gone, and when they do it'll be a nightmare. They're not here now, though, so I'm not gonna let them ruin our set." He pushes himself up defiantly and scans the stage, looking pleased with his assessment until his eyes reach me. "Who's this, then?"

A beat passes—the others regarding one another in silent deliberation. In the darkness, it's hard to discern the nuances of the unspoken history between them. From the periphery of the stage and the edge of their group, however, I'm obviously an outsider.

"This is Phoebe," JP says finally. "The friend I was telling you about? I invited her to watch us perform."

Luke scowls. "From the stage?"

Feeling unwelcome, I move to stand, but before I can get to my feet Neveah steps forward. "She's our guest, Luke. She stays here on stage with us."

As a thread of understanding strains between the bandmates, a spark of kinship ignites between me and Neveah. There's no obvious reason for her unsolicited support, but I'm grateful for it just the same. At the front of the platform, Luke blows out an exasperated breath. "Okay. Fine. Then let's do this." He taps the mic against his thigh to check for feedback.

Behind him, Zaq slips the strap of his bass around his neck and plugs it into the amp. "You got the setlist, Juan Pablo?"

JP pulls a few folded sheets of notebook paper out of his back pocket and hands one to each of his bandmates.

"Almost the same as last time. Just rearranged a few of the songs to help the flow."

Luke nods and lifts the mic to his face. "Check, check," he says, his lips precariously close to the mouthpiece. Instinctively, I start picturing all the previous singers' lip goop clinging to the surface but force myself to focus on JP's final preparations instead. I will not let my germaphobia, or Luke, ruin this night.

After making a few tuning adjustments, JP throws a hand signal to one of the guys behind the bar and the stage lights rotate into position. I'm still very much in the darkness, sitting just beyond the glow. He tucks his chin to his violin and raises his bow before casting his gaze in my direction.

"Break a leg," I mouth.

Neveah counts them in, and without so much as an introduction, they begin to play.

What follows is realistically the most surreal experience of my life. For the better part of an hour, it's just me and the band and the music. They play stripped-down renditions of old Coldplay, a couple reworked Beatles tunes, some George Ezra, and a bunch I don't recognize, all featuring JP on the violin. Watching them vibe off one another, anchored together by the swell and release of the harmonies fills me with such longing, there isn't room for my anxiety. It's completely shut out until a wobbly woman in four-inch heels and a bedazzled halter top trips over one of the amp's extension cords and topples onto me, spilling her fruity concoction into my lap.

I'm vaguely aware of the music dying away—first the violin, then the bass and drums followed by the vocals. The woman is screeching about a twisted ankle, and how someone's going to pay for her drink and medical expenses.

Two bartenders appear at my side, one with a mop and the other with a roll of paper towels, but all of them are white noise compared to the distinct voice inside my head urging me to get away.

Which I would gladly do if I weren't so paralyzed by fear.

I close my eyes and cover my head with my arms in an attempt to shut myself away from the situation. In addition to being completely covered in someone else's germs, the night is ruined, and it's all my fault. JP and the others will never forgive me for interrupting their performance. I add this failure to the mental list of reasons I have for hating myself.

This makes number 1,493.

In the midst of my self-loathing, I feel someone beside me and am temporarily placated by JP's voice.

"I'll take the paper towels, thanks," he says to the bartender. "Just, uh, point me in the direction of the lady's, will you?"

"To the left," she says. "Down the hall."

I'm acutely aware of the attention I'm drawing, hiding beneath my arms like a toddler having a tantrum. I'll never recover from the embarrassment. Never be able to show my face to JP or his friends or anyone on this side of town ever again. My only hope is the drunken woman's ongoing tirade is comparatively overshadowing.

"Phoebe?" JP's voice is close. He's whispering in my ear. "Just stand up and follow me. I'll get you to the restroom where you can clean yourself up." I'm considering both his offer and his motivation for being so thoughtful when he speaks again. "This is not a big deal. The spill is barely noticeable, and our set was just about over anyway. Everything is going to be okay."

I take a deep breath, forcing myself to repeat his words.

"Everything's going to be okay?"

"Yes."

"You promise?"

"I promise."

It feels as if every eye in the club is watching as I shuffle behind JP to the restrooms on the far side of the venue. On the way, I chance a glance down at my jeans and 'Just Throw Something' Clay Times t-shirt and am surprised to discover the spill is far smaller than I anticipated. And thanks to its alcoholic content, it also smells faintly like hand sanitizer—a reassurance that any transferred germs are unlikely to survive.

Unlikely but not guaranteed.

At the lady's room, JP forces open the door and leads me inside past a handful of other women at the sinks retouching their lipstick.

"You're not allowed to come in here with me," I say, stunned by his boldness.

He scoffs. "Christ, Phoebe, what are they gonna do? I'm not just gonna leave you alone in a public restroom. You may never come back out."

He's right about that. The urge to curl up on the floor in the fetal position and rock myself into oblivion has never been so strong. I'd probably be there already if the floor wasn't covered in bodily fluids.

Without another word and despite the glowers from the other women, JP unfurls a wad of paper towels from the roll, soaking it under the faucet before handing it to me.

"Wipe," he instructs.

I take the towels and begin dabbing at the red stain on the bottom of my shirt and top of my jeans. Surprisingly, it begins to fade. Once the towel is spent, JP hands me another, and when the discoloration is almost completely gone, he instructs me to wash my hands.

"If it'll make you feel better, go ahead and squirt a little hand sanitizer on the spot just for good measure."

I glance at him, eyes narrowed. "You think you know me so well," I say, meaning it as a joke but relishing in its truth.

He shrugs. "Do what you gotta do, but don't think you're getting outta the rest of the night."

What was there to get out of? I'd ruined the set. The night was over.

I dry my hands on a fresh paper towel. "What's the rest of the night?"

He opens the door, and a waft of thick air, rank with perspiration and stale beer overwhelms me. Maybe it would be better just to stay in the bathroom for the rest of my life. "After our performances, we always go to this greasy spoon for late-night breakfast. It's a great little place, and coming along will give you a chance to get to know the others."

I weave my arms protectively across my chest. "Like they're going to be interested in getting to know me after I just ruined their set. Especially Luke."

Two plastered women tumble past us into a stall, and I'm quite certain one of them is about to be sick. I have no intention of being around to witness it.

"You didn't ruin the set. The klutz with the cocktail ruined it. And she could've just as easily spilled on me." He's trying to make me feel better, and it's working.

"Yeah, but you wouldn't have had a meltdown." Now it's his turn to give me side-eye. "I'm wearing my brother's new Rag and Bone sneakers. You gotta know if she'd spilled on them, I woulda lost it."

A gagging sound echoes from one of the stalls.

"You guys are really going for breakfast?"

"Yes. But you don't have to eat anything. Just come with us. It's a tradition."

The woman begins puking in earnest, and I follow JP out the door.

CHAPTER 17
week three

There's an all-night diner on the corner of 2nd and 86th. Patrons are divided between a handful of booths and the counter, and we snag a six-top in the back corner of the restaurant where there's room to stow the guys' instrument cases in a nearby corner. After JP brushes off our seats with a paper napkin, a cheery waitress wearing a hairnet and overly sensible shoes rushes over with five waters and a stack of menus.

"Ah, the Neon Wingnuts have arrived for their post-performance sustenance. How was tonight's show?" She passes out the menus and gives me a once over.

JP takes a huge gulp of his water before answering. "It was great, actually. The crowd seemed to enjoy our sound and the manager asked us to come back next month."

Like JP, the others guzzle their waters, lips against glasses without even the sanitary protection of a straw, and I wait for one of them to say something about how their set ended with a meltdown of catastrophic proportions, but they don't.

She nods at me. "New bandmate or groupie tagalong?"

"Groupie tagalong," I confirm, uncertain as to whether I

should be embarrassed by my status. "And they were amazing tonight. They should definitely record their stuff."

"Been telling them the same thing for months. Then maybe I'd get a chance to hear them." She takes her pen out from behind her ear and pulls her notepad from her apron pocket. "What'll it be tonight? The usual?"

Neveah gives her the thumbs up. "Yup. One of each." She pauses, glancing across the table at me. "Unless you want something other than breakfast food. We just get a bunch and share. There's always plenty so you're welcome to dig in."

Regardless of the satisfactory sanitation rating posted on the door, it's downright laughable to imagine myself eating anything prepared in the kitchen, much less off of other people's plates. "Thanks, but I think I'd just like a bottled water. I'm not very hungry."

The waitress marks it down without giving me a second glance, and I feel as if I've been given a free pass. "Suit yourself. The rest of the food should be out in just a few minutes."

Alone with the band for the first time all night, JP next to me on one side of the table and Zaq, Luke, and Neveah on the other, I'm excited by this opportunity to get to know them all a little better. JP is close enough for me to feel the heat radiating off his smooth, bronze skin, but I suppress the urge to shift away, wondering instead what it would be like to touch it.

"Hell of a drum break between O Fly On and Warriors tonight," Zaq says to Neveah, stirring the ice in the bottom of his glass with a straw.

"Like the cowbell I added?" she asks, a smirk playing at the corners of her mouth.

"Yeah," he says. "But I was a little worried about the guy

who kept calling out requests from the bar. I was afraid we were gonna have another 'Cowboy Bill' incident like we did at the Indie Rock Festival last spring."

They laugh, most likely remembering, and JP turns to me. "We performed at this outdoor festival back in April, and this one drunk guy we dubbed Cowboy Bill kept screaming over and over again for more cowbell. He wouldn't shut up, and eventually Neveah just gave him what he wanted. It ended up destroying our entire set, though."

"We definitely won't be invited back again next year," Luke says with a huff, checking his phone for what seems like the hundredth time. "Same with Club 73 after tonight's fiasco," he adds, glancing in my direction.

I knew all the inclusivity JP promised wouldn't be a reality. People tolerate me until they don't, and I get the feeling Luke may be losing his patience already.

Instead of agreeing with him, though, Neveah settles back in her seat with a roll of her eyes. "Nah. The manager didn't seem upset about how the set ended. But I did overhear him say something to JP about his speed work on Sunday Bloody Sunday." She gives him a wink. "It was amazing, dude."

Beside me, JP blushes slightly, and I can't help but notice how he immediately redirects the conversation back to Luke who's checking his phone once again. "Any word from your Dad? I thought for sure you'd have heard something from him by now."

"Nothing yet," he says, lowering his voice as he leans forward, elbows resting on the table. "He's probably still so busy screaming at my mom they haven't even noticed I'm gone." He sighs before taking a sip of his water. "Maybe I'll get lucky enough to sneak back unnoticed this time."

Zaq scoffs. "If I were you I'd be trying to play your folks

against each other. Your dad might not feel the need to ground you all the time if he's getting something he wants from you."

Luke shrugs and takes another swig of his drink. "The only thing my dad wants is for me to hurry up and turn eighteen so I'm no longer a financial burden."

Neveah nudges him affectionately, and I'm struck by how supportive they're being with him. No pretenses. No judgment. Just acceptance and unconditional support.

JP's friends are pretty amazing, even with all the deliberate physical contact.

I'm picking on my cuticle, trying to imagine what I could possibly add to their dynamic when Zaq turns the conversation to me.

"So, Juan Pablo tells us you don't touch people." He unwraps the paper napkin from around his utensils. "That's gotta be tough, huh?"

"Seriously, Zaq?" JP scolds like a protective parent.

"What? Isn't that what you said?"

My hands are folded carefully in my lap, and although I've made myself as small as possible, instinctively tucking my limbs into the safety of my personal space bubble, if I'm going to let other people in I can't withdraw from them any longer. Physically or emotionally. I need to be willing to open up about myself. Ever since JP confided in me about his brother, Andre, I've been wanting to tell him about Toby, so maybe now's as good a time as any to confide in him about the origin of my anxiety.

"It's fine," I say to JP, throwing Zaq a smile. "And it's true. I don't touch other people. Not on purpose anyway."

Neveah nearly chokes on her water. "Not even your family?"

I shake my head. "Especially not my family. The whole not touching thing started because my brother Toby caught Covid from me, and it almost killed him." I tell them about the damage his lungs sustained as a preemie, how susceptible it made him to the coronavirus, and how vulnerable to infection he remains to this day. "We used to be inseparable. But once I realized I was a threat to his life, I decided it was best to keep my distance. I stopped touching to keep him safe."

JP throws me a sympathetic glance. "That must be tough. I hated having to be apart from Andre."

"Don't your parents realize why you're staying away?" Zaq asks.

I sigh. "Oh yeah. They know. It made my dad super happy when I started keeping my distance."

"You're kidding?" Neveah says, brows furrowed.

"It was hard for him, I guess, having a kid almost die, and even though he didn't always come right out and ask me to leave Toby alone, I knew the difference between what he was saying and how he was saying it. When I started avoiding Toby, the tension at the corners of Dad's eyes disappeared. The wrinkles softened. He was relieved. And, honestly, so was I."

I think of Dad, squeezing my shoulder and beaming down the first time he saw me actively move across the room away from my brother. 'That's my girl,' he'd whispered. 'Gotta work together to keep the little guy safe.' It was the first time I remember him winking at me like we were conspirators in a secret alliance. 'You're a really great big sister, Phoebe.'

I look across the table at the others now. "Once I saw how happy Dad was when I avoided Toby, it only made sense that I should stop touching him altogether. And stop allowing him to touch me."

Keeping my distance wasn't too hard at first—watching him play with his plastic dinosaurs in the sudsy water from atop the vanity instead of the edge of the tub at bath time or sitting on the opposite side of the kitchen table instead of beside him as he picked over his plate at dinner. I became the master at finding excuses for why he couldn't hang out with me even when I had nothing else going on. The longer our separation progressed, however, the more challenging evading his advances became. Regardless of how far away I positioned myself on the sofa to watch Disney Channel with him, he'd eventually scootch beside me, cuddling against my shoulder with his mop of dark hair. More often than not, to keep him safe I was forced to leave the room.

I had no other choice.

'Phoebe, don't go!' he'd whine as I hurried off to my bedroom. Hearing him call my name, knowing he only wanted to play, crushed my soul. But it was impossible to explain to a six-year-old that I was a veritable bastion of mobilized germs just waiting to infect him. Staying apart was in his best interest, and my heart couldn't bear the responsibility of another hospitalization.

I clear my throat, forcing myself to continue through the painful memories. "Unfortunately, once I headed back to school after the initial lockdown, keeping him safe proved to be far more challenging. I always wore my mask, made sure to keep my hands away from my face, and thoroughly scrubbed them with soap and hot water five-hundred times a day. It wasn't foolproof, but it was all I had." I glance around the table at their shocked expressions. "To this day, Toby still suffers in a lot of ways because of me. His lungs have never fully recovered so he can't even go to school like a normal kid. Doing my part to keep him healthy now seems like the least I can do."

"That's intense," Zaq says, looking genuinely concerned.

I shrug. "More isolating than anything. It's hard to maintain relationships with people when you're afraid of being infected, and literally everyone and everything is a potential contaminant."

Neveah leans across the table on her elbows as if I might make more sense if only I was a few inches closer. "But you're here now?" she says. It comes out more as a question than a statement.

"Only barely," I reply.

Their food arrives—four platters loaded with pancakes, scrambled eggs, hash browns, and sausage links—and the waitress sets them in the middle of the table, family-style. She disappears briefly, returning with a stack of empty plates which she passes around to each of them.

She even sets a plate in front of me. "Just in case."

The others dig in, picking up sausage links with their fingers, using their own forks to slide hash browns onto their plates. Salt and pepper is passed from hand to hand. The ketchup and syrup make the rounds as well. It's an absolute free-for-all, and I can almost see the pathogens delighting in this dispersion opportunity.

The others, of course, cannot.

Watching them devour their meals, licking their fingers and laughing about the way Luke's voice cracked inopportunely in the middle of Viva la Vida, I can't imagine what it would be like not to see the germs. To live in blissful ignorance, unaware of the danger lurking on every surface. Microorganisms carrying random head colds. Debilitating stomach viruses. Aggressive cases of conjunctivitis. All lying in wait, poised to infect.

The way the food smells, though, is Pavlovian, and my stomach grumbles in outrage at being ignored. Clearly, my brain is the only organ concerned about the threat of contamination. My stomach could care less.

As if an afterthought, the waitress returns for a third time with my bottle of Dasani. JP glances at me. "D'you want a napkin or something to wrap it in?"

The others are watching us now—their eyes boring into me, curious as to whether I'm gonna take the damn bottle. My gaze drifts to JP's face where visible concern pulls at the corners of his mouth. I've always wanted to be normal but never so much as I do in this particular moment.

I let out the air burning a hole in my lungs, then reach for the bottle and take it. "Thanks, but I'm good."

JP's eyes widen at my boldness, and the pride I see inside them is the only thing keeping me from passing out.

"Look at you," he says through a mouthful of pancakes. "You're totally doing it."

The lid twists off easily, and I set it to the side. If I'm going to take a sip I need to do it now before I lose my nerve.

There are no germs.

And even if there are, they won't kill me.

At least I hope they won't.

My lips connect with the surface of the bottle, and I tip back, letting the water flood the inside of my mouth. It's cold and refreshing, and before I realize what I'm doing, I've chugged the entire thing, far more parched than I thought.

Completely drained, I set the bottle on the table and shift in my seat, fishing my hand sanitizer from my back pocket. I squirt a little into the palm of my hand, relishing not only the physical coolness of it against my skin but the emotional relief it brings as I rub it between my palms.

Beside me, JP begins a slow clap. Neveah joins in.

Heat rises to the tops of my ears.

"So, either JP's a liar, or what just happened was a pretty big deal," Neveah says.

JP grins sheepishly at me. "I told them about your reaction to the kids at the coffee shop. You know, just so they'd be prepared."

It seems ridiculous taking a water bottle from a stranger and drinking from it would be cause for a celebration, but this is my life, and ridiculous is the norm.

"Walter's gonna freak when I tell him." I slip the Purell back into my pocket. "I haven't done anything like that since..." I try to remember the last time. "Since I went to my friend Macie's birthday party just before the pandemic. I ate cupcakes with my fingers." My stomach lurches at the thought. "Believe it or not, I haven't been to a party since."

For the first time since the food arrived, Zaq comes up for air, his fork hanging between his plate and his mouth. Little bits of scrambled egg cling to his beard. "You haven't been to a party since 2020?"

I think back. "Actually, it was probably 2019."

Now Luke's stopped eating as well. "No high school keggers?"

I shake my head.

"No sleepovers?" Neveah asks.

"No. Nothing."

Pity would be an appropriate response to my admission because I'm nothing if not pathetic, so I'm both shocked and strangely hopeful when they react with outrage instead of sympathy.

"That ain't even right," Zaq says, forked balled in his fist. "Somebody shoulda done somethin' for you by now."

Neveah nods in agreement. "Yeah, I mean, what good is therapy if it doesn't help enough for you to do fun stuff like go to parties?"

I force myself to smile. "I'm a lot better than I used to be. Freshman year was the worst. I switched therapists twice and ended up getting pneumonia, even with all my precautionary measures. There was one stretch when I didn't leave my room for a solid month."

Now it's JP's turn to look infuriated. "Your parents just let you hide away in your room?"

Memories of the fear associated with my ninth-grade bout of pneumonia come rushing back. The indisputable knowledge there was no absolute way to avoid contamination paired with the arrival of winter break (extended for a week by a blizzard) resulted in a perfect storm of anxiety. I had to be forcibly dragged into the building when school finally resumed in the middle of January.

It was not my finest hour.

But this wasn't on my parents. I was the only one responsible for my actions.

"My mom and dad didn't let me hide away. I didn't give them a choice. I was willful. Am willful." I study their faces, looking for an indication of understanding. "In the end, though, it turned out to be one of the best things that ever happened to me. My pneumonia cleared up. No one else got sick. And my refusal to get out of the car at school led the principal to bring in Roz, the best therapist I've ever had. She's the reason high school hasn't been as isolating as it could've been.

Zaq looks unconvinced. "That's better even though you

still don't go out with friends?"

It's hard to argue with his analysis of the situation, and it feels like something of a win that he feels comfortable enough around me already to say it aloud.

"I don't go out with anyone," I reply.

Neveah swallows a bite of eggs. "You didn't," she corrects. "Past tense. Because you're out right now. With friends."

Maybe she's using the term 'friends' loosely. Or maybe she means I'm out with JP and his friends. But semantics aside, the warmth of her declaration oozes through me like molten chocolate in cake, infiltrating every cell of my body.

"You know where we should take her?" Zaq asks as if I'm not even sitting at the table, continuing without waiting for a response. "To Teens Take the Met on Wednesday."

Kids from school go every year to The Metropolitan Museum of Art's teen-only event, but all I ever took away from listening in on their conversations was that it's something I'd have no interest in attending. Thousands of people corralled into the museum like livestock? No thank you.

I start to object. "I don't think…"

Zaq raises a palm to silence me, and after downing another forkful of pancakes, continues. "No. Wait. Hear me out. My dad's friends with one of the curators. It's how Neveah and I got invited to play at the Balcony Bar for the parents. What if she could get us in early, before the rush? Then you could just stay until it gets too uncomfortable."

The last thing I want is to cause another public scene. My freak out over the cocktail spill was bad enough, but at least the room was full of nothing but strangers. If something similar were to happen at the Met, there's a good chance people I know would be there to witness it. Not to mention the propensity teenagers have for filming other people's awkward moments. Can you say overnight internet infamy? I can picture the meme already.

I'm about to tell them no thanks, but JP's staring at me with such focus, it's almost as if the course of his life is somehow hinging on whether I agree to spend the evening with them at the stupid museum. Soulful eyes and adorable dimples have never influenced my decisions in the past, and I don't intend to be swayed now, but saying no is not in line with my ultimate goal of letting other people into my life.

"Do you really think your dad could work something out for me?"

He grabs another pancake from the communal plate. "I'll ask him in the morning."

CHAPTER 18
week four

I'm surprised to see a light on in the family room as I enter our apartment and ease the door carefully shut behind me with my foot. After parting ways with the rest of the band at the diner, JP rode the subway through Manhattan with me until I reached a station where I could catch the PATH into New Jersey. He said he didn't mind doubling back to where he lives in Corona.

My heart melts a little now thinking of how he smiled at me when we said goodnight.

"Phoebe? Is that you?" Mom whisper calls to me.

I hurry down the hall to where she's hunkered down beneath a blanket and a reading lamp with the latest issue of Time magazine.

This raises immediate red flags. She doesn't even like Time magazine.

"You didn't have to wait up," I say, falling onto the couch beside her.

She scrunches her nose. "Ugh. You smell like grease. Where have you been all night?"

I tuck my nose into my shirt and take a whiff—a pungent

concoction of sweat, grease, and hand sanitizer. I need a shower. "After the set, we all went to a diner uptown."

Her eyes widen. "And you ate?"

"I drank a bottled water."

She studies me, eyes stopping at what remains of the cocktail stain on my t-shirt. She wants to ask but falls short, probably afraid of what sort of explanation I'll give. "These kids were nice to you? Didn't give you a hard time about not eating with them?"

"They were amazing," I tell her, leaving out the part about being ignored by Luke. "A few of us made plans to meet up again Wednesday night."

Instead of embracing my enthusiasm, a mixture of intrigue and concern distorts her face in the dim shadows of the reading lamp. "You're not going to another bar, I hope. You're only sixteen-years-old. It's not appropriate even if it is open mic night."

I won't give her the satisfaction of knowing I wouldn't step foot in another bar for all the Purell in Manhattan. Instead, I share just the facts. "We're going to teen night at the Met. One of the guys thinks he can get us in early so it won't be as crowded."

She eyes me skeptically as I heave myself off the sofa and make my way toward the shower. "And if he can't get you in before the crowds, you still gonna go?"

I hesitate at the bathroom door before turning back, wishing she could be less pessimistic and more of a cheerleader. "I dunno. I guess we'll see."

***

Although Mom didn't exude the desired enthusiasm over my Wednesday night plans, I'm certain Walter will, which is why I'm practically bursting at the seams by the time I get to the store after pottery class on Monday.

"How was your weekend?" he calls from the stacks when he sees me come through the door.

"You first," I tell him. "I assume you have some proof of your night out with Beverly."

His smile beams brighter than the afternoon sun streaming through the store's front windows. "As a matter of fact, I do." He produces his phone from the pocket of his tweed trousers. "Take a look at this."

He holds out the screen displaying a selfie of him and Beverly mugging together on the lawn at Shakespeare in the Park. He's even wearing his Renaissance hat.

"You found it," I say.

"It was in a trunk upstairs."

"What did Beverly think?"

He swipes his thumb across his phone, scrolling through a few more photographs before holding it out again. This time Beverly's the one wearing the hat.

"I take it your night out was a smashing success?"

He's grinning at his phone like a kid who just found out he's going to Disney World. "We had a marvelous time. I haven't laughed so much since Rita was alive. And I'm not gonna lie—it felt really good."

"I knew you could do it," I say, amazed by the change in him since Friday afternoon. I'm hesitant to broach the subject, but I wouldn't be a good friend if I didn't at least ask about any setbacks. "Your anxiety wasn't too bad then?"

He returns his phone to his pocket and makes his way to his seat behind the counter. "You know, it's funny, for as anxious as I was before, my apprehension virtually disappeared once I left to meet her. It's almost as if the anticipation was the most stressful part, not the experience itself." He pauses then, logging onto his computer. "Truth be told, I did feel a little worried at first, sitting, waiting for the play to begin, but Beverly is so charming, she helped ease my nerves."

I can imagine them together on the lawn, catching up on the first six decades of their lives, bringing each other up to speed. I can imagine how distracting it is to lose yourself in someone else's world because JP and his friends seem to be providing a similar diversion for me.

Walter's staring through the computer screen, not at it, and his far-away look answers my next question before I even ask.

"Does this mean the two of you will be going out again soon?"

His eyes cut to me, a mischievous smile on his lips. "She invited me to go with her to the Tenement Museum on the lower east side for some special engagement on Thursday night. I guess she's big into genealogy and some archivist is going to be on-site with information."

"Two dates in less than a week. Sounds pretty serious," I tease.

"They aren't dates. They're outings. But she did stop by earlier today to drop off these." He pulls a plate of sugar cookies covered in plastic wrap from under the counter. "I guess when you reach a certain age you can't waste a lot of time on the 'getting to know you' phase. Nothing to it but to do it." He peels back the cover and picks up a cookie. "Want one? They're delicious."

I laugh at his old-fashioned expression but pass on the treat. "You gonna be okay to join her at the museum?"

He takes a bite and shrugs. "Probably not. It's gonna be hard. But if I did it once I can do it again, right?" He polishes off the cookie with an unexpected look of determination on his face. "Now, I kept up my end of the bargain. You better have kept yours."

I pull out my phone to show him proof of my night out with JP just as a harried-looking mother with three preschoolers underfoot tumble into the store.

"Don't touch anything!" she cries to her scattering children before handing Walter a slip of paper. "I'm looking for this book. Please tell me you have it in stock."

Walter chuckles, emerging from behind the counter. He throws me a look that says 'keep an eye on the rugrats' as the mother follows him into the stacks.

I trail the cacophony of unbridled youth to the back of the store where I find the oldest of the three children climbing the step ladder Walter used during his hat expedition. I slip on a latex glove from my back pocket and grab a picture book from the closest shelf.

"Hey, friends," I say, capturing their attention. "Anybody up for a story?"

The littlest one, who can't be more than two, toddles in my direction. I plop down on the floor, and she sidles up beside me.

"Book," she says from behind her pacifier.

I scooch to the left, just out of her reach. "That's right," I tell her, waving the others away from the ladder. "Come listen to Where the Wild Things Are with us."

I blow out a breath of relief as the oldest, a boy, backs down the final rung and rushes over to our impromptu story circle. "I love that book," he says, showing me his terrible claws.

His younger sister drops to the floor in front of me. "Me, too."

Once they're situated so everyone can see, I open the front cover and begin to read. They roar their roars, gnash their teeth, roll their eyes, and show their claws along with the Wild Things, laughing all the while. When I reach the part about Max wanting to be with someone who loves him best of all, the littlest girl pulls herself onto my lap.

It happens so quickly, there's no time to react. No moment to slide away or brace myself. There's just the weight of her, heavy and content against my chest.

When panic keeps me from continuing with the story, the boy expresses his displeasure by kicking at me with his foot. "Why'd you stop?" he asks. "You're not finished."

A tempest rages inside of me, fueled by the anxiety over her bare legs touching mine. Her skin is smooth and creamy, without blemish or bruise, and I force myself to look away, breathing my way through the early stages of the panic attack. I remind myself she's healthy and nothing bad will come as a result of this benign contact. She's just a little girl in search of a safe place.

Just. Like. Me.

With as much strength as I can muster, I continue, lifting the book for them to see. My arm shakes under the weight of it, and the pages flutter. I swallow hard, forcing levity into my voice which trembles as I start anew.

When I finish, instead of popping up, the little girl settles in further, sucking steadily on her pacifier. I resist the urge to cuddle her in my arms. Resist the urge to lay my cheek against her head. Resist the urge to bury my nose in her hair, the scent of Johnson's Baby Shampoo reminiscent of bath nights with Toby all those years ago.

But I also resist the urge to dump her out of my lap onto the floor.

Could this be progress?

"Read more stories," the boy squeals as I set the book to the side.

"Maybe another time," I hear his mother say. She and Walter are standing together beyond the closest shelf. His eyes are wide with disbelief.

My heart leaps at their presence which signals my stay of execution. "Okay! Time to go," I say a bit too cheerily as I begin to stand. "Everybody up!"

"Thank the nice girl for reading you a story," the mother instructs, as her offspring fall into line behind her on their way to the front of the store.

"Thank you," they sing out obligingly.

"You're welcome," I reply, wondering if Walter can hear the remaining tremor in my voice.

They're barely onto the sidewalk before his interrogation begins.

"One night at a bar with some new friends and now you're allowing rogue children to sit on your lap? Did this JP fellow drag you off to a weekend of conversion therapy or cast some sort of magic spell?"

He follows me to the bathroom where I furiously scrub my hands and legs with soap and hot water. "No. Nothing like that. And I didn't let her sit on my lap. She did it on her own without permission."

"But you didn't stop her. And you let her stay."

I dry off with a handful of paper towels and consider his appraisal of the situation. I did let her stay. And it wasn't entirely awful. "She seemed healthy. And you saw how sweet she was. I couldn't just shove her off, could I?"

He raises an eyebrow. "A year ago, you wouldn't have hesitated to shove her off."

He's right. A year ago, I wouldn't have even offered to read to them. I would've hidden in the storage closet.

"This friendship with JP seems like it's having a positive effect on you."

"And Beverly seems to be having a similar effect on you."

He turns away, pulling at his mustache. "They're forcing us out of our comfort zones, that's for sure."

CHAPTER 19

week four

There's a park not far from our apartment where Toby likes to practice flying his drones. In preparation for the upcoming regional tournament, he's been tinkering with a sleeker set of rotor blades and is excited to test them. So instead of heading off with Dad after dinner like he usually does, I offer myself as an alternative copilot.

Along the walk to Hamilton Park, he prattles on about brushless motors and carbon fiber frame stiffeners and rubber dampeners. I nod in pseudo comprehension, trying to follow along, but it doesn't matter if I don't know the difference between an 'A' blade and a 'B' blade. The skip in his step proves he's excited just to have me along.

The air is mild and less muggy than it has been in several weeks, and the park is packed by the time we get there. Dozens of teenagers shoot hoops at the basketball nets. Kids chase one another around the play equipment. People walk dogs of every size and breed.

And I try not to think about the germs.

"When's your next race again?" I ask once we reach the gazebo where he begins unpacking his drone from its case.

"Not 'til fall. The last weekend in September, I think." He slides the drone carefully out of its protective cover and checks a couple of fittings before setting it on the ground. He slips two fresh D-cell batteries into the remote and powers it on.

"I was thinking I would go with you to your next one if you'd like me to come along."

He looks up warily from his controller. "For real?"

"Yeah, well, I've been making a bit of progress with my anxiety lately, and I'm trying to challenge myself."

He turns his attention back to the remote. "Like with that guy you went out with the other night?"

His comment stings. My outing with JP must still be a sore subject. "Yes and no," I tell him truthfully. "It's not all about him. In fact, yesterday at work a little girl sat on my lap, and I didn't freak out. Or at least I only freaked out on the inside."

He looks at me, wounded, and I know he's thinking about how long it's been since I let him sit on my lap.

I busy myself retying my ponytail in an attempt to avoid his gaze and contemplate how I can explain my motivations without sounding like a jerk. "Listen, I'm trying to let people into my life, and this includes you. It's not easy for me to be out here at the park, but I'm here doing the best I can."

His drone lifts off the ground, sailing above our heads. He weaves expertly around two trees, cutting between the branches before shooting into the air. "Get my tablet out of the bag," he instructs eyes to the sky.

I hesitate. He knows I don't touch other people's belongings.

"I thought you were here to help." His voice is firm. Too firm for a nine-year-old. "I need to practice flying using the tablet. If you won't get it, you should go home and send Dad back to do it instead."

His bag rests against the gazebo step. The zipper is open, and I can see the tablet nestled inside.

I try flooding my brain with rational thoughts:

Nothing bad happened as a result of having a cocktail spilled on my shirt.

Nothing bad happened as a result of drinking bottled water from a restaurant.

Nothing bad happened as a result of having a little girl sit on my lap.

Nothing bad will happen now.

In one swift motion, I reach into the bag and pull out the tablet. Electricity buzzes inside of me, running the length of my arm to my fingertips and back again. I fight the urge to drop it but hold on. "What do you need me to do?"

He glances over at me, only taking his eyes off the drone for a split second. The corners of his lips curl into a faint smile before addressing me as if he's a tiny, asthmatic drill sergeant. "Turn it on. Find the drone camera app. It's at the top. A blue one with a propeller icon inside. Open it up and press the connect button. Then come hold it in front of me so I can see."

I do as I'm instructed, my mind screaming for a shot of Purell like a drowning victim gasping for air. Focusing on the task at hand helps distract me.

Power on.

Find the app.

Connect to the drone.

Show Toby.

"I think I've got it."

The image on the screen transmits directly from the

camera on Toby's drone, giving us a glimpse of what it's like to be aboard.

He's smiling in earnest now, adjusting his focus from the drone in the sky to the tablet's camera view. I don't know whether to attribute his change in attitude to my perseverance or the thrill of flying, but I suspect it's a little of both.

"This is how I steer during a race," he explains. "It looks way different from up there, huh?"

"Is it harder or easier to fly from the drone's point-of-view?"

He shrugs. "Just different. And Dad says I have to wait 'til Christmas to ask for FVP glasses cuz they're super expensive. That's why I'm stuck doing it this way."

The image on the screen shows the cityscape surrounding us in miniature, like the train gardens at the fire department at Christmastime—rowhomes, traffic, treetops, and the roof of a nearby library.

For the last couple years, the school library and the books inside have been one of my few safe-havens. I can hide away amongst the shelves, protected from the judgment of my peers. I can pursue friendships with characters between the pages of a book even if I can't sustain relationships in real life. It's the place where, after infecting Toby with Covid, I set out in search of answers for how I could protect him from getting sick ever again.

Mrs. Langford, the librarian, was instrumental to the cause. "What can I help you with today, Phoebe," she asked me from behind a stack of returns the day I began researching.

"I need to know about avoiding contagions," I'd told her.

She eyed me skeptically but rose from her chair. "Contagions, huh?" she said. "I think we have some good stuff over in the research section."

I followed her through the stacks. "Okay. But I want real information. Not the fake stuff I keep finding online," I'd explained. "Whatever you have about infectious disease spread."

I left the library with a backpack full of books so heavy I could barely hoist it onto my shoulders. After reading straight through study hall and opting out of lunch, I had a much better understanding by the end of the day. I returned all but one of the books on the way out the door during dismissal.

Mrs. Langford grinned as I slid the rest into the return slot. "Did you learn everything there is to know about contagions already?"

"Yes," I told her. "And I'm never going to make anyone sick again."

She chuckled, which part of me considered insulting. From what I'd spent the day reading, viruses and bacteria were serious business. Anything capable of killing little brothers was no laughing matter.

I returned home wiser. The library books had not only provided a comprehensive education on pathogens, but they also confirmed I was harboring dangerous germs inside my body, as indicated by my current sore throat. I was a ticking time bomb waiting to go off, and if I blew up all over Toby, there was no guarantee he'd survive another illness.

Something had to be done.

That night, instead of watching reruns of Avatar: The Last Airbender with the family, I shut myself in my bedroom and slipped the stolen library book out of my backpack. Unlike the others which were written solely for physicians and researchers, *Your Germs, My Terms* included a section for layman in the back, making it an especially valuable resource.

Included in the appendix was a list of all the ways to keep from getting sick. I took out my Danny Phantom notepad and matching pencil from my desk drawer and turned to the first page. At the top, I wrote: HOW TO AVOID GERMS. Below, I began my list:

1. Germs come in through the eyes, nose, and mouth. Don't touch those parts no matter what.

2. Don't share: toothbrushes, juice boxes, lollipops, tissues, Chapstick, or anything that touches my eyes, nose, or mouth.

3. Cover sneezes and coughs with a tissue or my elbow. Don't use my hands.

4. Wash my hands all the time or use hand sanitizer.

5. Touching spreads Germs. Don't touch.

Your Germs, My Terms inspired me to view the world at the microbial level. To see germs collectively as enormous, hulking monsters committed to destroying everything in their path—including my little brother.

Now, looking at our city from the drone's point-of-view, I'm surprisingly comforted by this new perspective. From high above the treetops, all the big things appear small. Cars the size of Legos. Buildings the size of shoe boxes. Germs so infinitesimally small, I can barely imagine them existing at all.

"Check this out." Toby directs the drone to a residential area where three boys play in a sprinkler. "They don't even look real, do they? More like avatars in a video game."

They do look tiny and pixilated like I could move them with a controller. "How high can you go?" I ask.

The boys on the screen grow smaller as he edges the drone a bit higher. "I can't go much further because it's hot out here. Thermals can make it tough to control."

Mesmerized by his piloting abilities, I watch in rapt admiration as he steers around buildings, above treetops, and under powerlines. The motions appear effortless, but I'm certain it's taking all his concentration not to crash.

As he brings the drone in on its final descent, I'm struck by how much less ominous the world appeared from above. As if nothing bad could happen in the picturesque landscape below. No Covid-related lung damage. No anxiety disorders. No accidental 'death by scaffolding.'

"This was fun," I tell him as we make our way along the sidewalk toward home. I've squirted our hands with sanitizer twice already and not wanting to press my luck, have restrained from offering a third time. "Think I could come with you again sometime?"

He grins up at me. "Yeah. But only if you promise to take the controller and fly."

CHAPTER 20

week four

After dinner on Wednesday, instead of joining Dad and Toby on another drone expedition, I lock myself in my room, stashing necessities for my trip to the Met: latex gloves, hand sanitizer, a granola bar, a bag of Toby's goldfish crackers, my student ID, my phone, and a metro card. Without thinking, I reach into my nightstand for one of my old cloth masks, but of course, the drawer is empty.

Mom threw the tattered remains of my last one away months ago.

The truth is, even if I had a mask to wear, the thin layer of cotton would do more to protect other people from my germs than other way around. I'm rational enough to understand this, but the thought of not having something covering my face around all those people still freaks me out.

Although Zaq's dad wasn't able to get us in before the event, he did manage to get us side-door entrance and access to some of the off-limit areas. JP texted around lunchtime promising to help me conquer microbial threats, both real and imagined, if I agreed to at least put in an appearance at the museum.

At this point, showing up is all I've agreed to.

After taking inventory of my stash one last time, I shove everything into my bag and call goodbye to my mom as I head out of our apartment.

"Don't be out too late," she says just before the door shuts behind me.

When I eventually make it to Midtown, JP's waiting for me at street level as I ascend from the subway tunnel below, leaning casually against a trashcan, jeans slung low. He smiles when he sees me and for the first time since agreeing to this ridiculous endeavor, I consider going through with everyone's plans.

"You're right on time." He falls into step beside me, pulling a piece of paper from his back pocket.

"What's that?"

He unfolds the sheet, revealing a highlighted map of the museum. "Zaq and Neveah will be performing in the adult's only area until 6:30, so I thought you and I could go through the museum together until they're done. This map shows all the rooms open to the public tonight labeled with their activities. You should pick the places you think might be the most interesting and least crowded. We can avoid the busiest places and activities we don't care about. Limited exposure and all." He holds out the map, and I take it tentatively with my bare hand. "Still progressing?"

"Oh, yeah. This is nothing," I tell him. "I let a little kid sit on my lap the other day."

He stops in the middle of the sidewalk in mock horror, bringing an unexpected smile to my face. "How'd that happen?"

I tell him about the impromptu storytime at the

bookstore Monday and how I've held two books, a doorknob, and Toby's tablet with my bare hands since.

"Impressive," he says without an ounce of sarcasm in his voice.

"Yeah, well, I'm not picking garbage off the street yet so don't get too excited."

Reading his map while avoiding run-ins with other pedestrians proves nearly impossible, so after several seconds I hand the paper back to him. "I have a rule about multitasking on the sidewalk. Can you give me the gist instead?"

We round the corner onto Madison Avenue as he begins outlining his plan for the night. "They're giving out temporary tattoos on the main level by the entrance, but I didn't think you'd have any interest in those."

"Definitely not," I confirm.

"Also, there are a couple places where they'll be giving out snacks—at the game arcade and silent dance party—so I thought it would be best to avoid those areas altogether. Where there's food, there's people, right?"

"Agreed."

"There's a bunch of creation stations like Upcycled Glass Engraving and Optical Toy Making, but I thought we should probably avoid those, too, since everyone will be sharing equipment."

It's only now occurring to me how much time and effort he put into this list and how much he's willing to give up to make sure I'm comfortable in my surroundings. He should be performing with the others instead of acting as my babysitter.

"You don't need to walk around with me," I tell him. "You shouldn't have to miss out on the fun stuff because of me."

He brushes me off with a wave of his hand. "It's no big deal. I went with a bunch of classmates from school to the last teen night, so I've already done everything I'd want to do. And besides, it's not like you're a burden or anything. I'm going along so you can have the experience."

A taxi's horn blares in the street beside me, and steam vents from the grate at my feet. The bustle of the city is as familiar to me as my avoidance rituals. What's foreign to me is someone else going out of their way to be inclusive of them.

I fumble for the best way to express my appreciation but come up woefully short. "Thanks."

"Don't mention it."

What follows is an awkward silence as the museum comes into view. I'm nervous for some reason now, not about embarrassing myself with my anxiety but with the thought of disappointing him. Surely, I'll feel comfortable participating in at least one activity.

"So, if snacks and dancing and hands-on projects are out, what's left?" I ask.

JP scans his map, pointing to a cluster of highlighted notes. "There's a poetry slam—participation optional—and an audio guide we can take around the art exhibits. The roof access will be open so it might be fun to go up there. We could also do the Collaborative Story Salon or watch the film screening." He pauses, glancing in my direction, his dimple chiseled into his cheek. "And if you're feeling really brave there's a sculpture opportunity."

Longing floods my soul. "What kind of sculpture?"

He shrugs. "Last time it was a carving thing. I don't know what it'll be this time, but I bet if we ask we could get you fresh materials." Although he says this as an aside, his tone suggests arrangements may have already been made.

"You think?"

"Zaq's dad might've already mentioned something to his liaison."

I swallow back a wave of unexpected shame. "He told her about my anxiety?"

"Yeah. I mean, he didn't go into specifics or anything, but the museum is happy to accommodate you. It's no big deal."

I don't know whether to be grateful or offended or embarrassed. "They're holding out fresh supplies for me?"

"Yep. All you have to do is tell them who you are when we get there." He bites at his nail, frowning slightly. "If you want to, of course. It's fine if you don't."

"No, it's... Thanks. That's really nice of you guys to do this for me."

A hint of color rises to his cheeks as he folds the map and stuffs it back into his pocket. "Seriously. Personal supplies are not a big deal." He pauses for a moment but continues when I don't respond. "You know the Silent Dance Party was started to help autistic kids feel included. Everyone wears wireless headphones so it's not as much of a sensory overload for people who have less tolerance for loud noises. It's cool, right, because everyone should be able to get their groove on."

He's telling me this, of course, so I'll feel less self-conscious about my accommodations. Surprisingly, it works.

"It's cool," I admit, wishing I could participate but knowing I'd never be able to bring myself to put on unsanitary public headphones.

We approach the Met where teens are lined up around the block already waiting to get inside, and my pace slows involuntarily. JP reaches out as if to take my hand but stops short. "I know it looks like a ton of people, but the museum is a huge place. I promise it won't feel crowded once we get inside."

I nod, taking slow, deep breaths as we make our way to the employee entrance on the side of the building. JP presents his ID to the door attendant, and after showing my student ID as well, we're ushered into the building.

CHAPTER 21

week four

I stopped going to museums after a particularly harrowing field trip to the Hayden Planetarium freshman year. It was dark and cramped and due to our unusually large class size, my teacher forced me to share a seat with Josh Evans who kept dangling a phlegm wad over my lap instead of gazing up at the Milky Way with the rest of the class. It wasn't my first encounter with someone who couldn't be trusted to understand—much less respect—my aversion to germs and without the structured rules of the classroom to protect me, I was left to my own defenses. After asking him repeatedly (and quite unsuccessfully) to leave me alone, I finally abandoned the seat we shared and moved to the floor.

Less than five minutes later, I was reprimanded by the planetarium staff for posing a fire hazard and received a verbal lashing from my teacher for not staying in my seat where I belonged.

I haven't been to another museum since.

Maleeha, our event liaison, leads us through one of the Met's back hallways to a service elevator which dumps us into the Arts of Africa, Oceania, and the Americas gallery. She directs us past a room full of indigenous wooden sculptures where I crane my neck hoping to get a better view of the intricate carvings on display.

"This way," Maleeha calls out, her floral hijab cascading across her shoulders when she notices I've fallen behind.

I hear the horde of teenagers before I see it, their voices echoing around the Great Hall. Laughing, screaming, singing—it's enough to make me want to crawl back into the service elevator for the rest of the night.

Maleeha leaves us to wait in a vestibule just beyond where the other kids are dropping off their bags and signing in but returns a moment later with special passes and maps. "These badges will allow you into some of the areas which will be off-limits to most of the other guests, just in case you need a quiet place to get away."

JP takes both of our passes, slipping them around his neck as if none of these special perks are a big deal. I, on the other hand, can't imagine what Zaq told his dad about me to warrant the VIP treatment. My meltdown at the bar must have left an impression on him.

"Okay, you two are all set. Have a great night." Maleeha points us in the direction of the Great Hall which is now swarming with rowdy teenagers.

"Would it be alright if we went back to the African section? A theater performance will be taking place there soon, right?" I ask.

She glances at her watch, a small scowl pinching her brow. "You're not technically supposed to be in the exhibit areas for another ten minutes or so, but I suppose it would be okay. If anyone should ask, just tell them you have my permission."

We thank her and waste no time retracing our steps back

to the Arts of Africa gallery.

I let out a sigh of relief once we're out of Maleeha's earshot. The beauty of our surroundings eases the lingering tension still tugging at my attention just beneath the surface.

"Amazing how something primitive can be so intricate and beautiful, isn't it?" JP ponders, pointing toward the closest sculpture.

"It's gorgeous," I agree, noting the complexity of the linework.

We stroll through the gallery together, commenting on the craftsmanship of this mask and the artistry of that tapestry. I try to imagine what sort of hands fashioned each creation. What each material would have felt like against their skin as they formed something out of nothing. What they would think if they knew their creative talent was on display for the world to see.

Behind us, the theater performance actors are completing their final preparations on the makeshift stage against the back wall.

Hands in his pocket, JP cuts his eyes in their direction. "Wanna stay for the play or you wanna test out just how far these passes will get us." There's a mischievous grin on his face, and as the first audience members wander into the room, I take a step toward the closest exit.

"Lead the way."

Late afternoon sun glints through the ceiling casting shadows across the tile floor as we meander down a courtyard lined with European sculptures carved from enormous slabs of granite.

JP sidles up beside a naked statue of Perseus wielding a sword in one hand and the slain head of Medusa in the other. After studying it for a moment, he squares his shoulders, striking an identical pose. "What do you think? Could I pass for a Greek God?"

Greek God? No. Ecuadorian God? Abso-frickin-lootly.

Before he can change his position, I pull my phone from my pocket and snap a quick shot. He's beaming at me from both the screen and across the room.

"Your turn," he says, pulling out his phone.

I scoff. There's no way I'm posing like a statue for him. "I can't."

He grins, scanning the other figures around the room. "You can. You must." He points to a woman who appears to have thrown herself on the ground in despair. "How about that one?"

"I'm not laying on the floor."

He harrumphs, moving down the line to another statue. "Fair enough. How about this one?"

This woman is glancing over her shoulder, arms clutched protectively against her chest. The plaque on her pedestal reads:

Venus Italica

Workshop of Antonio Canova

(Italian, Possagno 1757–1822 Venice)

"She looks nervous, doesn't she? Like she wishes she could get away." I say, more to myself than to JP.

He narrows his eyes, considering us both as I stand beside the marble woman. "She looks a lot like you. I mean, you're not naked, but you're wearing the exact same expression. And your body language isn't far off either." He captures my image with his phone before I have a chance to position myself beside the statue the way he did and holds out the screen. "See?"

He's right. Our shoulders are hunched; knees bent, ready

to make a quick escape. And our faces, the way our eyes suggest vigilance in the face of constant peril. Do I always look this way?

"Let me do a different one," I say, noticing a less sullen-looking statue toward the end of the hall.

JP reads the inscription beneath the woman's feet. "La Crainte des Traits de l'Amour," he says with a nearly perfect French accent. "It suits you."

I position my hands, mimicking the statue, and cast my gaze down to the right, as if there's a small child beside me as well. "Okay, smart guy, what's it mean?"

"It roughly translates to 'The Fear of Cupid's Darts.'"

I lift my chin just as he snaps the photo. "And you think it suits me?"

He frowns, motioning for me to return to my original position before taking another shot. "Yeah. Don't you?"

In a moment of uncharacteristic boldness, I reach out to place my fingertips against the cool permanence of the granite, wondering what the sculptor, Jean-Louis Lemoyne, would've thought of a girl like me. Would his rendering of my likeness reveal the same apprehension so skillfully chiseled into this woman's face?

I slip my sanitizer from my pocket and squirt both hands before vigorously rubbing my palms together. "I'm not afraid of love," I say more firmly than I intend before stepping into the next room—a blue hallway lined with nothing but ornate side tables.

I'm still staring blankly at an intricately inlaid sideboard when I feel JP step into the room. A beat passes before he speaks but when he does his voice is tentative. Hushed. I don't think he means for me to hear him say, "You might be."

JP isn't the first person to suggest my pathological fear of contamination is something my mind constructed as a way to protect me from the pain of loss. Before moving to Chicago, Roz suggested the mere threat of losing Toby might've reprogrammed my brain, giving me the perfect alibi for keeping others at bay. Germaphobia breeds isolation. Isolation from others ensures I'll never be forced to create emotional attachments.

Is my fear of germs actually a fear of pain? A fear of love?

I shrug. "So, what if I am?"

His shoes squeak across the floor, quieting when he reaches my side. He pretends to study the table. "My mom would be so pissed if I set a glass down on that without a coaster."

"Mine, too."

He chuckles to himself as if remembering something. "This one time when I was little, my dad got all three of us—my older brother Mateo, Andre, and me—these giant snow cones from a street vendor outside our building. Mateo and I drank ours down, but Andre complained his was too cold and set it on Mom's favorite antique sideboard. The next day Mom found a condensation ring worn into the finish, and Andre got this tongue lashing of his life." He pauses then, reaching out to run his fingers across the inlaid mosaic on the table in front of us. "You know the funniest part? Andre told me later that was the best day of his life, getting yelled at by Mom like that. Made him feel like a normal kid, even if it was only for ten minutes."

Tears prick my eyes, but I blink them back. I can't think of a single appropriate thing to say.

"For a long while, Mom covered the damage with a doily. After he died, though, she put it away. I guess she doesn't mind seeing the ring anymore. I guess she doesn't mind being reminded of him." He pauses, clearing his throat. "Your mom decorate with doilies?"

Somehow JP manages to redirect the conversation from serious to silly, taking me from tears to smiles in five seconds flat. "No," I tell him, grateful for the lighter topic of conversation. "She's a modern minimalist. We have so few tchotchkes our apartment echoes sometimes." I glance over at him still staring at the sideboard. "My grandma has lots of them though. They were her mother's. My mom calls them her 'dust collectors.'"

He laughs, finally turning to face me. "Our apartment is like a shrine to 1945. It's so weird. I wouldn't be surprised if some of my mom's junk ends up in a museum someday. A doily museum."

"Maybe they could make room for them here," I say, following him into the Wrightsman Galleries where we begin quizzing one another on the portraits we recognize from art history class. We're having so much fun trying to out-do one another, I don't realize we've stumbled into the American Art gallery. A handful of teens are sitting around a large table with clay and sculpting tools scattered between them.

"Oh." I hesitate by the door. "Is this the workshop?"

JP nods toward the table. "Yeah, I think so. And it looks like they're sculpting clay faces this time." He raises an eyebrow and bites at his bottom lip. "This is the part where you should go get your supplies, assuming you're interested in participating with me."

I get the feeling he has something riding on this. Like he's made a bet with the others about whether he can convince me to participate. It's the first time I've thought about Zaq and Neveah all night. I wonder briefly when they'll be joining us. It's nice having JP to myself.

"My supplies, huh?" I spot a bearded guy with an administrative badge at the sign-in desk. "I think I will get them, thank you very much."

He suppresses a smirk and heads for the far end of the table where two adjacent seats are available. I take a deep breath as I approach the man whose nametag reads: 'Brian— Teens Take the Met Chaperone.'

"Hi, Brian. My name is Phoebe Benson, and my friend Zaq's dad reserved some separate sculpting materials for me to use. He said I should check in here to get them."

He grins at me, his cheeks raising into swollen apples. "Well, of course. I have them put aside for you right here." He reaches into a box beneath the table to reveal a Ziploc bag with my name scrawled in Sharpie across the top. It's stuffed full of supplies—shapers, spatulas, texturers, scrapers, burnishers, and of course, a large ball of clay. "So glad we were able to help you out tonight."

I thank him and make my way over to JP, noting how my interaction with Brian made me feel less like a burden and more like a treasured artifact—another to add to the MET's collection.

"So?" JP says as I sit beside him.

"So, what?"

"So, whose face are you gonna make?"

I chance a glance at the lump of clay in front of him. He's already hollowed out eyes above a rudimentary nose. It looks ridiculous. Honestly, Toby could do a better job. "I dunno. I hadn't thought about it. I didn't know if I would even make it this far."

He returns to his misshapen visage, attempting to fashion a chin by pinching the bottom of the lump. "I'm making

Light Yagami."

I scoff. "The anime guy?"

"Yeah. Why? You got a problem with Death Note?"

"No. It's cool. It's just… you're doing it all wrong. Your proportions are completely off. Can you find a picture of him on your phone?"

He drops the clay glob which looks nothing like Light Yagami and pulls up Google on his phone. "Here," he says sliding it toward me.

The protagonist of the manga series fills the screen, all tousled and heart-shaped. "The secret to creating a proper face is getting the proportions right. For a standard face, the eyes are about halfway down the head. For an anime face, though, they're a little lower."

His dimple is back. "Show me."

My plastic baggy of supplies is practically screaming for me to open it, but I'm almost certain the instruments aren't brand new, and I have no way of knowing whether the last person who used them was sick. Whoever it was could've coughed on the wire shaper. Or put the boxwood tool up his nose. Or had a raging case of conjunctivitis.

After unzipping the bag to remove the plastic-wrapped ball of clay, I unroll it, relishing the lump against my skin. It's cool and lifelike, pliable like flesh. I resist the urge to close my eyes and imagine as I work it between my hands.

"Once you've created the basic shape, you'll want to carve out the eyes in their proper position to give you a good starting point," I instruct, urging JP to follow along with his own lump of clay. "Light isn't super stylized so his eyes are only slightly larger than a normal person's would be. Like this, see?"

He attempts to imitate the roundish eyes I've carved into

my head on his own. They're a little too large and a bit too wide, but otherwise not entirely awful.

"His nose is long and thin and should reach into the bottom quadrant of his face," I continue, rolling a small cylinder of clay between my palm and the table. "Not too much clay," I warn, "or the nose will be way too big."

Once we've set the eyes, nose, mouth, and ears, our last step is to sculpt Light's massive mop of hair. JP watches wordlessly while I add strip after strip of clay to the head, replicating locks of hair. He sets about creating strands of hair for his Light, carefully cutting ribbons from my flattened-out section of clay. As we work together, side by side, our eyes meet, and I see something in them. Something buoyant and expectant. His smile makes me feel like an ordinary girl capable of doing ordinary things. As I reach out to slice my final strip of clay, his hand brushes against mine, hovering between us in midair.

Dread and longing flood my system in equal parts, and when I glance over to meet his gaze it's obvious there was nothing accidental about the encounter. He brushed my hand on purpose. But why would he do that when he knows, HE KNOWS, how I feel about touch?

"Oh God, Phoebe, I'm sorry," he says as if coming out of a daze. "You've been making such great progress, and I thought…"

Part of me wants to scream at him for being so careless. For forgetting himself. For brushing into me when he knows I don't want to be touched. But then it occurs to me that maybe—just maybe—he thought I was ready to make an actual physical connection.

I take a breath. Close my eyes. Begin counting back from ten.

I am not going to lose it.

I am not going to lose it.

I am not going to lose it.

"Phoebe?" He's staring at me now, worry lines tugging at the corners of his eyes.

"It's okay. I'm okay," I tell him, fishing my hand sanitizer from my pocket.

"You are?" He sounds incredulous and more than a little hopeful.

"Yeah. I mean, I need to go find a restroom to wash up, but I'm not leaving if that's what you're worried about."

"You're not?"

"No. I don't think so." I hesitate as the sanitizer performs its magic between my palms, working to suppress the irrational fear bubbling to the surface. "We should just... You should just be more careful. For the rest of the night. So we don't accidentally bump into each other again."

"Oh, yeah. Absolutely."

"Unless it wasn't an accident. And then maybe next time you could ask first." My heart's thumping. I can't believe I'm saying this. "Not that I'm ready to start touching, but at some point I might be, so you should probably keep checking in."

He nods and looks away, falling silent as I begin cleaning up my supplies. There's an awkwardness between us now, and I hate it.

"You know, your Light didn't turn out half bad," I tell him truthfully, looking at our nearly completed projects beside one another on the table—Light One and Light Two. "You sure you haven't taken a sculpting class before?"

He shakes his head, but I can tell he's secretly pleased with himself. "Nope. You must just be a good teacher. You should do it more often."

Heat warms my face. It feels nice to share something I love with him. It feels nice to be appreciated. "Thanks. Maybe I will."

We're still cleaning up our supplies, not talking about our physical encounter, when Neveah and Zaq arrive.

"Light Yagami, huh?" Neveah says, clearly impressed by our sculptures. "Not bad."

Zaq throws a conspiratorial glance at JP. "And you used the Met's supplies after all, huh Phoebe?"

"Yeah. Thanks for the hookup," I tell him, slipping the last of my tools back into the bag. "It was a lot of fun."

Neveah smiles at us. "The night's still young, though. Who wants to head up to the roof?"

JP glances nervously in my direction, still uncertain about where we'll go from here, both physically and metaphorically. I don't know where we're heading either, but the rooftop seems like a good place to start.

"Lead the way," I tell Neveah, smiling at JP. "Just need to hit the restroom to wash this clay off my hands before we go."

CHAPTER 22

week four

Days later, I'm still thinking about how liberating it felt dancing with JP and his friends on the Met's rooftop terrace as I smooth a rough section on one of the candlestick holders I'm finishing for class Friday afternoon. About ten inches tall and fluted in several places to create a proper base, knop, shoulder, and sconce, I notice only a slight variation between the two lamps once the imperfection is fully removed.

Making a matched pair of anything in pottery is hard. Like ridiculously hard. Because thrown pottery is inherently unique, making two pieces look identical takes skill.

And I totally nailed it.

While I enjoyed the challenge the project presented, it's taken me every bit of the week to finish so there hasn't been spare time for any additional projects until today. A quick glance at the clock on the wall confirms there are still forty-five minutes left until the official end of class. As I carry my candlesticks over to Arrush for final inspection, I consider whether I want to stay today or skip out early. If I skip out, I could take the long route to see JP. But if I stay...

These look incredible, Phoebe," Aarush gushes as I set ₁e candlesticks on the table in front of him. "I bet your mother is going to love having them on her dining room table."

I force myself to look into his face and accept his compliment with as much grace as I can muster. "Thank you. I'm sure she will." Although the truth is Mom displays very little of my work. Too much pottery makes the house look 'cluttered.'

"Would you like to stay a bit longer? You could start next week's project or create a little something on your own again." He hesitates as if he's just remembered something and rises to his feet. "Speaking of that… the jar you made last week is back from the kiln. Let me grab it for you."

My allegiance is torn. Do I leave early so I can deliver the jar I made for JP's tips to him before work, or do I stay and allow myself a few minutes of extra time with a fresh batch of clay?

"I think I'll stay," I tell Aarush when he returns with my jar.

By the time I return to my wheel, there's only half-an-hour left until the end of class. I break off a small clump of clay from my personal stash and relish its smoothness beneath my fingertips. This wet clay is my favorite type of greenware because it's the most mailable. The most like human skin. By the time a project is ready to be fired in the kiln it's either leather hard or has become bone dry—losing its appeal. And after it's fired? Forget it. Then it's just another lifeless object, incapable of change. While it retains some moisture, though, it can still be anything. Still has infinite potential. But the kiln's fire destroys all that, turning it to solid bisque.

On the counter beside Aarush, my candlesticks remain unfired, and if I wanted I could still reform them into something else. By next week, though, after the kiln, they'll only ever be candlesticks. Looking at them now, thinking about how much I've changed in the past few weeks, I'm forced to admit maybe Walter was right. Maybe I am still greenware.

Encouraged by the thought, I focus on the new wet clay in my hands. I've gotten over caring what Eleanor thinks of me from her neighboring wheel and close my eyes unabashedly, blocking out my other senses so I can concentrate fully on the sensation of the clay molding itself against my palms. For several moments, the clay remains its own entity, but it doesn't take long before I'm imagining the clay is something else.

JP's hand.

I'm certain there must be calluses on his fingers, a byproduct of playing the violin. I wonder what those calluses would feel like against my palm. Against my arm. Against my cheek. The wheel slows as I back off the pedal, and when the clay finally comes to a stop, I rub the pads of my fingers against it. If I close my eyes, I can almost feel the rough patches of his skin, like dried candle wax.

The memory of the way he brushed against me at the Met sparks a pang of regret.

"See you all Monday," Aarush says to my classmates who are packing up around me, breaking me from my trance. After stripping the clay off the wheel and tossing it back into the pile, I finish cleaning my workspace, wiping everything down with a wet paper towel.

"Have a good weekend," he says to me when I pass him in the doorway.

"I will," I say. "And you, too."

It's after three o'clock by the time I hit the sidewalk so there's no time to take the long route to work. Wrapped in tissue paper, JP's tip jar is nestled at the bottom of my bag, and I'm disappointed I won't have a chance to give it to him until next week.

The entrance to the 6 is busier than usual as I approach, and I stop at the top of the stairway and mentally prepare myself to enter the tunnel.

And that's when I hear it. Someone's playing the violin.

Cutting my breathing ritual short, I take the steps two at a time, deftly maneuvering around a group of women in yoga pants on the way to the local studio and two teens carrying skateboards. My metro card is stuck in my pocket, and I struggle to dislodge it as I reach the turnstiles. My hand sanitizer is in the way, and as I slip my latex glove out of my pocket, the metro card falls to the ground.

Oh my God. Holy crap.

Beside me a brutish-looking guy curses under his breath as he pushes past me, accidentally kicking my card under the turnstile as he passes through. My heart is pounding against the inside of my chest as I consider my options, none of which are optimal.

1. Leave the station and walk thirty plus blocks to Dust Jackets where I can borrow one of Walter's cards for the trip home.

2. Put on my glove, pick up my card off the ground, and proceed through the turnstile.

3. Curl up in a corner and die.

Although the corner does look mildly inviting, the thought of walking halfway across Manhattan in ninety-degree heat makes my decision for me. In one swift motion, I slip on my glove, pluck my card off the ground and swipe it through the reader. When I look at it all I can see are millions upon millions of germs swarming all over its surface, a tiny infantry of invaders. In a moment of rare decisiveness, I turn my glove inside out over the card in much the same way as I've seen doctors do on television shows, encasing it inside the impermeable latex shield before tying the end shut like a balloon. It occurs to me I'm going to have to retrieve the card for my trip home from work, but I decide to deal with it when the time comes and toss it into my bag.

The sound of the violin continues down the hall, and once I recognize the melody being played, I know exactly who it is.

"JP," I call out when I'm within earshot. "What are you doing here?"

He waves to me with his bow and starts in my direction. "I'm here to see you."

"Me? Why?"

He shrugs. "Because it's faster for you to take the 6 to work, and I can play wherever, so I might as well play in a place where I get to see you every day."

I'd never considered this before, assuming instead the Q was somehow his line and the 6 was mine. Knowing he changed his routine for a chance to see me quickens my heart in a far more desirable way than dropping my metro card on the ground. "That's really sweet. And it's nice seeing you, too. In fact," I say, remembering what's in my bag, "I almost headed over to the Q today to find you. But now I'm glad I didn't."

"You did?" He looks chuffed.

"Yeah. I have something to give you." I reach into my

bag, pull out the tip jar wrapped in tissue paper, and hand it to him. "I made this."

He tucks his violin and bow under his arm and unfolds the wrapping. He runs his fingers across the glazed surface and traces the letters– T I P S—I carved into the front. Once he realizes what it is, his face breaks into a grin. "This is awesome."

"Yeah. I mean, I know you have your case which is probably a better way to collect tips in the subway, but when you play other places, like events and things, I thought a jar might be nice."

"Really nice," he agrees, rewrapping the tissue around it. "And I can't believe I have a Phoebe Benson original. I mean, when you're a famous artist, this thing is gonna be worth a ton. I might be able to retire on what I make off it."

I know he's teasing but the words fill me in a way Aarush's don't. They fill me in a way I've never been filled before.

I glance at the train schedule above our heads. The southbound should be arriving in less than two minutes.

Part of me wants to wait for the next one.

JP tucks the jar carefully into his bag. "I was going to text you today if I didn't see you for some reason." He clears his throat. "Luke, uh, invited everyone to go bowling Sunday night and wanted to make sure I invited you, too."

Luke, who could barely contain his annoyance with me at the diner? The guy who found a convenient excuse not to come with the rest of us to the Met? That Luke is inviting me to go bowling?

It seems unlikely he actually wants me along, but I'm fairly certain I know what's going on.

1. Luke invited everyone else.

2. JP asked if I could come along, too.

3. Luke agreed but only because, given my aversion to touch, he's hoping I'll decline his invitation.

It's a safe bet since the thought of touching a bowling ball held by thousands of other people makes my skin prickle. And then there are the shoes. He must know I'll never take him up on this offer.

"There's no way I'm going to a bowling alley," I say.

He nods and raises a hand in acknowledgment of my refusal. "I kinda figured that would be the case. But this offer is a special and unique opportunity you won't be able to pass up." His voice sounds like a Telemundo infomercial salesman. I almost expect him to finish with 'but wait, there's more.'

"I'm listening." I catch a glimpse of something resembling relief in his eyes.

"Luke's uncle owns a bowling alley out in Queens and they close early on Sundays. Luke said we could go there after-hours so it would be just the five of us. Or seven if Neveah brings her cousin and Zaq brings his boyfriend."

Commuters swarm around us, and I'm exasperated by JP's apparent lack of understanding. "You know, being around crowds of people is only one of my issues." I extend my arms to indicate the commotion going on around us. "The touching is a problem, too. The bowling balls. And God help me, the shoes…"

'Yeah, no, I get it." He fiddles with his bow. "And I think Luke has a way to address your germaphobia, but only if we go there when it's closed to the public."

An image of us bowling together pops into my head, and I have to admit it's not entirely awful. "His uncle won't mind?"

He shrugs. "Nah. Luke knows how to get in. He's done it before. I don't think it'll be a big deal. And besides, if you don't come now, when am I ever gonna get to show you my killer hook shot?"

I chew the inside of my cheek. There is no reality in which I ever imagined myself bowling, and yet... "I'm not touching some filthy communal balls. They're disgusting."

He grins mischievously but lets my inadvertent innuendo slide without comment. "I'll talk to Luke. We'll figure something out." He lifts his chin, eyes hopeful, as the train roars into the station, and I can't help smiling back at him. "Is that a yes then? You'll come with us?"

I think of the spilled cocktail and storytime and dropped metro card I somehow managed to move past without incident. "It's a maybe. Text me later after you've talked to Luke about the ball and the shoes."

CHAPTER 23

week five

When JP texts me Saturday afternoon to assure me both the ball and shoe situations have been addressed, he also insists on meeting me at the 23rd Street station where we'll be able to catch the F into Queens. I try to convince him it's unnecessary to come all the way into Manhattan to pick me up, but he claims he's going to be in the area anyway.

"I'm picking up a new E string at my favorite supply store nearby. Plus, it'll give us more time to hang out."

I'm surprised by how relieved I am to see him sitting on the worn wooden bench under the green-tiled '23rd Street' sign as the train reaches the platform. It's strange seeing him sans violin case and without it I can't help but notice the way his vintage Black Sabbath t-shirt cuts snugly against his chest. I wonder briefly what it would feel like to lay my head against it but quickly toss the thought aside.

We proceed along the familiar route I take into Queens whenever my family visits my grandma. Along the way, JP explains the intricacies of proper bowling etiquette.

"Only one person can be on the lane at a time. You gotta give space, you know, so the other bowlers don't get distracted. And you're only allowed to take your turn when the bowlers on either side of you have completed their turns, but you won't need to worry about that since we'll be the only ones there."

"About that," I say, still unconvinced this whole plan is sound. "You sure it's okay we're doing this?"

The train rattles against the tracks as we emerge from the East River tunnel. Fading sunlight washes into the car, brightening JP's face.

"I guess. Luke says when he was little, before his parents hated each other, his entire extended family used to go there after hours on Sunday nights. He says he can get us in without any trouble. And since it's closed, we'll be able to bowl in our socks."

I interrupt him. "But we're stealing a ball?"

He sighs. "We're not stealing. We're just borrowing a new one from the pro shop for you to use tonight. We'll put it back when you're done, and no one will be the wiser."

It sounds easy coming from JP, as if breaking and entering isn't technically what we're planning to do.

"And we're sure Luke's uncle is okay with us going in?"

He shrugs. "As far as I know. I mean, I don't see why not."

I can think of a dozen reasons why not, but I don't say anything. If JP's cool with it then I figure I should be, too, especially when there are more important things to worry about than Luke's uncle.

My utter lack of bowling experience, for example.

"I'm probably gonna suck," I admit aloud as we pull away from the Queensbridge station. I'm not sure why I want to impress him, but I do, and as heat spreads across my cheeks, I turn my attention to the world opening up around us—

rowhouses and corner markets and gas stations—to avoid having to return his gaze.

"Everybody sucks at first," he says, his voice reassuring. "I think I was like ten before my mom finally let me play without the bumpers."

I scrunch my face in confusion.

"Most places have bumpers they put up for people just learning how to play. Used to be they were just inflatable tubes along both gutters so the ball would bounce back into the lane, but they were a pain to set up so now they use metal rails that slide up out of the gutter. I'm sure Luke will know how to pull them up if you wanna use them."

"You think I'm gonna need them?"

He chuckles, considering his own hands. "I think I'm gonna need them. I haven't bowled in forever. Probably not since middle school. I'll ask him to put them up, just in case."

He's insisting a bit too much, the way Toby does when he's trying to convince us he's not on the brink of a respiratory episode. In JP's case, I suspect he's a far better bowler than he's letting on, what with the education he's attempting to give me and all. Still, that he's willing to ask on his behalf to spare my embarrassment warms my heart.

Twilight is fading by the time we hop off the train, casting dark shadows down alleys. The dense Manhattan skyline has given way to sparser suburbia with its squat buildings and corner bodegas. We walk beside one another in agreeable silence as Luke and JP shoot a handful of texts back and forth confirming the location of the bowling alley and instructions once we arrive.

I spot Neveah the moment we round the corner to the bowling center's delivery entrance, her dreadlocks piled on the top of her head with a colorful wrap. She waves frantically upon seeing us and begins walking in our direction, her leather strapped sandals flip-flopping against the pavement.

"You made it," she says brightly, looking past JP directly at me. The tone of her voice suggests there'd been some question as to whether I would show up.

"I did," I reply, hoping I don't look as nervous as I feel.

JP glances further down the drive. "You the first one here?"

"Actually, no. You're the last ones here. Luke, Zaq, Devyn, and Calvin are already inside. And there was a little mishap with the alarm, but I think Luke got it sorted." She turns to the door, wrenching it open before stepping inside. "Come on, you gotta see this place."

JP catches the door before it closes, holding it open for me. He doesn't say anything as I hesitate on the sidewalk, cool air from inside prickling my skin. He just stands there, waiting, his face free of emotion, unaffected by the unfathomable number of germs inside the bowling alley, a place where people sweat and eat and use the bathroom without washing their hands.

I force myself to ignore them as I step across the threshold.

It takes a few seconds for my eyes to adjust to the dim interior. A few safety lights glow eerily around the alley, casting dark shadows across the polished hardwoods. Voices echo from somewhere in the distance. Luke calls to Zaq. He calls back. And there's a girl's voice I don't recognize.

"The main bank of lights is in the office, and the office door is locked," Luke calls.

Footsteps pound across the space. Zaq curses under his breath. "Here, just let me try it."

Beside me, JP takes in our surroundings—the disco ball overhead, the dayglow carpeting, the kitschy wall murals—and nods approvingly to himself. He's about to say something when a loud crash from the far end of the building sends him sprinting in the direction of the office. Not wanting to be left alone, I start after him, maneuvering between snack bar tables and ball racks until I reach the hallway where everyone else is standing. In addition to the people I already know, there are two others JP told me to expect: a guy I assume is Zaq's boyfriend, Calvin, and a girl who looks so much like Neveah, it must be her cousin.

"You broke the lock?" Luke cries in frustration.

"It's not a big deal." Zaq shrugs. "We can just move the padlock a little higher and patch the hole in the door."

Luke's face reddens, and he takes a deep breath through his nose. "It's a very big deal." He snatches the broken lock from Zaq's hand. "And I'm gonna catch hell for this. I knew coming here with you guys was a bad idea."

As the level of behind-the-scenes coercion which must've taken place between Luke and JP reveals itself, an enormous wave of guilt washes over me. This whole outing was JP's idea, not Luke's. And somehow JP convinced him to coordinate all of it for my benefit. Now the door's broken, Zaq and Luke are fighting, and it's all my fault.

If I wasn't so needy JP and I could just go bowling together like regular people, and he wouldn't feel the need to pressure his friends into breaking into a secured office after hours like a bunch of common criminals.

Concern and remorse must be written all over my face because when I catch JP's eye he immediately looks away as if the smudge on the floor below him is the most interesting thing he's ever seen.

Neveah takes a step forward, running her hand against the door's rough edge. "It's an easy fix, but dude, you could've at least tried unscrewing the latch first."

Zaq shrugs, pushes the door open, and steps into the office, flicking on the light. "I'm sorry about the door and promise to help you fix it, but when was the last time I did anything with finesse? You know me, I'm the master of brute force and awkwardness. It's how I get things done." He winks at his boyfriend, Calvin.

Without another word of acknowledgment, Luke shoves past him, heading straight for the control panel on the far wall. He flips the main switch, illuminating the entire bowling center. Scoring monitors wink on above each alley down the line and the ball returns hum with life. "Okay. You came here to bowl. So, go bowl."

Zaq and Calvin take off for the lanes hand-in-hand, leaving the rest of us standing awkwardly outside the office door.

"I, uh, thought you said you'd grab a new ball for Phoebe to use," JP says, stepping into the room.

I've never wanted to disappear inside my skin more than I do at this moment. I want to tell him his efforts are unnecessary—I can just sit to the side and watch. I don't need to bowl. I don't want to cause any more problems.

Luke sighs. "Yeah. There should be some over here in this cabinet."

While the others mill about the office, Luke wrestles open a metal cabinet with the grace of a drunken sailor. Beside me, the girl who is Neveah/Not Neveah taps the pads of her fingers against the pads of her thumbs in rapid succession, humming quietly to herself.

"Phoebe, this is my cousin, Devyn," Neveah says. "She

has OCD."

Devyn looks up from her self-imposed treatment to say hello just as Luke extricates a box from the bottom shelf. "There's a brand-new, germ-free ball inside here you can use. Ten pounds should be about right." He pulls off the lid, revealing the bright orange ball inside. "Go ahead. Take it. Just try not to scuff it up, okay? I won't be able to buff out any deep scratches."

I consider putting on one of my gloves, but if the ball's never been used there shouldn't be any need. I slip my thumb and two fingers into the holes and lift the ball out of the box. It feels strange to be holding something other than clay.

"How's it feel?" JP asks. "Too heavy? Too light?"

I'm Goldilocks tasting the porridge. "No. It's just right."

"Well, good. Then let's get this party started."

Back in the huge expanse of the bowling center, JP hovers beside me as we take off our shoes like he's waiting for me to come to my senses, realizing where I am and what I'm doing. At the center lane, Neveah wipes down the ball return and the seats with Clorox wipes.

"Sanitizing was Devyn's idea," she says as I approach, giving a nod to her cousin.

"I appreciate it," I say to both girls. "Every little bit helps."

Once Luke raises the gutter bumpers, I'm encouraged to go first, and after ricocheting across the lane twice, my ball knocks down four pins. My success is met with fervent cheers from behind. My ball seems to take forever to roll back down the shoot, and I wonder how annoyed everyone is going to get having to wait on me all night.

I tumble four more pins with my second roll, and I can't help being secretly pleased with my score.

Or the fact I'm having a good time.

"You know," Zaq says as I join everyone back on the benches, "there's no reason we all need to bowl in one lane. The place is ours. We can each have our own."

Everyone agrees this is a tremendous idea and in less than two minutes we've spread out over six lanes, with Zaq and Calvin opting to bowl together. Devyn takes the lane to my right, JP the lane to my left.

"Time for us to get strikes," he says winking at me.

I don't get a strike, but I do manage to pick up a spare. The pins crash around us, and I wait for my ball.

Devyn moves to the edge of her lane. "Neveah says you have an anxiety disorder. Specifically, germaphobia?"

I nod. "Yeah. That's what the therapists tell me."

She holds her hot pink ball against her chest and gives me a weak smile. "You know, the term germaphobia was coined by William A. Hammond in 1879 when he described a case of obsessive-compulsive disorder exhibited in repeatedly washing one's hands."

It sounds as though she's been hanging out with Walter. "I didn't know that," I admit. "And I thought I knew everything about my cursed affliction."

She laughs at this. "I know more than any one person should about OCD. There's this guy in my group who can name every phobia in the order it was added to the DSM-5."

My ball has returned, but I don't pick it up. "That's impressive." I hesitate, wondering if it's appropriate to ask about the nature of her group. I decide to go for it.

Devyn gives me a knowing smile. "I go once a week to group therapy. It's a bunch of high schoolers with different mental health issues—depression, anxiety, OCD, ADHD, eating disorders, autism. You name it, one of us carries the diagnosis." She slides her fingers into the holes of her ball and turns her attention back to her lane. "You should come with me sometime."

I return to my own game, throwing the ball wildly down the lane as I consider her invitation. It might be nice to have someone to talk to other than Walter, but I feel guilty just thinking about it. He and I are good together. I don't need anyone else. I mean, I'm bowling for crying out loud.

"You want some help?" JP asks after yet another one of my balls careens off the end of the lane without hitting a single pin.

A glance at his monitor reveals he's finished his fourth frame and already has a score of seventy-six. I don't even know how that's possible considering I have a score of twenty-seven.

He crosses the invisible barrier between our lanes to stand beside me, his biceps flexing under the weight of his ball. Demonstrating his technique, he explains, "You want to start back here and as you approach the line bring your arm forward, wrist straight. Keep your whole body lined up so everything points to the center of the lane."

Behind him, Luke appears to have gotten over his anger, laughing with Zaq and Calvin as each of them pirouette down their respective lanes like a trio of possessed ballet dancers. As distracting as they are, for some reason, I can't take my eyes off JP. The way he's smiling at me. The way he looks as if he'd like nothing more than to take my hand and demonstrate his technique using my body instead.

The memory of our encounter at the Met returns—a flitter of longing associated with his touch. Surprisingly, the same unfamiliar desire stirs within me now. The need to touch and be touched. The primeval compulsion for human contact.

Do I want to let him touch me?

Do I want to touch him back?

I'm still weighing my options, talking myself through the mental gymnastics crucial to making such a decision when my thoughts are interrupted by the deafening wail of a police siren coming from just outside the front door.

CHAPTER 24

week five

Behind me, Luke is trying desperately to explain to Officer McNeil how and why we came to be in the bowling alley.

"Listen, kid. All I know is when the alarm was triggered and no one answered the security company's call, it was sent to dispatch. Now I have the seven of you with no tangible proof you are who you say you are or whether you have permission to be here. What I do know is you've broken into a private business which is a criminal offense. I don't have any choice but to take you all in. You can call your families when we get there."

I'm certain my face mirrors the horror visible on everyone else's.

None of us wants to go to jail.

"Try my uncle again," Luke pleads for the third time.

"We've called the number you gave us. Several times. There's no answer."

"What about one of the managers. Maybe we can get one of them to vouch for me," Luke says.

Officer McNeil scoffs. "You got their numbers?"

Luke's shoulders slump. "No. But I might be able to find them inside."

"Fat chance," the officer says to Luke before speaking into the walkie clipped to his shoulder. "This is thirty-three. Bringing in seven suspects on a 10-23, break-in in progress."

JP's gaze fixes on mine. He knows what I'm thinking. He knows I'm less worried about an arrest record than I am about the legions of microbes I'm sure to encounter inside the patrol car and at the precinct.

Could I possibly be more ridiculous?

"You two." Officer McNeil points at Neveah and Zaq. "Go with Officer Eifert. And the two of you," he continues, pointing at Devyn and Calvin, "go with Officer Neilson." He thumbs his finger at the rest of us. "The three of you are coming with me to the station so we can get this whole thing sorted out."

He opens the patrol car door for us, and it's stupid, but I can't help being relieved I wasn't forced to touch the handle. Luke goes first, shooting an icy glare in my direction before scooting across the back seat. There's only a second to respond with my own look of remorse and shame before the police officer takes a step in my direction.

"You're next, missy," he says when I don't immediately follow Luke. "Get in."

Behind me, I feel JP's presence. "It's gonna be okay," he whispers. "You don't have to touch anything. Just get in, and I'll be right beside you."

My hands are palsied with tremors. All I can think about are all the filthy, disgusting criminals who've come before me. How many have thrown up back here? Relieved themselves? Bled from open wounds?

"Now," the officer barks, officially losing any patience he

might've had with me at the start.

JP turns to him, and with a tone he probably has no business taking with an officer of the law says, "She suffers from an anxiety disorder. You're freaking her out. Just give her a second." Without waiting for a response, he returns his attention to me. "Put your hands on your lap and slide across on your butt. Your shorts will protect your legs."

Our eyes lock and the intensity of his determination compels me into the car. If he says it's going to be alright, it's going to be alright.

Right?

The seat is plasticky and slightly sticky, and I have to scooch instead of slide to the middle of the seat. JP slips in behind me and in his haste, our shoulders accidentally brush against one another. I wait for the rush of panic. For the fear to kick in. Instead, our brief physical connection comes as a welcome relief.

We're in this together.

I'm not alone.

It's me and JP... and God help me, millions and millions of germs.

I manage to avoid touching anything with my hands the entire way to the precinct. Once we get there, though, we're ushered through a side entrance into an in-processing area where we're made to surrender everything we're carrying. I'm forced to hand over my hand sanitizer and my latex gloves— the only things protecting me from the threat of the outside world.

As the admitting officer drops them into a bag with my other possessions and carries them away, I close my eyes and attempt to visualize something calm. Something joyful.

Something to make me forget where I am and what I'm being exposed to. My thoughts immediately go to JP and the way he makes me feel when we're together. Like I'm more than just the sum of my anxieties. Like I'm whole and worthy both because of them and despite them. Clinging to this sense of belonging, I'm able to hold it together until a female officer approaches donning a pair of her own latex gloves.

"I'm going to pat you down," she says, "starting with your head and working my way to your feet.

Until that moment, I'd been balancing on the tip of a needle. Now, there's nothing left but to burst into tears. "No. Please," I beg her, my voice trembling. "I'm not hiding anything. I just don't like being touched. Can you do something else instead?"

"Honey, this is standard procedure. You need to comply or you can be charged with resisting an officer."

Beneath me, my entire body trembles almost to the point of spasm, and my lungs fill with sand. Everything around me appears hazy and dark around the edges, as if I'm in a cheesy made-for-TV movie, and I'm about to fade out of a scene. Beside me, JP's not looking so great himself—his brows stitched tightly together, gaze wary. Sweat stains spread beneath his armpits, and he's picked a cuticle raw. Scanning the room, the others don't look much better, especially Luke, who's tapping his foot so forcefully, I'm afraid he's going to rub a hole through the linoleum floor. Still, when JP sees me crying, begging for clemency, he takes a step in my direction, as far as the officers will allow.

"Phoebe," he says quietly. "Just close your eyes and pretend what you're feeling are your own hands or something else that's completely sterile. Once you get through it, they aren't going to do anything more than talk to us. Just tell them the truth, and when they finally get a hold of Luke's uncle, he'll explain everything, and they'll let us go. Seriously, the only way they can keep us is if someone presses charges, and there's no way his uncle will make us stay here. Just get through this and everything will be fine." His voice is steadier than his frazzled posture would suggest causing a small glimmer of something like relief to spread through me.

Unfortunately, that flicker is immediately squelched by the reality of our situation.

1. The police have taken my lifelines, a stranger is about to frisk me, and gloves or no gloves, I don't want to be touched.

2. I am going to need to call my parents to let them know I broke into a bowling alley, trespassed onto private property, and am currently being detained by the police in Queens.

3. All of it is completely my fault.

And then, I pass out.

CHAPTER 25

week five

Dad shows up just before midnight to retrieve me from the precinct. He's alone because Mom didn't think it was a good idea to expose Toby to the scandal of my indiscretions. At least that's what he tells me as we cross the police station parking lot on the way to his car. "But seriously, Phoebe, what in God's name would compel you to break into a bowling alley? Why wouldn't you all just ask permission?"

I wish I had a logical explanation for him, but I don't even have the strength to make something up. The stress of being patted down—and fainting—before coming to in a room with three unsheltered kids, a junkie who was practically foaming at the mouth, and a drunk girl who threw up twice, not ten feet from where I was sitting has drained me of any desire to explicate myself.

Luke's uncle arrived two hours after our initial detainment and assured the arresting officers Luke was his nephew, and as such he wouldn't be filing charges against any of us. But by then the damage was already done.

After barely making it through the experience, I've

decided I'm never, ever putting myself in a position to let anything like this happen again. Maybe I didn't have friends before I started this little social experiment of Walter's, but I lived my life on my own terms which included no unsolicited contact. I also didn't get arrested and thrown into jail, exposing me to far more potentially deadly pathogens than I'd otherwise be subjected to during an average day. The precinct was certainly crawling with Hep-A, Norovirus, strep, MERSA, ringworm...

I shudder to think.

"Well, I just hope you learned your lesson." Dad jingles his car keys in his hand. "It's lucky your friend's uncle didn't press charges." He unlocks the car door and pulls the handle for me. "And you are definitely grounded, young lady. You won't be going out again with these friends of yours for a very long time."

"Don't worry." I slide into the passenger's seat. "My going out days are officially over."

***

After a silent trip across the city, Toby's asleep by the time we get home, but Mom's waiting with a cup of hot tea at the kitchen table.

"Sit down, Phoebe," she says when I walk in the room.

I motion toward the bathroom. "Can I take a shower first, and then we can talk?"

"No. I'm tired. I want to go to bed. Sit."

I swallow hard. My head's pounding. "Could I stand instead?" She's angry but there's a hint of compassion in the tone of her voice. "It's just, I'm contaminated is all."

She nods. "Fine. You can stand. But you need to know how disappointed we are in you."

I'm unable to look her in the eye. Disappointed is assumed. I mean, how many parents would be like 'great job getting arrested for trespassing.'

"I know. I'm sorry I let you down."

"Well, it's not like we shouldn't shoulder some of the blame. This might not've happened if we hadn't allowed you to go with them to that bar. I should've trusted my gut about these kids from the beginning. They're obviously not the sort of people we want influencing your decisions."

Dad stands behind Mom at the table and lays his hands on her shoulders—an act of solidarity or surrender. I'm not sure which. "It's just… we can't understand why you even agreed to go with these kids to the bowling alley in the first place. Why you would think trespassing was a good idea. You don't even know how to bowl."

I take a deep breath and blink back tears, suddenly defensive. My friends are not bad people. And JP is not a bad influence. "The others only trespassed because of me. They can go bowling anytime they want during normal hours without having to break in, but they decided to trespass after it was closed so I could go with them. They thought it would be better if I could go without all the other people around. They were trying to be good friends."

My dad looks slightly less irritated. "While it's kind of them to include you and consider your needs, it still doesn't explain why you didn't just ask permission instead of breaking in."

"You'll have to ask Luke because I have absolutely no idea. I assumed we had permission until the cops showed up."

"Really?" Mom asks skeptically.

"Yes," I reply since it's mostly the truth.

She stands from the table, sighing as she carries her mug to the sink. "You're grounded, you know, for the rest of the summer. No going out with anyone else. You can go to pottery class and work, but that's it. Otherwise, you're here at home."

"So back to life as usual. Got it," I say under my breath. "Am I excused?"

***

After a long, hot shower utilizing half a bottle of antibacterial body wash, I take my contaminated clothes and dump them into the washing machine knowing I may never wear them again. By the time I get to my bedroom, my phone has blown up with messages from Zaq, Neveah, and JP.

> *Zaq: just wanted to tell you how sorry i am about tonight. i know it totally sucked for you. hang in there huh? ervthings cool.*

> *JP: Hey. You ok? Worried about you. Please let me know.*

> *Neveah: are you ok? so worried about you. let me know you're ok.*

> *Neveah: where are you? you ok?*

> *JP: You're scaring me Phoebe. Please talk to me. I'm scared for you.*

> *Neveah: can u meet tomorrow? just to chat? need to know you're ok.*

JP: Phoebe...
JP: Phoebe...
JP: PHOEBE!!!!!

I sit for a long moment staring at the screen, reading and rereading the messages from my new friends. I want to respond reassuringly—tell them I'm okay, and it's no big deal. But I'm not okay. And it is a big deal. What I need to tell them is we can't be friends anymore because I won't be responsible for their reckless behavior. I won't be the person who forces them to change their plans, redirect their agendas, or take stupid risks in the hopes of giving me an authentic teenage experience.

They broke the law so I could be involved, and we were all arrested because I couldn't go bowling with them legally like a regular person.

I compose several responses in my head, but in the end, I power off my phone and climb into bed without replying at all.

CHAPTER 26

week five

Walter's in the back of the store with a customer when I show up for work Monday afternoon. I'm late because I took the Q instead of the 6 to avoid JP. Now I'm sweaty and exhausted and in no mood for the inquisition I know is coming.

My phone buzzes in my pocket for the eleventh time in the past half hour. I know it's JP. I know he's wondering why he didn't see me at the subway. And also why I haven't returned any of his texts or calls since leaving the police station Saturday night.

"Both of these books are excellent resources for indoor gardening," Walter says to a young couple following him down the aisle. "Indoor Gardening for Novices is a more entry-level read while Urban Jungle is great specifically for small indoor spaces like city apartments. I don't think you can go wrong with either choice."

"I think we'll take them both," the shorter of the two women says winking up at her partner. "We need as much help as we can get."

"It's true." The chic-looking blond laughs. "We killed a

ficus. Who in the world is hopeless enough to kill a ficus?"

I slip between two shelves as they approach the counter, still chuckling about their collective horticultural ineptitude. Perhaps if I can begin my sorting before Walter notices I've arrived I'll avoid having to fill him in on my disastrous weekend.

My stack of books is right where I left it Friday afternoon. I slip on my glove and set about logging new inventory into the database, but I only make it to the fifth title before I hear the bell over the door signaling the women's departure.

In less than ten seconds, Walter's by my side. "So, how was bowling? Did you get any strikes?"

"No," I tell him flatly, taking another book from the stack. "I got arrested."

"Excuse me?" He leans against my table. "You got arrested?"

I continue entering the book's title into the system to avoid making eye contact. "Yeah. It was horrible, and I don't want to talk about it if it's just the same to you."

His astonishment bores into me, begging to be addressed, and just when I think he's going to pry me for information, he straightens himself and starts to the front of the store. "Suit yourself," he says. "And by the way, I've got another delivery coming tomorrow so if you could finish those today that'd be great. Might have to work a little more expeditiously, though, since you couldn't be bothered to make it to work on time today."

The stench of his passive-aggressive attitude lingers long after he's safely perched behind the counter at the front of the store. I pick up the next book, Love's Tender Embrace, and flip to the copyright page so I can input the publishing information into the system. Another Harlequin—no surprise there with a title like that. I flip through the first chapters where the main character, a beautiful (albeit mildly unhappy) middle-aged woman meets the man she'll fall in love with, break up with, and eventually reunite with for her happily-ever-after by the last chapter. I wonder what these two love birds will need to overcome? A jilted ex-girlfriend? A secret love child? A disapproving family?

Anything but mental health issues because obviously no relationships ever recover from those.

I chuck the romance at a nearby shelf, and it crashes to the floor. I hate the stupid book and its stupid message that if you can make it past life's stumbling blocks, everything will work out in the end. For those of us with anxiety disorders, nothing ever works out because life is just a series of never-ending obstacles, one after another.

I key in the information about the next book and the one after, but by the third, it's obvious I don't have the strength to concentrate on the task at hand, however tedious it might be.

Walter slides his readers to the end of his nose, as I approach. "Thought you didn't want to talk about it."

"I don't. But I think I need to."

He pats the seat of the chair beside him, an invitation onto the therapist's couch.

I sink into the seat. "It was awesome—the bowling part I mean. I sucked so bad, but it was still fun because it didn't matter, you know? It was just fun being a part of what was going on around me, like in it as opposed to watching from the sidelines."

He smiles but doesn't interrupt. He really should have his license.

"Anyway, I guess Luke never actually got permission for us to be there, and then he accidentally set off the alarm and didn't answer the phone when the monitoring company called to make sure everything was okay. They assumed the alarm was legit and called the cops. They found us when they arrived, and when we didn't have any proof we were allowed to be there, they took us to the station until it could be sorted out."

Walter's worked his face into a neutral expression, but I can still make out a glimmer of mischief behind his carefully fabricated façade. There's a part of him who's happy I got into trouble like a regular kid. "And I assume since you're not still behind bars you were able to get things taken care of?"

I nod. "Yeah. Luke's uncle showed up after a couple of hours and explained everything to the police. But Walter, oh my God, it was the worst place ever. I barely survived."

He peers over his glasses at me. "They touched you."

My heart quickens involuntarily at the thought. "Yeah. Big time."

"And there were lots of gross people?"

"The grossest," I confirm.

"But you're still here."

A beat of silence passes between us, our eyes locked onto one another. I get what he's saying, I do. But no. Just no. "I can't do this anymore."

He turns from me, adjusts his computer screen to account for the sun glare. "Do what?"

"Let people into my life. I mean, I did what you wanted, right? I met JP. I met his friends. I let them in. And guess what happened. We all got arrested."

"No one got arrested because of you, Phoebe. They got arrested because your friend Luke was too stupid to ask for permission. And because he set off the alarm. Neither of those things is on you."

I slide my arms across my chest. "Luke's not my friend, especially after calling me a freak the other night."

"He said that to you? I thought you were friends. Wasn't this whole trip to the bowling alley his idea?"

I'd initially ignored the off-handed comment Luke made while we were all in the holding cell together, about how this was the last time he was gonna go out of his way for some freak. But the truth is, his words stung because thanks for the reminder, jerk.

I pick at a loose piece of thread along the frayed edge of my jeans shorts to avoid looking Walter in the eye. "JP told me bowling was Luke's idea, but he lied. He pressured Luke into letting us in because he feels sorry for me. None of them would have been in any position to get arrested if it wasn't for me and my stupid anxiety. It's just like at the Met when JP skipped all the cool stations to walk around the exhibits with me. I'm a leach, Walter. All I do is cause problems."

"And he told you this? JP said he wished he could be doing lots of other fun stuff, but now he can't because he's saddled to you?"

The bell over the door chimes as Beverly breezes into the store with a plate full of baked goods. "Hello, Walter. Hello, Phoebe," she trills.

Walter looks between us, his allegiance split. Finally, he turns to me. "Did it ever occur to you, Miss Benson, perhaps these friends of yours simply enjoy your company and don't consider making accommodations for you a sacrifice?"

Beverly purses her lips, setting the plate on the counter. "It sounds as though I've interrupted you two. I'll just leave these here and come back later."

"No, no." Walter reaches out to take her hand. "I think Phoebe and I were just about finished anyway."

I agree, smiling sweetly at them before retreating to my inventory pile.

It's almost closing by the time I hear Beverly call a cheerful goodbye as she leaves the store. A moment later, Walter's by my side, retrieving stacks of books off the floor that have piled up around me. "D'you think at all about what I said before?"

I shrug.

"I'm sure none of them blame you for what happened."

I'm glad he can be so certain.

"Have you at least reached out to JP? Met at the subway station? Given him a call?"

I glare up at Walter. I have no idea why he can't accept the truth. Being friends with me is a burden no one should have to bear. Probably not even him. "No. I haven't. Because I'm grounded for the rest of the summer. But I don't care. I'm letting them all off the hook so they can go back to their regular lives where they don't have to take my needs into constant consideration."

Deep lines furrow between his brows. "I can't stop you from doing what you think is best. But I, for one, think you're making a horrible mistake."

CHAPTER 27

week five

Aarush shows up to class Wednesday morning with a runny nose. And I'm not talking about an occasional sniffle—I'm talking about frequent, full-on snot blowing maelstroms. We're supposed to be constructing a piece incorporating words or letters this week, but with his constant sniffing and blowing and sniffing and blowing, I've barely worked on my design at all. What I'm doing instead is monitoring Aarush for proper handwashing technique after each trip to the tissue box. So far, I give him a C-.

The clay, which until this moment has always been my escape, lays in a lifeless mass atop my wheel. I squeeze a few drops of water from my sponge to rewet the surface, but as I press the pedal to make the lump turn beneath my hands, there's absolutely no relief. Instead of being transported to a place where touching is safe, I'm still right in the second-floor walkup pottery studio where touch is not only unsafe, it's downright dangerous, especially with Aarush spreading his mucus-y particulates around like confetti.

By the time we break for lunch, my stomach is so knotted I can barely sit upright, much less think about eating. I'm short on sanitizer, having already used most of my bottle as a precautionary measure against Aarush, so while everyone else grabs their lunch bags and gathers at the worktable to eat, I throw my bag over my shoulder and bolt out the front door without cleaning my station or offering an explanation for my hasty departure.

Relief washes over me as my feet hit the sidewalk, but as amazing as it feels to be free from Aarush's germs, I know the euphoria will be short-lived. Sure enough, by the time I reach the corner, guilt and shame have already set in. A week ago, instead of leaving, I probably would've looked for other solutions. I might've asked to move my wheel to a more isolated corner of the room. I could've confided in Aarush about my issues, and perhaps asked if he could wear a mask or use some nasal spray. But I didn't. Instead, I did what I always do which is relieve my anxiety in the easiest possible way—by running.

Completely unfazed by any negative opinions Aarush and my classmates might have about me now, I turn south on Lexington, picturing the unfinished project I left drying on the wheel. The reality of having to start over doesn't upset me. Not even a little.

I freeze midstride.

If nothing else about what transpired this morning bothers me, this final realization gives me pause. Never in my life have I cared so little about my art. I've always found a way to move past my anxiety to create.

Looking up at the street sign above my head, I'm surprised to discover I've walked five blocks since leaving the studio. I'm utterly adrift.

I'm also ravishingly hungry.

There's a turkey sandwich, a yogurt, and a Ziploc full of

grapes in my bag, but there's no place to sit, and no one to eat with. Heading to Dust Jackets is out of the question because my early arrival would require an explanation, and Walter and I have barely spoken since I told him I was giving up on making friends. There's no way I'm going to tell him how pathetic I was, running away from class because I was too weak to properly defend myself against Aarush's runny nose.

Without purpose or direction, I turn down 77th Street and head for Central Park. Heat radiates off the blacktop, forcing me to the shady side of the street before I can retreat beneath the marginally cooler canopy of the park. There are benches by the bronze Alice in Wonderland statue just down the path, but when I arrive all of them are occupied with resting joggers, slack-jawed tourists, a group of nannies wielding half-a-dozen strollers, and a random unsheltered guy who's sound asleep like he's at the Holiday Inn. There's one seat available at the end of a bench beside a man and woman discussing the accuracy of their respective Fitbits, but the empty stone wall towering above them all looks far more inviting.

I tell myself I'm only electing to go there because unlike most of the benches, the wall is still fully shaded, but I'm a horrible liar.

Cross-legged on the flagstone, I open my lunch bag and pull out my sandwich. With the precision of a neurosurgeon, I peel back the plastic bag to reveal the top of the sandwich, making sure not to accidentally touch any of the actual food with my fingers. After several bites, I push the bread up from the bottom, exposing another inch of the sandwich. The sequence continues—bite, bite, bite, push, bite, bite, bite, push—until only the last edge of crust remains. I've found the best way to eat the end of a sandwich is to slip my hand inside the nearly empty bag and use it as something of a glove to pop the last bite into my mouth. The yogurt, of course, is easy because it can be eaten with a sterile spoon. The grapes, however, take a great deal more finesse to eat without using my fingers.

The grapes are green because Toby prefers green to red. Given a choice, I'll always take red, but it's not a hill I'm willing to die on, so green is what Mom buys and I don't complain. I pull open the bag and use my fork to spear one of the grapes. If you've never tried to impale a round object, let me assure you it's as hard as it sounds which is why I'm not surprised when the first grape falls off the fork onto the ground.

I sigh. Life would be so much easier if I'd just use my stupid fingers like everyone else.

But Aarush was sneezing and blowing, and I haven't properly washed.

I stab another grape, this time with more conviction, making sure it's securely on the fork before pulling it out of the bag. This one makes it to my mouth as do the next four. During the next attempt, however, a shrieking infant distracts me, and as I thrust the fork back into the bag, it deflects off one of the grapes, piercing my palm instead. The searing pain causes my hand to open involuntarily, dropping the bag to the ground.

Two dozen grapes roll down the hill to the concrete below. One of the nanny-brigade minions toddles over to where several of the grapes have landed and squats to pick one of them up.

"No, don't!" I cry out, my voice heavy with dread and disappointment. "You can't eat those now! They're dirty!"

Instead of backing away sensibly, the two-year-old glares up at me as if I've just stolen his favorite stuffed animal before bursting into tears.

"No, please don't cry." I fumble with the remains of my lunch, furious with myself for spilling the stupid grapes to begin with.

"Oh, Liam, what happened?" one of the nannies asks, scooping him up off the ground and drying his tears with her shirt.

"Grapes," he says between sniffles.

Now she's the one glaring at me. "No," she tells him sweetly. "No grapes, but you can have some crackers from my bag instead. Meanwhile, someone needs to clean these up."

The someone she means is me, of course, but as she carries Liam over to where the other children are playing, I know there's no way I'm picking those grapes up off the ground. Even from my perch on top of the rock wall, I can see the brown flecks of dirt covering them. And with the number of dogs I've seen walk through, I know the ground is covered in fecal matter.

There's a good chance the grapes are covered, too.

I'm still sitting there, trying to come up with a plan for picking up the grapes using my plastic baggies as gloves when I hear someone calling my name further down the path.

"Phoebe? Is that you?"

I turn toward the reflecting pool to see Neveah and Devyn heading in my direction. They're dressed in coordinating bohemian skirts and tank tops, and Devyn has an artist's portfolio tucked under her arm. At first glance, they look carefree as a summer afternoon, but Neveah's brow furrows as they approach.

"What are you guys doing here?" I ask, unnerved by the coincidence of running into them.

"They're fumigating our building and forced us out of our apartments for the day. We've been searching for somewhere quiet for Devyn to sketch." She hesitates, climbing the wall to sit beside me. "Is something wrong, though? You look like you're about to cry."

The moment she speaks this truth aloud, solidifying it into the universe, it's as if she's permitted me to act. Tears fall before I'm able to blink them back. "I just... I'm having a hard day is all."

The girls settle in beside me, Neveah on my left, Devyn on my right. Neveah nods down at the ground below us. "The grapes piss you off or something?"

I can't help but smile at the mess I've made. "The bag fell out of my hands because I stabbed myself trying to eat them with a fork. Now I need to pick them up so people don't squish them beneath their shoes, but I haven't quite worked up the nerve."

Without a beat of hesitation, Neveah grabs my crumpled lunch bag and slides down the hill. One by one she deposits the grapes inside. "A fork, huh. Sounds like a recipe for disaster if you ask me." She gets on her hands and knees, reaching beneath the bench for a particularly wayward grape. Once she's collected them all, she returns to her place beside me. "Well, that's one less thing to worry over. What else is ruining your day?"

On my right, Devyn taps the pads of her fingers together in rapid succession. I do my best to ignore her soothing ritual as I explain to them how Aarush's relentless nose blowing pushed me over the edge.

"That's gross," Devyn says. "I don't blame you for

leaving."

I shrug, trying to figure out how to explain the experience without sounding like I need to be institutionalized. "It's just a cold and my brain knows catching it wouldn't be the end of the world. It's not like I'm completely irrational, you know what I mean? I just couldn't endure the exposure. It got too messy inside my head is all. So much for all the progress I was making, huh?" I wring my napkin between my hands, embarrassed by the false indifference of my tone. "Anyway, what's going on with you guys?"

Ignoring my attempt at small talk, the girls are silent for a moment, and I can almost feel the shame of their judgment. All the risks they took for me, all the stuff they gave up, for nothing.

"About your progress," Neveah says finally, lifting her chin to meet my gaze. "Have you talked to JP recently? He's worried about you. I mean, the rest of us are too, it's just... he's especially upset he hasn't heard from you since, you know, that night."

... even after everything he did for you, I finish her sentence in my head.

I blow out a long breath, casting my eyes to the ground. "I knew the whole 'letting people into my life' thing was gonna be tough, but it was way harder than I ever imagined. I just don't think I'm ready to expose other people to all my issues yet. Maybe in a few months... or a year. I don't know." I'm rambling now, trying to talk my way out of the conversation without making things worse between us. "No one else should be forced to deal with my baggage. It's not fair to anyone, especially you guys. You've been so nice to me, and I've caused nothing but trouble."

Neveah turns away, but Devyn sees fit to respond.

"You're not your anxiety, Phoebe. And Neveah and the others wouldn't have invited you if they weren't willing to do whatever it takes to help make things easier for you."

"But why?" I interrupt. "Especially now after I got you all arrested?"

Neveah scoffs. "Luke got us arrested because he screwed up the alarm. It wasn't your fault."

We sit in silence for several moments. I don't know why Neveah is trying to spare my feelings. And I can't imagine a world where people would choose to spend time with someone like me. It just doesn't make any sense. Luke is right about me being a freak. I don't even want to be around myself most of the time.

"Thanks for picking up the grapes," I say at last. "They'd probably be squished all over by now if it wasn't for you."

"Don't mention it," she says, an unmistakable hint of sadness in her tone.

Feeling a sudden urge to flee, I throw my bag over my shoulder and rise to my feet. "I, uh, should probably be getting to work. There's a new book shipment coming in this afternoon so lots to shelve." My voice is forced, and I can tell by their disappointed expressions they know I'm lying. "It was good running into you guys. I'll see you around I guess."

"Yeah. See ya," Neveah says as I take a step back into the grove of trees behind us. "Think about stopping to see JP at the station, though, will you? Or at least send him a text or something, okay?"

"Okay," I call over my shoulder even though we both know I probably won't.

CHAPTER 28

week five

After fleeing Aarush's head cold and chucking my grapes across Central Park, things do not improve. The death spiral of my inner monologue only intensifies.

At work, I decide to spray down the new box of inventory with Lysol when it arrives just to be safe because I can't be certain the books aren't coming directly from the quarantine unit of a hospital wing. When Walter catches me with the can of disinfectant he only sighs and warns me not to damage the pages.

Between decontaminations, I lock myself in the bathroom each time the bell jingles at the front of the store. The last thing I want is to be forced into another impromptu storytime. After making the toddler cry at lunch, I'm clearly in no condition to be around children. Or anyone at all for that matter.

Determined to get out of my head, I pull three random books out of the box to play a quick round of Guess the Gifter.

Superfudge.

Junie B. Jones and the Yucky Blucky Fruitcake.

What to Expect When You're Expecting—Fifth Edition.

This one is just as easy as the last time I played, but before I can dig a little deeper into the box to find what I hope are more difficult selections, my mind creeps back into familiar territory—Aarush and his raging head cold. Obviously, he must've contracted his illness from someone, so it only stands to reason a mid-summer pathogen is running rampant through the city. I, for one, have no intention of becoming its next victim.

A quick scroll of the CDC website on my phone yields no confirmation of my suspicions. But perhaps the pestilence has just begun to spread. It might be merely a head cold now, but by the time it mutates and spreads across all five boroughs, it'll be too late to contain. And everyone knows colds can easily develop into pneumonia and pneumonia is the eighth leading cause of death in the United States.

Especially for kids like Toby.

I wonder briefly if there's someone in the media to alert.

I'm still sitting there in the middle of the stacks staring off into space when I hear the click of Walter turning the front door latch, locking the store for the night. I glance at my phone. He's three hours early.

"I'm having Beverly over for dinner tonight," he calls back to me. "But you know how I feel about cooking so I'm heading to the East Village to pick up sweet potato knish from Yonah Schimmel's. She's never had one. Can you believe that?"

I've never eaten sweet potato knish. Or cheese or broccoli or beef knish. The byproduct of only eating my mother's cooking for so long. This benign realization is not unlike so many of the others I've had over the years about all the things in life I'm missing out on, but for some reason, this particular loss sparks something inside of me, and it isn't disappointment.

It's anger.

I clear a path to the back door for him, shoving my book stacks against the wall with obvious irritation. "So that's it then," I say as he approaches. "You're completely fixed now? You meet one new person who solves all your problems, and now you're free to come and go as you please, anxiety be damned?"

He stops midstride, recoiling as if I've punched him in the gut. I stare at the liver spot on his left temple while he recovers sufficiently from my outburst to respond. "No, Phoebe. That's not it at all."

"Really? Because it seems to me Beverly's your new magic elixir. And I'm glad for you. I am. But you'll have to excuse me if your friend therapy didn't work as well for me. Hanging out with JP didn't solve my problems like you thought it would. I guess we can't all be as lucky as you are."

He takes a step forward, reaching out, but I'm well-rehearsed in the choreography of this particular dance and back away just out of range. He lowers his hand, defeated. "Phoebe, it's not like that…"

All the frustration and sadness I've been dutifully suppressing over the past several days bubbles to the surface, and now there's no way I can prevent them from spilling over. "Yes, it is. It's exactly like that. We've always been a team, Walter. The two of us together against all our stuff. But now you're all better and you don't need me on your team anymore. You have Beverly, so I guess I'm on my own."

The pain in his eyes is sincere, but I'm too angry to care. "Phoebe, come to dinner with us tonight so you can see how it is between Beverly and me…"

A small, sharp laugh escapes me. I don't know where it comes from, and I don't know why I'm laughing when I feel so much like breaking down. Maybe it's the stress of the day or maybe it's the absurdity of my situation. Because let's face it—I've just been invited to tag along on a date with a sixty-four-year-old man and his new girlfriend. Things could not be more depressing.

"Thanks anyway, but I'm going to pass on being a third wheel. The truth is, I've got a bit of a sore throat and should probably just go home." I shove the last stack of books into place. "In fact, I might not be into work tomorrow. Or the next day."

He eyes me skeptically. "Maybe your throat is just parched. Did you drink enough water today?"

I make a show of grabbing my neck, rolling my head to the side. "No, it's my lymph nodes, too. They feel swollen. But don't worry, I'm sure you'll get along fine around here without me. Maybe Beverly can sort books since she's so good at everything."

A look of resignation crosses his face, and he steps past, placing his hand on the doorknob as if he's going to leave without me. At the last second, though, he turns. "Seems unlikely you would catch something with all your precautionary measures, but I guess you know better than me. It is strange, though, you haven't exhibited these sorts of avoidance behaviors in quite some time. One setback now, though, and suddenly they've returned. It's such a shame. I thought the two of us had rounded a corner... together."

Without making eye contact, he opens the door and braces it with his foot, waiting for me to follow him into the alley. Disappointment oozes from his pores as the humid evening air raises an immediate sheen to my skin. "If I don't see you, have a nice weekend. Hope you'll be feeling better by Monday." His voice is diplomatic. Boss-like.

"I'll let you know," I tell him as I turn to leave, unable to stand in such close proximity. As he heads down the alley toward the back stairwell of his apartment, something breaks inside of me. Because losing JP and his friends is one thing. Losing Walter, the closest confidant I've ever had, is something different altogether.

CHAPTER 29

week five

At home, I avoid the usual 'how was your day' chit-chat with Mom by feigning a sore throat and after a quick shower, I retreat to the relative security of my bedroom. Down the hall, Toby and Dad laugh about which vegetables would make the best supervillains while Mom tells them both to eat their snow peas or no dessert. My stomach grumbles having subsisted the entire day on a turkey sandwich and yogurt, but there's no way I can be with the entire family right now, not even for a chance to eat Mom's lo mien. I'll just have to sneak out to the kitchen a bit later for leftovers.

Amid a fruitless Google search for local pathogen outbreaks, someone knocks at my door. Without waiting for an invitation, Toby barges in with his drone bag and a handful of comic books, throwing himself on my floor. He sniffles several times before wiping his nose with the back of his hand, and immediately, I think of the night I got arrested. Somehow, I must have spread jail cell pathogens around our apartment when I got home. I probably infected him with my contaminated clothing or touched something of his inadvertently with my bare hands. I don't remember anything specific, but there's honestly no other reasonable explanation.

I should've known all of my reckless galivanting with JP and the others would eventually get my brother sick.

If he dies, I'll never forgive myself.

"I'm meeting Trevor and Prisha at the park tonight to practice for prelims. Wanna come?"

Hearing his stuffy voice and seeing him casually sprawled across my floor, nonchalantly flipping through the latest issue of The Mighty Thor, several ideas float through my head in rapid succession:

Me: Where did Toby get the idea it's okay for him to come into my room?

Other Me: From you, dummy, when you let him stay the last time.

Me: Well, it looks like I already made him sick, and since I was exposed to more dangerous microorganisms today, he should definitely get out.

Other Me: You have no way of knowing whether you're the one who infected him. He hangs out with his racing friends all the time.

Me: Yeah. But I might have. And what if I'm contagious with something different right now? Something worse? I should stay away from Toby, and he should stay away from me.

Other Me: He's not made of glass. A cold won't kill him.

Me: Tell that to his damaged lungs. The last time he had pneumonia they collapsed, and he spent two days in the hospital.

Other Me: The hospital stay was a precautionary measure, and after a few nebulizer treatments he got better.

Me: Shut up. I hate you.

I turn my attention to Toby, closing my computer's browsing window. "Didn't Mom tell you I have a sore throat?"

"So, take some aspirin," he says without looking up.

"I have a headache, too," I lie. "And my pottery instructor's sick so I'm probably contagious. You need to get out."

This gets a rise out of him but instead of getting up he merely gazes at me through his lashes. "You're afraid of making me sick?"

I nod. "Duh. It sounds like I already did."

"Well, I'm not afraid of getting sick. And my runny nose isn't your fault. I probably caught it from Trevor last week. We've been sharing a controller."

"Oh, have you," I say in my sternest big-sister voice. "So, I guess you don't care about ending up in the hospital again or missing out on your big race next month? If you were smart, you would stay away from your friends for a few days until I can properly research the spread of this current outbreak."

He stares at me stone-faced as if I'm speaking a foreign language, but instead of recognizing a lost cause when I see one, I continue blathering on, hoping to get through to him. "Seriously. You should stay home tonight. For your own good."

"I'm going," he says with a defiant roll of his eyes. "And I already told the others you were coming, too, so now you're gonna make me look like a liar if you don't show up."

Sweat pools under my armpits dampening my t-shirt. He's already sick, and nothing I say will stop him from going out with his friends. I should probably go along to help protect him, but there's no way I can force myself back into the world tonight. "You can tell them something came up."

He straightens, and for a moment I think he's leaving. Instead, he tucks his legs beneath him so he can see me properly, face-to-face.

"You're not really sick, are you?" he asks with a sniffle. When I can't even look at him—much less respond—he continues. "I thought you liked coming to the park with me. I thought you were ready to try flying on your own. Or are you done letting me into your life already?"

I wonder sometimes if Toby's premature birth did something refractive to his soul. Like maybe he was given a mature, robust nature to compensate for a body that was destined to be frail. There's no other explanation for the unassuming presence of wisdom he exhibits at such a young age.

Nevertheless, I dismiss him with a wave of my hand. "A bunch of stuff happened. Stuff you wouldn't understand."

"Like what happened at the bowling alley when you got arrested?"

My eyes widen. I didn't think he knew about my arrest.

He likes surprising me, and a smirk plays at the corner of his lips. "I'm not deaf, you know. Mom and Dad were super loud when you called them from the police station that night. The whole building probably heard them fighting about what to do. Mom was super pissed at Dad for taking your side. Anyway, is that why you're pretending to be sick? So you can stop having friends because being with them got you arrested?"

A painful mass hardens just below my ribcage as all my anxiety balls itself into a single point of focus. All the stress of being in the police station comes rushing back—the exposure to the vomit, having my sanitizer taken away, and of course being touched by a stranger all over my body, her hands coming in direct contact with my bare skin. To say it was the most excruciating experience of my life is not an overstatement.

But is it possible I've been subconsciously blaming JP for everything as Toby suggests?

All these days I've been telling myself they couldn't possibly want to be friends and would be better off without me. I've been playing the role of martyr, sacrificing my happiness for the good of the group. Is there a chance, however, I've concocted this whole narrative about not wanting to burden them with my issues because it lets me off the hook, allowing me to go back to my isolation where there's far less risk of exposure?

Not to mention far less risk of having my heart broken.

"Maybe it is," I tell him finally. "I mean, getting arrested was awful. I never want to be put in a situation like that again. So, it's probably safer if I just keep to myself from now on, don't you think?"

He's staring at me, one eyebrow raised in scrutiny. "It sounds stupid and boring to me." He closes his comic book and shoves it in his bag. "Didn't you have fun with those kids? Didn't you have fun with me?"

I remember the last time JP and I were together, the way I considered what it might be like to let him touch me. Allow him to lay his hand against mine to help with my bowling technique. I remember how at that moment I felt truly alive for the first time in my life. Lighter. Freer.

Unburdened.

In all the years I've been trying unsuccessfully to cast off the anchor of anxiety moored to my soul, it never once occurred to me that instead of struggling on my own to remove it, I could be asking the people around me if they'd be willing to help me carry it. Of course, people like Luke might not want to help and that's fine, but JP and Devyn were willing. Maybe others would be as well.

The only real question is: Do I have the strength to find out?

"Yes, of course, I have fun with you. But it's all been too much too fast, I think. I'm not properly equipped to deal with all this new… stuff." The words feel shallow, like a cop-out, and the look on his face says he knows it.

To help him more fully understand the hopelessness of my situation, I tell him about Aarush's cold, and how I spilled my lunch on the ground, and how Walter and I have been fighting. I tell him how instead of being relieved JP's finally stopped texting me twenty-five times a day, now I'm obsessively checking my phone to make sure I haven't missed something new from him. "I'm totally messed up in the head. And it's not like I want to go back to not having any friends, but I don't know how to go on from here. I don't know how to not be me."

Without a word, he gathers his comic books into his arms in what appears to be resignation, and a rush of relief washes over me.

He gets it.

"Thanks for understanding," I say.

Halfway to the door, he turns around, looking as though I've just slapped him across the face. "I don't understand, Phoebe. I don't know why you're just giving up. And I was really looking forward to hanging out tonight, but now you've ruined it."

I open my mouth to respond, but there's nothing to say.

I've broken his heart.

Ten minutes later, he leaves the apartment with a slam of the door. I watch from my bedroom window as he exits the building and walks alone down the sidewalk to the park. I'm still staring after him when my phone buzzes on my nightstand.

I grab for it, checking the screen and swallowing down a lump of disappointment when there's still nothing from JP. What I find instead is a text from an unknown number.

> *hey phoebe this is devyn. hope you don't mind neveah gave me your number. i wanted to invite you to my therapy group. we meet at the community center on warren st in brooklyn saturdays at 11. see you there?*

I reread the message a second and a third time before sending my response.

> *I was pretty sure everyone had already given up on me. Honestly, I was about to give up on myself. So thx for the invite. I'll see you Saturday.*

CHAPTER 30

week five

I don't go to pottery class or work on Thursday. I don't go to pottery class or work on Friday. I ignore Mom's admonishments through my bedroom door about wasting money on both counts because I'm pretty good at knowing when I need some time to myself. A chance to reboot and get things sorted in my head.

"There's no reason you can't go out into the world with a cold," she says. "People do it all the time."

"That's not at all comforting," I reply without opening the door.

On Saturday, I wait for Mom to head out on her weekly trip to the farmer's market before poking my head out of my room. The repetitive theme song of Toby's favorite videogame drifts down the hall, and I'm pretty sure Dad's already out for his morning run. I edge down the hall into the family room, hoping to sneak past Toby, but he pushes pause and looks up from the screen as I enter the room.

He's still in his pajamas, and there's a trash bag full of dirty tissues on the floor next to his inhaler. His cold has moved into his chest now, but the preemptive nebulizer treatments Mom's been giving him seem to be helping. At least that's what I'm telling myself.

"Hey, Toby. When Mom gets back will you tell her I picked up an extra shift at Dust Jackets to make up for the days I missed, and I'll be gone until after lunch?"

He shifts the controller in his hands and resumes his game. "Text her yourself." His voice cuts through straight to the bone, and I worry he might be mad at me for the rest of my life.

The train is below the East River when it hits me—I'm voluntarily going to group therapy with a bunch of strangers because I've alienated everyone else in my life. If this isn't desperation, I don't know what is.

The community center is a modest three-story brick building with several planter groupings outside filled with daylilies and brightly colored daisies. The front door is plastered with tape residue and flyers about everything from bingo night to a 'build your own window garden' seminar. The door isn't automatic, but large and unwieldy with a huge wooden handle. From the sidewalk, I'm still debating with myself about whether to pull out my glove when an elderly couple pushes their way out. After the woman passes through, the man gives a nod, ushering me inside.

I thank him, grateful for small acts of unwitting charity.

There's a whiteboard easel just inside the lobby where the day's activities are listed. I scan the list, hoping there's not some weird secret code for our group I won't recognize, like how Walter told me 'friends of Bill W.' is Alcoholics Anonymous. Luckily, under the listings for eleven o'clock, Adolescent Mental Health Discussion Group is clearly labeled.

I follow the signs to room 211 on the second floor, but once I get there, I can't force myself through the door. Inside, a handful of other teenagers stare down at their cell phones and sip Starbucks, yet watching them leaves me strangely hopeful. I'm not naïve enough to think these other struggling kids will be the ones to finally help me conquer my germaphobia after all these years. But they might help me figure out how to simultaneously navigate both my anxiety and my new friends.

Footsteps echo down the hall, and before I can turn around to see who it is, Devyn calls my name.

"Phoebe! You're here," she says walking up behind me. "I'm so excited you came. You're gonna love this group. The other members are a lot of fun, especially Rashad. He's the best."

I thank her again for inviting me, and after she steps past me into the room, I have no choice but to follow her across the threshold. Sunlight streams through the large bank of windows on the far wall onto an unoccupied circle of chairs someone has painstakingly arranged. Devyn waves to a few of the other kids and grabs a cookie from the plate beside the door.

"OCD perks—all the free cookies I can eat. Want one?"

I purse my lips. They look homemade. I'd actually love one. "Nah. I'm good." I omit the explanation about not eating food from unknown sources.

She nods in understanding and swipes another cookie as a middle-aged man in a Nike t-shirt and grey athletic shorts claps his hands in the center of the chair circle.

"Hey folks, it's about five after so let's take our seats and go ahead and get started. Any volunteers for the first check-in?"

Everyone meanders to their seats, and Devyn leaves the chair beside her open for me.

"I'll go first," she says once everyone is settled. "Most of you know I'm Devyn, I suffer from OCD, and my primary issue is repeated checking which makes me late all the time, often to this group." She pauses while the others chuckle, acknowledging the truth of her admission. "My goal for this week was to reduce each of my checks by one, so instead of checking beneath my bed four times before leaving my room, I only checked three times. It was hard the first few times to skip the extra check, but by the fourth day, it wasn't quite as stressful. And, as you can see, I made it on time today."

The rest of the group claps politely, and a guy to our left raises his hand. "I'm Reggie. I suffer from depression, but I had a pretty good week all in all—got outta bed and went to work every day, so that's something. Also, I've been walking my neighbor Frank's dog while he's been on vacation, and I definitely feel better after I go. I don't know whether it's the exercise that's helping or spending time with Chuckles—he's the dog—but I think I'm gonna ask Frank if I can keep walking him when he gets back. Or maybe my mom will let me get a dog. I dunno. That's it. Thanks, everyone."

More clapping. Smiles. Nods.

"Rashad here. ADD. My week sucked big. My grandma died…"

Murmurs of apologies float around the room. The girl beside him takes his hand.

"Thanks. Thanks a lot. I mean, yeah, it was sad losing her. She'd been sick, though, so it wasn't like it was a surprise or anything, but still, it threw the whole week outta whack and you guys know how much trouble I have when my routine gets messed with. Anyway, I'm sure next week will be better."

Everyone claps but when no one else speaks up, the group facilitator turns his attention to me. "Thanks to you all for sharing. And now, if I'm not mistaken, I think I see a new face." He nods in my direction. "My name's Paul, and I'm a certified group therapist. Usually, when we get a new member we ask if you'd feel comfortable sharing your name and something about yourself—as much or as little as you'd like. And, of course, you're welcome to pass altogether. Our group is a safe space—no participation required."

My eyes cut to Devyn who's gazing at me expectantly. I've never spoken to a group like this before. Rarely to my family and only to therapists one-on-one. I only hope the others are as accepting of me as they seem to be with one another. "Thanks, Paul. My name's Phoebe. Devyn invited me to come today, and I'm glad to be here. I suffer from a specific anxiety disorder—germs, contamination, sickness, that sort of thing. I don't touch—objects or people—which might not seem like a big deal, but it's isolating. After a couple years of therapy, I've stopped trying to get better. I understand anxiety is always going to be a part of my life, so I'm not here for you guys to try and fix me. I'm here because I'm lonely and more than a little scared that I'm never going to be able to manage my anxiety in a way that allows me to let other people fully into my life." I take a breath, letting the truth of the past several weeks settle over me before going on. "Recently, I started putting myself out there, but I screwed everything up, and now the three most important people in my life are mad at me. I don't want to give up on them, and I guess I don't want to give up on myself either.

The others wave and say hello, smiling broadly as if my presence is something to be celebrated. Perhaps it is— another soldier joining the ranks.

Paul pulls a folder from beneath his chair. "Well, Phoebe, you've come to the right place. A lot of us can appreciate how you feel, and I think today's topic might get you started in the right direction." He passes a stack of papers around the circle to his left. "This morning, we're focusing on nuts."

"This should be good," one of the older girls quips. "Especially since Rashad loves talking about his."

Devyn giggles beside me, and even I can't help but smile at the double entendre.

"Thank you for that, Katie, but we will not be referencing any genitalia this session. The anacronym NUTS stands for Negative Unconscious Thoughts. Once you get a copy of the paper, you'll see that today we are going to be naming our NUTS, cracking our NUTS and counting our NUTS."

"Last time I checked I still just have the two. Lefty and Righty," Rashad says, eliciting another round of giggles from Devyn.

Ignoring Rashad, Paul continues. "A negative unconscious thought is any destructive internal dialogue you have with yourself concerning your mental health. Feelings of inadequacy, self-loathing, disappointment, that sort of thing. Let's take a few minutes to name a few of your NUTS, and then those of you who feel comfortable can share."

There's a squirrel with a giant acorn on the sheet of paper in my gloved hands. Below the squirrel it reads:

Name

Crack

Count

There are five lines below NAME where I'm supposed to be listing all the negative unconscious thoughts inside my head. Beside me, Devyn is already feverously scribbling down her NUTS.

I haven't even gotten a pen out of my bag.

The squirrel stares back at me, taunting me with his giant acorn. "You can't even fill out this stupid form," he says.

I smile back at him and write: 'I'm incapable of doing simple tasks.'

After that, the rest of the list practically writes itself.

'I'm not good enough.'

'I don't deserve to have friends.'

'People don't like being around me.'

'I'm a burden.'

Screw you, I think to the squirrel.

When it's time to crack our NUTS, we're supposed to list evidence for and against our negative thoughts, answering whether the ideas we have about ourselves are true or false.

I scan my list. I'm capable of doing simple tasks, and I don't honestly believe I'm not good enough. Everyone deserves to have friends, so I must, too.

When I consider evidence for whether people like being around me, I'm forced to admit they must, otherwise why would Devyn have invited me to group therapy with her?

Why would JP and his friends have invited me out with them to begin with?

This leaves me with the final NUT which is proving to be the most difficult to crack. There's no denying my anxiety forces me to make accommodations and by default, forces other people to make accommodations as well. The forced sanitary measures. My refusal to eat food prepared outside my home. The avoidance of crowds.

Toby might be the only kid in his class who's never been to Disney World, and it's not for lack of wanting.

The final NUT stares back at me uncracked, but I get the sense that complete nut obliteration is not what we're going for here. Growth takes time, and besides, four outta five ain't bad, right? If I don't have anything to work on going forward I wouldn't have an excuse for coming back.

And I already know I want to come back.

I chance a glance at Devyn's paper. Her top four NUTS are covered by her arm but her fifth—'The world will fall apart if I don't arrange my shoes properly'—is visible. Her eyes are squeezed shut, and she's tapping the pads of her fingers to the pad of her thumb in rapid succession. Watching her struggling to harness her demons using simple repetitive motions, it occurs to me I would never see her coping mechanism as an inconvenience.

I would never see Devyn as an inconvenience.

"Okay, folks," Paul says, rousing everyone from their sheets, "time to share. Anyone want to tell us how the NUT cracking went?"

Several others volunteer, telling us about their negative thoughts, and how those thoughts impact their daily lives— trapping us inside ourselves and preventing us from being who we're supposed to be.

"When you have a NUT you can't crack, what should you do?" Paul's eyes dart around the circle. "Any thoughts?"

Devyn speaks up. "We can state our affirmations?"

He smiles at her. "Try again, but this time say it like you mean it."

"We can state our affirmations," she says again, with a bit more conviction.

"Should we do it now, one at a time around the room using the NUTS you couldn't crack?"

Beside him, Rashad stands, clearing his throat. "Even though I suck at focusing, especially when there's stuff I can't control, I deeply and completely accept myself."

The girl beside him goes next. "Even though I hate the way my body looks right now, I deeply and completely accept myself."

Reggie stands. "Even though I sometimes feel like there's nothing to live for, I deeply and completely accept myself."

By the time the affirmation reaches me, my hands are shaking and damp with sweat. I take a deep breath, my voice trembling. "Even though I see myself as a burden, I deeply and completely accept myself." Saying the words aloud is harder than I expect, but the tightness in my chest releases, and I'm able to steady my breathing.

As I listen to Devyn's affirmation it occurs to me for the first time in my life I am perfect and whole just the way I am. And if that means other people need to make accommodations for my coping mechanisms, then so be it. None of us comes into a relationship without some sort of baggage.

Toby's lungs are damaged. Because of him, we can't go on family runs or bike rides. We'll never climb to the top of the Statue of Liberty together. And he gets a free pass on having to carry the groceries up the stairs with the rest of us.

Mom is a neat freak. We all have to keep our bath towels straight on the racks and can't set down a cup without a coaster. She never displays my art because it makes the house cluttered, and she won't let my dad go to bed at night until all the dishes in the sink are clean.

Dad can't make decisions to save his life. We spend hours choosing what to watch on Netflix together, and every afternoon he stews over what we should have for dinner each night. We went without a family car for almost two years because he couldn't decide what model sedan he wanted.

And I have germaphobia.

So what?

So what if we watch movies in the family room instead of at the theater? Who cares if we celebrate birthdays at home instead of at a fancy restaurant? Why are my life adaptations any different than anyone else's?

They aren't.

I've made compromises for Mom and Dad and Toby without question my whole life just as they've made special considerations for me. It's what families do.

Maybe it's what friends do, too.

After the meeting, Devyn walks with me to the first-floor lobby of the community center. It's lunchtime and my stomach growls so loudly it echoes off the walls.

"You hungry?" she asks with a laugh as we push through the doors onto the street.

I place a hand over my stomach and giggle. "Starving. And it takes me an hour to get home from here. I may not make it."

She shrugs. "Well, I'm only fifteen minutes away. You're welcome to come to my place for lunch. I think we have some cans of soup or maybe we can make grilled cheese sandwiches?"

There's something in the invitation, a longing in her voice perhaps, which prevents me from immediately dismissing her. I love soup and as long as I wash the bowl and spoon first, there's no reason to decline. "You have clam chowder?"

"You mean the best soup of all time? Um, yeah."

"Oh, good." I smile. "But I was probably coming even if you didn't."

On the trip to her apartment, Devyn tells me about the onset of her OCD. "When I was twelve, I was playing on the jungle gym at the park with my little sister and her friends. I was showing off and climbed on top of the monkey bars to stand on them. While I was up there my foot slipped, and I fell. I don't remember exactly what happened, but the other kids said I hit my head hard on the metal bar on the way down. I was knocked out and had a pretty bad concussion. Spent a few days in the hospital. Anyway, when I finally came out of it, everything was different."

I nod along in agreement. I know how quickly your whole life can change. Mine's been split into two distinct segments since the pandemic—before Covid and after. I've been living in this stagnant reality for so long, I've never stopped to imagine there might be more change in my future. But it feels as though I might be at one of those turning points now.

Before friends and after.

"I started having the compulsions, like the spam filter on my brain stopped working, you know? I would get stupid thoughts like: 'if I don't check to make sure all the lights are turned off the building will burn down.' Before the accident, I wouldn't have thought something so ridiculous, and I certainly wouldn't have acted on it. But now I don't have a choice. I have to check the lights or I literally cannot go on with my day."

"It's the same with my avoidance behaviors," I tell her. "I totally get it."

She smiles over at me as we come to a traffic light. "Outside of the group, I've never had anyone to talk to about any of it." She hesitates, kicking a bottlecap off the curb onto the street. "At least not anyone who really understands."

Although JP and Neveah are good allies, they'll never truly appreciate what it means to be driven by compulsion instead of free will. But Devyn and I, we get each other. And so maybe someday we won't need another person to vent to about our mental health frustrations, but until then, maybe we could have each other.

"Anyway," she says as we start across the street. "Enough about me. What I really want to talk about is what's going on between you and JP. You gonna reach out to him or what?"

The mention of his name elicits an involuntary tightening in my chest—the rift between us may already be irreparable. "You think he still wants to talk to me?"

"He told Neveah the other day he wishes we'd never gone bowling that night. Said it ruined his entire summer."

The tightening releases just a bit. There are dozens of reasons he might feel that way. "And you think it has something to do with me?"

"Girl, it has everything to do with you."

CHAPTER 31
week six

Aarush has fully recovered from his cold by Monday's class, and without having to worry over him I'm able to finish the previous week's assignment before starting on the final project of the summer—an engraved piece.

I know exactly what I'm making and who I'm making it for. An apology of sorts.

After class, I bypass the 6 and book it down 96th Street to the Q, hoping to catch up with JP face to face. I've texted him half-a-dozen times since my conversation with Devyn on Saturday, and I even broke down and called him last night, but he hasn't responded to any of my messages, and even my call went right to voicemail.

It figures, now that I've decided to try the whole friendship thing again, I can't get a hold of the one person I want to be friends with the most.

Without stopping to take a proper cleansing breath, I race down the stairs into the tunnel. When I don't immediately hear his violin, I pick up my pace, accidentally knocking into a teenage girl on my way to the turnstile. I mumble a hasty apology as I take off down the platform, voices echoing off the tiled walls, drowning out the pounding of my sneakers against the concrete floor. I strain, listening for a single note, but there's nothing. No Bach. No Tupac. No Carly Rae Jepsen.

I round the corner, still hoping perhaps he's talking to someone or taking a break between songs, but only passengers line the platform. Not a single performer in sight.

Where the hell is he?

My stomach knots with disappointment. I wasn't expecting the pain of regret to feel so acute.

Oh, God, I think. *What have I done?*

On my way back out of the station, I shoot a quick text to Walter letting him know I'm on my way but will be late. I set off at a jog for the 6, deftly maneuvering around pedestrians until my shirt is plastered to my back, and I'm forced to slow to catch my breath. Along the way I find myself silently praying he'll be there, as anxious to see me as I am to see him.

But he's not.

Tears prick my eyes, and I bite my bottom lip to keep them at bay as I scan the platform a third time. He's absolutely, positively not here. He's avoiding me. The train rumbles into the station, and I climb aboard, taking a seat in the corner where I can be alone with my grief.

By the time the Dust Jackets marquee comes into view, I'm desperate for Walter's counsel. He's the one person I can talk to about anything and everything. The one person who understands what it's like to be me. But when I lean against the door to push it open, my shoulder crushes against an immovable force. I try again, pressing down on the handle with my elbow.

The door is locked tight.

Inside, the lights are off, and specks of dust float aloft on sunbeams. The front computer is tucked safely out of view beneath the counter, and a stack of envelopes lay on the floor just below the mail slot.

Walter never opened the store today.

Something is terribly wrong.

The deodorant I swiped under my arms this morning has officially worn off, and as I cut down the nearest alley to the back of the building, I can smell the day's stress gushing from my pores. Climbing the stairs, memories of the last time Walter failed to open the store come rushing back, and I can't help but wonder what condition I'll find him in now.

Did something happen on his date with Beverly?

Am I going to find him huddled in a corner again?

I approach the door to his apartment and knock gently at first, calling his name quietly so as not to disturb his neighbors. There's no movement from inside. No shuffling of feet. No call for me to go away or leave him alone. I knock again, this time with the butt of my fist and a bit more conviction.

"Walter! Are you in there? It's Phoebe. Is everything okay?"

A car horn blares in the distance. I try for the knob.

Locked.

"Walter! This isn't funny. I know you're angry with me but please let me in. We need to talk."

Behind me, the door across the hall creaks open, and an exhausted-looking woman with a baby on her hip peers out at me. "You looking for Mr. Haimovich?"

My heart quickens involuntarily. "Yeah. Have you seen him?"

She gazes down at her infant as if she's not sure whether

to tell me what she knows. When the baby starts to cry, she throws me a guarded glance. "All I know is I heard an ambulance out front and voices here in the hallway last night. Woke the baby who decided she didn't want to go back to sleep so now we're having an especially cranky day. If he's not answering the door now, they were probably here for him."

My head swims with this new information. "Did you hear what they were saying out here?"

She shakes her head. "Nope. Couldn't make out what they were saying over this one's screaming. Good luck finding him, though." With that, she slips back into her apartment and shuts the door.

I release a deep breath, trying to piece together what I know about Walter. Being taken away in an ambulance last night would account for him not opening the store or answering his door today. I pull out my phone to call him and realize he never responded to my earlier text about my delay. He *always* responds.

With trembling hands, I place a call to his cell. After four rings it goes to voicemail.

I try again with the same result. This time, I leave a message. "Walter, it's Phoebe. The door was locked at work so I came upstairs to your apartment but you don't seem to be here either. Your neighbor told me she heard an ambulance here last night, and I'm hoping it wasn't for you. Anyway, call me when you get this message. I'm worried about you."

I disconnect the line, and my legs wobble beneath me, no longer able to support my weight. The stress of the afternoon—from running between stations and not finding JP, to Dust Jackets being closed and Walter's disappearance—is all too much, and I crumple onto the floor.

Walter, where in the world are you?

I consider calling Beverly since she was the last person I know he was with, but then I remember I don't have her number. I don't even know her last name. Without her, the only thing left to do is start calling hospitals.

After shifting uncomfortably against the wall, Google Maps confirms there are four major hospitals on this side of the city: New York Presbyterian, Lenox Hill, Mount Sinai, and Metropolitan Hospital. The closest is Lenox so I call there first.

"I'm sorry, Miss, no one by the name Walter Haimovich has been admitted here. Have a nice day."

The line goes dead. I waste no time contacting NY Presbyterian but meet with the same response. Walter isn't there.

I'm losing hope by the time I dial the third number.

"Mount Sinai reception. How may I help you?" a pleasant, grandmotherly voice answers.

"Yes, I'm calling to see if someone by the name of Walter Haimovich was admitted last night. He might've been brought in by ambulance."

The line hums with indistinct conversations from the hospital lobby. "Yes, Ma'am. I have him right here. He was admitted last night."

Relief and dread flood my system in equal parts. "Is he okay?" I ask.

"Well, now, I'm not at liberty to say one way or another. HIPPA regulations and all. But if you can get here in person, I'm sure we'll be able to figure something out."

My mouth goes dry. There's *not* enough Purell in the world to get me to step foot in a hospital. "Does he have an extension you could connect me to, just so I could speak with him?"

I hear the receptionist tapping furiously at her keyboard. "I'm afraid not, Ma'am. There's no room assignment on file at this point. Have you tried calling his cell phone?"

"Yeah, I…" There's nothing left to say to the woman. There's only one way to get to Walter, and she can't help. "It's fine. Thanks anyway."

The air is thick, matting my hair to the back of my neck and making my thoughts sticky. They're all gummed up inside my brain, pasted to one another so I can't make sense of what I should do next. All I know is I can't sit in the hallway of Walter's building for the rest of my life. I need to go find him. I need to make sure he's okay.

But there's no way I can do it by myself.

I stare at my phone, screen dark in my hands. I need someone to talk this through with. Someone who'll understand.

Only one person might be able to help.

Hey it's me. I'm sorry to keep bothering you but I don't have anyone else to call. Walter's in the hospital and I don't know if he's ok. I need your help.

CHAPTER 32
week six

The time between hitting send and my phone ringing are the most nerve-wracking fifteen seconds I've experienced in a long time. More difficult than getting a cocktail spilled on me. More stressful than getting arrested. I hit accept by the second note of my ringtone.

"Phoebe?" JP says before I can say hello.

Hearing him speak my name with such desperation releases a bit of the tension wound up inside of me. He's going to help. It's going to be okay.

"Hey. Hi." My voice trembles. There's no mistaking the regret etched in those two words, and as anxious as I am to find out what's going on with Walter, I recognize the need to clear things up between us first. I fumble for the right words. Something to eloquently express the remorse I feel over my behavior. "I'm sorry. I'm so sorry about everything," is what I come up with.

In my mind's eye, I can see him pursing his lips on the other end of the line. Taking a deep breath. Composing himself the way he does before playing a particularly difficult arrangement on the violin.

"I thought we were friends, Phoebe," he says, his voice clipped.

The word friend conjures up images of my childhood in the years before Covid. The days when school was full of jump rope and hair braiding. Filled with lunch swapping and freeze tag, birthday parties with ice cream cake and frequent trips to the playground.

When I lived my life from the inside instead of from the outside looking in.

"We are friends," I tell him.

"Are we?"

A question mark hangs at the end of his statement, punctuating the entirety of our relationship. If I am his friend, I certainly haven't been a good one, at least not for the past couple of weeks. Selfish would be a more apt description.

"Yes," I tell him resolutely. "We're friends. Good friends."

He hesitates, blowing air into the receiver. "You know, it's not okay, the way you've been treating me. It's sucked being ignored by you. I get it, though. I get why you flipped out, and I get why you were afraid to answer my texts. And I've been ignoring you back to show you how it feels because I've been angry. And more than a little hurt." He clears his throat, his tone changing subtly. "But we don't have to talk about all that now. Tell me what's going on with Walter."

The lump in my throat dislodges, and I wipe my eyes with the underside of my t-shirt before replying. At least he's talking to me. It's a start. I tell JP what the neighbor said about the ambulance and the voices in the hall, and how I tracked Walter down to Mount Sinai Hospital.

I explain about my afternoon—about not being able to find him or Walter.

A beat passes. "You were looking for me?"

I sniffle, refusing to wipe my nose with my sleeve. "Both stations. The 6 and the Q." I can almost hear him smiling across the line.

"And Walter's at Mount Sinai?"

"Yeah." I rub the sweat from my palms onto my thighs. "But they wouldn't tell me what's wrong. I'm really worried about him."

"Nothing like this has ever happened before?"

I shake my head. "No. Never. And he hasn't been sick that I know of." Images of snotty Aarush and sick Toby come to mind. "Unless I transferred something to him last week from my pottery instructor. He was super sick, and I was trying to be careful around Walter. We got into this fight, and maybe I transmitted something to him inadvertently. That was Wednesday, and the incubation would be two to three days and depending on how virulent it was—"

"Ah Dios mío, Phoebe." JP lets out a huge groan. "I can almost guarantee whatever's wrong with Walter has nothing to do with you. This isn't your fault. No one expects you to protect everyone all of the time. You get that, right?"

Yes.

No.

Maybe.

He sighs. "Just go to the hospital and find out how he is. You know he'll be happy to see you, and you'll feel better once you know he's okay."

My bottom lip trembles. This is not the answer I'm hoping for. I can't do this on my own, especially if it turns out Walter's not okay. I need JP to go for me. Or at least come with me. "There's no way I can go inside a hospital. It's just... too much."

He's moving now. Something rustles against the earpiece, and I hear his footsteps clomping down the stairs. "That's crap, and you know it. You can go see Walter, you just don't want to. Because being inside a hospital is gonna make you uncomfortable. But here's the thing about friendship—you can't just be there when it's easy and bail when it gets tough. And right now, Walter needs you."

His assertion feels like a kick to the chest where my heart pounds heavily, struggling to keep pace with my emotions. He's right, of course, giving me a lot to unpack not only about my relationship with Walter but with him as well.

But I am not going inside a hospital.

I can't.

No. No. No. No. No.

"Maybe you could just go check on him for me?"

A door slams. He's out on the street. "No. I can't. Walter needs you to be his friend. Now's your chance to be one. Text and let me know how it goes."

And with that, the line goes dead.

Tears pool in the corner of my eyes, but I refuse to let them spill over as I slip my phone back into the pocket of my cargo shorts. There's a possibility Walter's in critical condition, and I'll never be able to live with myself if I don't at least attempt to go see him. To tell him I'm sorry, and I love him.

I think back to the last time I forced myself to do something I thought was impossible. How did I do it?

One. Step. At. A. Time.

If my ultimate goal is reaching Walter, the only way to get there is by breaking the trip into achievable bite-sized chunks. And so, the internal bargaining begins—an auction of sorts where I bid against myself until I can go no further.

Forcing myself to my feet, I set my first goal: make it down to the street.

Once I arrive in the alleyway behind Walter's building, I set my second goal: make it to the subway station.

At the subway station, I talk myself onto the train.

At 96th Street, I talk myself off the train onto the platform.

I continue in this manner all the way to the front entrance of the hospital where my resolve deteriorates like a puff of smoke into the breeze. I know the truth. There are germs inside the building, along with the potential for catching something.

I don't want to get sick, but more than that I don't want to make my brother sick. There's no way I'm going through these doors without first devising some sort of plan. If I contract something contagious, I'll need someplace to go.

I can't stay at home.

I can't go to Walter's.

I can't go to JP's.

But who else is there?

A moment later, I dial the only other person I can think of.

"Hello?" Devyn says across the line. "Phoebe?"

"Yeah. Hey. It's me." I hesitate, knowing how absurd the conversation we're about to have will sound to her. Still, I force myself to go on. "I have a favor to ask."

"Sure. Anything. What's up?"

"I'm worried about getting sick."

"Okay."

"And if I get sick, I'm gonna need someplace to stay."

There's a pause. "What makes you think you're gonna get sick."

"Probable exposure."

"Okaaaay." Her drawn-out response alerts me to her skepticism.

"So, can I stay with you?"

"Phoebe, what in the world is this really about? Tell me what's going on."

It's a long story so I give her the condensed version before asking, "Please, can I stay if something happens?"

"Yes. Of course. You're always welcome to stay here," she says after the briefest hesitation.

"Really?"

"Yes. Really. Now go. And let me know how it turns out, okay?"

I agree to keep her updated and hang up.

With preparations in place for the worst-case scenario, all that's left is to force myself into the building. Crossing the hospital's threshold is going to be akin to entering the ninth circle of Dante's Inferno, but I need to make sure Walter's okay, so walking away is not an option. Still, there's got to be something I can do to help me feel more comfortable about walking through the door.

Every drop of liquid in my body has sweated through my pores leaving my mouth as arid as the Sahara Desert. I can't swallow. I can barely breathe.

And then it hits me.

I don't need to do this alone. I might not have JP beside me, but I'm in the middle of Manhattan, one of the most populated cities in the world. If I need help, all I need to do is muster the courage to ask one of the dozens of people milling around the building.

I survey the scene for the healthiest, least intimidating option and spot a dad-ish looking guy playing peek-a-boo with another woman's toddler. Any man who'll hide behind his hands for someone else's kid is a good guy. I take a deep breath as I approach.

"Hey… hi," I stammer. "My name's Phoebe, and I don't want money or anything, but I was wondering if you could help me out." He doesn't jump at this Good Samaritan opportunity, but he also doesn't tell me to go away, so I continue ad-libbing. "My grandfather is sick, and I need to go see him, but I've had a bit of a cold and was wondering if you'd be willing to go inside and grab a surgical mask for me to wear? You know, just as a precautionary measure."

He raises an eyebrow as if he can't decide whether I'm a little batty or just overly considerate. "A surgical mask?"

"Yeah. I just, you know, don't want to get into any trouble."

He smirks, his eyes dancing, and just when I think he's about to blow me off, he rises to his feet. "You got it, kid. Be back in a sec."

I nod. I can't believe it worked.

The second the glass doors slide shut behind him, the urge to flee intensifies. Once the guy returns with the mask, my next goal will be to enter the hospital. At that point I'll have two options: go inside or run away.

I know if I run Walter would forgive me. I'm just not certain I'd be able to forgive myself.

There's an empty spot on a nearby bench recently vacated by the mother and her toddler, and as I walk toward it I begin making deals with myself. I'll stay on the bench until the man comes back, and if he doesn't have a mask, I'll leave. If he does have a mask, I'll decide what to do then.

Two minutes later the guy appears by my side with two surgical masks and a handful of sanitizing wipes. "Here's everything they would give me." He holds the stack of items out for me to take.

"Thanks," I say. His return has me flustered as if my mind somehow couldn't conceive of a scenario in which he'd actually come back with the mask as requested. I pull two latex gloves out of my side pocket, and after slipping them on, take the stuff from his hands. "I really appreciate you helping me out." I'm self-conscious now, not wanting him to witness whatever comes next.

Thankfully, he must sense my unease and releases me with a wave of his hand. "Anytime," he says as he walks away.

Faced with the most difficult leg of the journey, the masks stare back at me through their plastic sleeves, taunting my anxiety. Without overthinking it, I pull the first mask from the bag and tuck the elastic bands behind my ears.

I swallow.

The second mask regards me with disdain. Mocking me. You can't be serious, it says. I already feel like Darth Vader, but that doesn't stop me from tearing open the bag, and in an act that feels a bit like willful defiance, I slip the second mask over the first. My breath stifles under the layers and perspiration beads along my upper lip. I look ridiculous, but I'm beyond caring. I consider rubbing a squirt of sanitizer between my gloved hands for good measure but decide that would be overkill, even for me. Instead, I take a few tentative steps toward the entrance.

Walter's in there. And he's probably all alone. He needs me to do this for him.

I take another step, and the automatic doors slide open.

I close my eyes and step inside.

At the front desk where I assume the dad-dude procured the masks, I steady my breathing to enquire about Walter's whereabouts. "I'm his granddaughter, Phoebe Haimovich," I lie, the tremor in my voice muffled through the material. "I was hoping to see him."

The receptionist asks me to spell Haimovich and after entering the information on her computer, directs me to the third floor. "He's just come out of recovery and has been taken to a private room. Check in at the nurses' station when you get up there to make sure he's able to receive visitors."

Ignoring her bemused expression, I thank her before allowing a wave of relief to wash over me.

Walter is alive.

Everything's going to be okay.

At the elevator, I stop dead. I haven't pressed a call button in years, and I have no intention of starting now. Especially inside a hospital. I decide to wait for someone else to do it, and there's an awkward exchange when the first woman who walks up beside me realizes the elevator hasn't been called. With a barely contained eyeroll, she presses it with her elbow, and we wait in silence for the car to arrive. The illuminated bank of numbers descends from six to five to four, and my heart is racing by the time it reaches the first floor. As the elevator doors open, the woman, a couple of hospital personnel, and a grumpy looking guy in a suit rush aboard.

I don't rush.

I don't even move.

Because if walking into the hospital was hard, forcing myself onto the elevator is worse.

"You coming?" one of the hospital employees asks, holding the door open with his arm.

What I need in this moment is for someone to physically drag me into the car with the other passengers. If JP was beside me, I'd make him do it. But he's not here.

In my head, though, I can imagine what he might say. I can almost hear him instructing me to hold my breath if I have to, and then he would hold his, too. He might even make a big show of puffing out his cheeks and making silly motions with his eyebrows, acting as though he's about to pass out. I carry this image of him into the elevator with me, concentrating on this mental deflection. Luckily, before the panic of the confined space completely sets it, the doors open, and I tumble into the third-floor hallway.

Piece of cake.

Now if only my feet would start moving.

CHAPTER 33

week six

At the nurses' station, I inquire about Walter's condition and am told he's awake but still being closely monitored. "We don't let infectious persons on the post-op floor, though, so you're going to need to go back downstairs," a fiery redhead named Tricia tells me.

"I'm not contagious," I explain. "I'm wearing the masks because I have an anxiety disorder, and I'm afraid of germs. They're to protect me from the patients, not the other way around. I know that's stupid because masks don't work that way, but my disorder is not rational."

She narrows her eyes at me. "You're serious?"

"Completely serious." I'm surprised by my boldness. "Now about that room number for Mr. Haimovich?"

Nurse Tricia runs a finger down her chart and eyes me skeptically. "Number 338. Down the hall, fourth door on your left. And as long as you're going, he was just given the clear for some liquids so why don't you take him this apple juice." She hands me a lidded cup with a straw.

I thank her but after taking a few steps toward Walter's room, I'm distracted by a splotch of dried clay on the toe of my left shoe. I come to a stop, staring at the clay as the reality of my situation sets in. The difficulty of forcing myself into the hospital pales in comparison to what comes next. After being such a raging idiot the last time we were together, I'm suddenly terrified of facing Walter. Fueled by jealousy and resentment, my indignation over his improvement and friendship with Beverly clouded my judgment and at the time, I couldn't see his frustration for what it was. Looking back now, though, when I picture him walking away, I recognize the slumped shoulders and tucked chin of rejection.

He only wants the best for me. It's all he's ever wanted.

But instead of being appreciative, I acted like a spoiled brat. I messed up with Walter just like I messed up with JP, and now the only thing left to do is work to fix what's broken.

I put one foot in front of the other to the end of the hall.

The door to the fourth room on the left is cracked and creaks slightly as I open it. Light from the hallway spills across a bank of monitors, an IV drip, and an adjustable bed where a disheveled Walter is propped up against a stack of pillows staring at the blank wall on the far side of the room. With a white sheet draped across his legs and oxygen cannula tucked into his nostrils, he's smaller and frailer than I've ever seen him. Both arms are connected to tubing, and the silence of the room is punctuated by the steady beep of a heart rate monitor.

His sunken eyes shift when he hears me enter the room. "Oh my God, Phoebe. You're here. You're inside a hospital. What about all the germs?"

I cross the room in three strides to the chair beside him, the face masks absorbing the tears spilling down my cheeks. It's just like Walter to come out of surgery and be more worried about my well-being than his own.

I sniffle, trying to compose myself. "Of course, I'm here. You're my best friend. I had to come, germs or no germs."

A moment passes, both of us staring at one another in disbelief. "Now don't cry," he says as I continue blubbering beneath my mask. "Everything's going to be fine."

"It is?"

"Yes." He offers me a tissue from the box on his night table.

Before I can refuse, his IV pump engages with a loud beep, startling me from my chair. Walter chuckles at my frazzled nerves, and I'm overcome by an urgent need to apologize before letting another moment pass.

He could've died not knowing how I feel.

"Walter, I need to tell you how sorry I am about everything. I didn't mean all that horrible stuff I said to you last week—about your relationship with Beverly and the two of us not needing each other anymore. I felt so bad about it, and I was planning to apologize at work today, but you weren't there. It feels weird bringing it up now, since you're sick and all, but I wanted you to know—I'm here for you, always." The lack of air underneath the mask is suffocating, and I'm forced to take a deep breath through my mouth. "Anyway, I hope you can forgive me, and I'm glad I found you. Why are you here, though? What happened?"

A sad smile plays on his lips as he regards me. "Of course, I forgive you. You don't need to apologize for being upset. It's normal. But I appreciate the sentiment just the same. All is forgiven." He shifts in his bed, pulling the sheet a little higher across his hips. "As for what landed me here, I woke up to use the bathroom in the middle of the night the way we old people do, and I was covered in sweat. By the time I got to the hallway I felt as though I was being run over by a train—short of breath, terrible chest pain. I knew right away something was wrong and called 911."

"Does your family know?"

He shakes his head. "I was barely conscious by the time the paramedics arrived, and I left my cellphone on the nightstand. I haven't called anyone because I don't memorize numbers anymore. Blasted technology."

I can't help but smile at his candor, his personality seemingly unaffected by the ordeal. "Don't worry about your phone. I'll go get it tonight and bring it back so you can call your daughter and Beverly to let them know you're alright." I hesitate, swallowing hard. "You are alright, aren't you? Did you have a heart attack?"

He brings a cathetered hand to his chest. "Apparently. The doctor told me he found a ninety percent blockage in one artery, and an eighty percent blockage in the other. Did something called an angioplasty on my old ticker. Put in a couple of stints to hold the arteries open. Doctor says I should be good for another twenty years, give or take." He chuckles to himself. "And to think all this time I've been worried about something bad happening to me out in the world, and I almost died sleeping in my bed. Life's funny, huh?"

Before I have a chance to respond there's a knock at the door. But instead of the nurse I'm expecting, JP pops his head into the room. "Hey, Walter," he says.

"Oh, Juan Pablo, you're here, too!" Walter exclaims. "What a pleasant surprise."

My eyes cut between the two of them as JP enters the room, a sheepish grin on his face. For a moment, my heart soars because I think he's come to see me, but then I realize what's going on. "Wait. Walter, you know him?"

"Oh, yes. Juan Pablo and I are well acquainted." Walter lifts his chin, an invitation. "You wanna tell her, or should I?"

JP drags a chair from against the wall over to where I'm sitting beside Walter. He bites at his bottom lip as if he's afraid of getting in trouble for what he's about to say. "I didn't know what else to do when you didn't respond to any of my calls or texts last week, so I went to Dust Jackets to look for you. Walter told me you were home sick."

Unbelieving in what I'm hearing, I don't know whether to laugh or cry. "You were stalking me?"

"No. I mean, not technically. You weren't even there, and I wasn't gonna be confrontational or anything. I was just worried. I needed to make sure you were okay, that's all."

"And?" Walter says, urging JP to continue.

JP rolls his eyes. "And Walter loaned me a few of his books about anxiety. Books with tips about how I can help make things easier for you, that sort of thing."

"Even gave him my copy of Loving Someone with Anxiety," Walter says, wagging his eyebrows.

I let all of this sink in. Walter and JP met and have been secretly conspiring behind my back, planning for some hypothetical future scenario in which JP and I are friends again? Does this mean JP might be willing to forgive me after all?

And also, Walter gave JP a book called Loving Someone with Anxiety?

Jesus, Mary, and Joseph.

"Wait a minute. Did you actually have a heart attack or is this some sort of joke?" I glance up at the ceiling in mock horror. "Are there hidden cameras in this room? Are you guys pranking me?"

Walter laughs, lifting his sheet. "I assure you the heart attack was real. You're welcome to take a peek at the sutures in my thigh where they ran the catheter up my leg into my heart."

I swallow back a wave of nausea. "I'll take your word for it, thanks, though."

Conspiracies debunked, the conversation quickly turns to what's next for Walter and the store and the type of help he'll need moving forward. Eventually, though, Walter's curiosity gets the better of him, and the discussion circles back to how I was able to talk myself into the hospital in the first place. How I successfully applied several of the methods from the books he's given me over the years.

JP's beaming. "She did great, didn't she?"

"I can't believe she got through the door. It's truly a miracle." Walter gives me a wink.

I roll my eyes in exasperation but am secretly as pleased with myself as they are. "Guys. I'm right here. Like, in the room, so if you're proud of me, feel free to say it to my face."

"I'm proud of you," Walter says.

"Me, too," JP says.

"Me, three," I say.

CHAPTER 34

week six

Since Covid, I haven't felt a single compulsion to hug anyone, except maybe Toby—no one can refuse his snaggle-tooth grin. Outside of him, though, resisting the urge to touch other people hasn't been hard. Besides being far too dangerous, most of my potential physical contacts remain strictly platonic anyway.

But there's nothing platonic about the way JP's looking at me as we leave the hospital together. His smile makes me want to touch him. Makes me wonder what the stubble of his face would feel like against my cheek. Even as the conditioned air of the hospital gives way to the stale humidity of the city, I long to press myself against him so I can feel his heat. But I can't. At least not now.

There's a lingering awkwardness between us as we fall into step beside one another on the sidewalk. I wish I could pretend the past two weeks never happened. I wish we could pretend we're just two normal friends off for an evening stroll to a friend's house to grab a cell phone. But we're not. Our story is far more complicated.

"You want me to go with you?" he asks. "It'll be dark by

the time you get to Walter's and make it all the way back to the hospital."

I shrug. "I'll be fine. I'm afraid of germs, not the dark, remember?" I mean it as a joke to lighten the mood, but it falls flat.

The lines of his face are taut as he works his jaw in frustration.

"I'm not asking because I think you need protection. I'm asking because I thought you might like the company." He stuffs his hands in his pockets and his chin falls in obvious frustration.

And then I see it. Is it possible I have it all wrong? Has he completely forgiven me? Are we friends again?

"Wait a sec." I pause at a traffic light. "Did you only come to the hospital so you could check up on Walter, or did you come to see me too?"

He sighs, staring at the crosswalk sign on the other side of the street. "Of course, I came to see you, too. Friends don't leave friends out to dry."

At that moment, a small herd of middle school boys heads toward us on their skateboards, and JP steps out of the way to let them pass. As they roll through, our eyes lock, and inside his gaze I catch a glimpse of everything unspoken between us, thinly cloaked behind his veil of disappointment. Friendship. Forgiveness. Understanding.

The potential for something more.

All he's done since the moment we met is try to make things easier. To convince me I should deeply and completely accept myself the way he already does.

The last of the boys crosses the street, and now it's just the two of us, enveloped inside the moment. If my life were being aired on the Hallmark Channel, this would be the part where I'd turn to him, raise myself on tip-toes, and kiss him with wild abandon. Where I'd suddenly realize all this germaphobia business is an utter waste of time, and that my life would be so much better if I simply shook it off like a butterfly emerging from her cocoon.

But my life is not being televised, and none of that happens. Instead, the moment passes us by, and I'm left with reality staring me in the face.

At least it's a reality where JP and I are still friends.

"I'd love for you to come with me to Walter's to get his stuff and back to the hospital. Hell, you can walk me all the way home if you want."

His dimple puckers his cheek. "Yeah?"

"Yeah."

We walk together to the 6, through the turnstiles, and onto the train. We traverse the last two blocks to Walter's apartment on foot and make the return trip to the hospital with Walter's phone.

And he doesn't leave my side until I'm safely back in Jersey City at the end of the night.

The two of us fall into something of a routine over the following week. After pottery class, we take the 6 to Dust Jackets together where we visit with Walter in his apartment while he recovers. The first few days his daughter Neomi is there, cooking and cleaning and driving Walter slightly batty with her neuroticism.

"If she asks me one more time if I've taken my pills today, I'm going to throw the bottle at her," he tells me on Wednesday afternoon, Neomi just out of earshot. "There's a reason I didn't move with her to Pittsburg, eh?"

Once Neomi is safely on the plane back home, Beverly

takes over for her as Walter's home healthcare nurse, making sure he has access to clean laundry, the remote control, and his stack of crossword puzzle books. On Friday, she invites me and JP to stay for Shabbat dinner.

"I'm making Walter's favorite, matzoh ball soup."

I glance at JP. He raises an eyebrow as if to say 'this will be the weirdest double date I've ever been on,' but he doesn't object when I accept Beverly's invitation for the both of us.

***

On Saturday, I wake up early in anticipation of my next group therapy session and am waiting for Mom at the kitchen table with cups of coffee already brewed when she arrives.

"You came in late from visiting Walter last night," she says, accepting her mug. "Everything okay?"

"He's great actually," I say. "He's up and moving around. Nothing strenuous but the doctor said he should be able to reopen the store Monday."

She slips into the seat beside me and takes a sip of her coffee. "I bet that's a relief. And it's good timing, right? Now that your pottery class is over for the summer, I'm sure he could use your help around the shop getting caught up."

I pour a bit of creamer into my cup. Walter and I have already discussed increasing my hours from now until the start of school. "Yeah. I'm also going to be running a weekly storytime for preschoolers to help drum up extra business."

She holds her mug aloft mid-sip. "You what?"

"I volunteered to host storytime. I did one a few weeks back, and the kids seemed to enjoy it."

Her eyes narrow. "Did you enjoy it?"

I hesitate, thinking back to the initial rush of panic accompanying the children's proximity. But this negative association is overshadowed by the pleasant memory of the youngest girl's smile as we read together. Looking back, the pros of the experience outweigh the cons, especially since no one ended up getting sick. "I didn't hate it."

"Hmm. Well, I'll be excited to hear how it goes. And, oh, while you're here to talk with, what's the deal with Tuesday night? Dad said something about an art showcase?"

I suppress the urge to roll my eyes. Toby must've mentioned it to Dad.

"Oh, it's no big deal. Aarush's cousin owns this coffee shop near the studio, and he's displaying all the class's pottery there Tuesday night. I think it's like a fundraiser, too, for the National Endowment for the Arts, but really, there's no reason you need to come. It's just a bunch of boring pottery."

She scoffs. "Nonsense. It's your boring pottery, and we want to be there to support you. What time?"

A rush of heat rises to my ears. "Seven, I think."

She pulls her grocery list from her purse and adds green onions and sticky rice. "Well, find out for certain, and I'll make sure Dad wears a tie. Maybe I'll invite Grandma, too. I'm sure she'd like to see your work."

Her coffee almost finished, she stands up and walks over to the pantry peering in to make sure she hasn't forgotten anything for the list. She crouches down, her back to me.

It feels safe to open up to her about the real reason for our contrived early morning rendezvous.

"There's something else I wanted to tell you about." My voice catches in my throat.

"Hmm?" She shakes a box of cereal to assess whether she needs to buy another.

"My friend Devyn's been going to these group therapy sessions every Saturday for kids with all sorts of mental health issues. And I know I'm grounded, but I wanted to let you know I'm going with her today."

She turns slowly on her heel, cereal box still in hand. "This Devyn was one of the kids there when you were arrested?"

"Yeah, but Mom, she's one of the reasons I didn't end up having a full-blown panic attack at the police station. And getting arrested wasn't her fault. Or anyone's fault. Like everyone else, she was just trying to be a good friend."

She clears her throat, unable to look directly at me. "And you want to start going to group therapy with her?"

"I actually already went with her last week. And I'm going to keep going every week, with or without your permission. I just want to be honest with you about it."

There's a long pause while she considers my confession, looking at me as if I've just admitted to killing puppies in my spare time. "Okay," she says at last, turning back to the pantry. "I appreciate your honesty. But you're still grounded so I expect you home right after the session is done."

She's not looking so I don't have to suppress the grin on my face. "Thanks, Mom."

CHAPTER 35
week six

I'm a few minutes early to support group and even though it's only my second meeting, crossing the threshold feels something like coming home. Devyn hasn't arrived yet, and as I return Rashad's wave from across the room, I wonder how long it took for her to arrange her shoes properly before leaving her apartment today. For all I know she could still be there, waiting for her compulsion to allow her to leave.

She still hasn't arrived by the time Paul takes his seat in the circle and invites the rest of us to do the same. There are a couple new faces from the week before, but the familiar ones seem genuinely pleased to see I've returned.

Katie pats the seat of the chair to her left. "You can sit here beside me if you want."

I thank her and settle in, still checking over my shoulder for Devyn and also Reggie, who I've just noticed is missing as well. With his history of depression, I worry maybe something's happened.

"Welcome, everyone." Paul sets his water bottle on the floor by his feet. "Glad to see you all this morning. Who wants to check in first?"

A girl I don't recognize raises her hand. "I'll go. Most of you know I'm Tracey. Generalized anxiety disorder. I wasn't here last week because my family was on vacation at the Jersey Shore. It was tough, worrying about all kinds of stuff—am I wearing enough sunscreen? Are we gonna get a table at Mom's favorite restaurant? Are my cousins going to kill each other over some guy? And it didn't help that my whole family was like 'Tracy, quit stressing everyone out, we're on vacation for Christ's sake,' but you all know how that is. When you don't get it, you don't get it. Anyway, I survived the week, so I'm proud of myself."

Everyone claps. Paul gives Tracey an affectionate pat on the shoulder. Devyn slips through the door and tiptoes to the empty seat beside me.

"Who's next?" Paul asks, greeting Devyn with a wave.

Tentatively, I raise my hand.

"Phoebe, right?" Paul asks.

I nod, and he instructs me to go ahead. "Hey. I'm Phoebe. Specific anxiety disorder. I'm germophobic and don't touch people." I lock eyes with Tracey who throws me an empathetic smile. "My week ended up great but started out horrible. My best friend had a heart attack Sunday night."

A collective gasp spreads around the room.

"Oh. No. Walter's old. Sixty-four. Not a teenager," I explain, smiling at their confusion. "He's fine now, but he was in the hospital for a little while before I knew what was going on. At first, I didn't want to go visit him, but my friend JP convinced me I needed to go. It was stupid hard, but I was so proud of myself once I saw how happy Walter was to see me." I pause to chew at the inside of my cheek. What happened next is personal—the way JP took over the part of my brain reserved for rational thought—but somehow, I feel as though it's safe to share. "And also, I've decided to keep letting other people into my life, as friends and maybe something more."

Rashad shimmies his shoulders at me from across the room. "So, there's probably gonna be some touching in your future, huh?"

I hadn't considered this; the physical contact most romantic relationships require. Not just hand holding but hugging and kissing and oh my God, all the rest. If I open myself up to the possibility of moving beyond a platonic friendship with JP, there's a good chance he's gonna expect all of that. Maybe not right away but eventually. What seventeen-year-old guy wouldn't, right? "Yeah, I..." I shrug, not knowing what else to say. "I guess I'll just figure out that piece as I go along."

"Well, you have us," Katie says. "A few of us are particularly well-versed in the romance department. I'm sure we'll be able to help you through it."

The rest of the group agrees, and for the first time in a long time, my future doesn't look quite so solitary.

CHAPTER 36

week seven

Two dresses hang beside my closet door—a lacy teal one I wore to my cousin's high school graduation last year and an off-the-shoulder green one Mom bought me for a dance I refused to attend and never wore out of the house.

"Wear the green one." Toby throws himself across my bed, a bag full of Twizzlers in his hand.

I'm secretly glad to see him. We've barely spoken since our standoff the other night, and it's nice that he's finally coming around. Old habits die hard, though, and can't resist giving him a hard time.

"What are you doing? How many times do I need to remind you, my room is off-limits?"

He doesn't budge and continues chewing happily on his candy. "Not off-limits."

"Yes. Off-limits."

He takes another bite, a mischievous grin on his face. "I heard you talking on the phone last night with that guy again.

Does Mom know you have a booooyfriennnnnnd?" He draws the word out so it has about eleven syllables. He knows I'm not supposed to be talking to JP since I'm still grounded, so now he's blackmailing me into letting him stay in my room.

Of course, it works.

"For your information, he's not my boyfriend. He's just a regular friend. And no, Mom doesn't know, so you're not gonna say anything. Got it?"

He rolls his eyes. "What kind of monster do you think I am?" He takes what's left of his Twizzler and pretends to jab it into his heart. "You cut me deep, Phoebe. You cut me real deep just now."

I ignore his Shrek reenactment and hold the green dress up to my chest, checking my reflection in the mirror. It looks pretty, a nice contrast to my fair complexion and ebony hair. It doesn't have pockets, though, so there'll be nowhere to stash my Purell and latex gloves. I'm rooting around my closet for a purse or smaller backpack when Toby calls my name. When I turn around he's standing in front of my desk with one of my papers in his hands.

"What's this?" he asks.

"Put that down," I say on impulse without even knowing what he's got.

Of course, he doesn't listen. "'How not to get germs. Number one. Germs come in through the eyes, nose, and mouth. Don't touch those parts no matter what.'" He looks up from the page, dumbfounded. "Did you write this?"

Anger and embarrassment bubble up. He has no right to touch my things and suppressing the urge to wrestle the paper from him is a struggle. What I want to do is leap over my bed and tackle him with my bare hands. No one has ever seen my germs list. Ever. And I don't care if I have to touch him to get it back.

I take a step toward him. "That's mine. Put it down."

"Number two. Don't share: toothbrushes, juice boxes, lollipops, tissues, Chapstick, or anything that touches my eyes, nose, or mouth."

"Toby, I'm not kidding. Give it to me." I toss my dress on the bed and lunge for him.

"Number three. Cover sneezes and coughs with a tissue or my elbow. Don't use my..."

Before he can finish I snatch the paper from his hands. A beat passes before I realize I'm not holding the whole thing. He has the top half, I have the bottom. I look down at my list, so carefully penned on my Danny Phantom stationery, and in a moment of clarity, I tear my half of the list a second time, relishing the satisfying rip.

Taking my cue, Toby rips his half a second time. And a third. And a fourth. By the time we're both finished shredding my list, all that remains is a small pile of confetti on the carpet.

We stare at one another for a long moment. A lone tear falls down my cheek and both of us are afraid to speak. Finally, after I wipe my face with the back of my hand, he says, "You wrote that stuff because of me, didn't you?"

"Yeah. But it's not your fault. It's not anyone's fault."

He sighs. "And now it's gone."

"It's not like I need it anymore." I kick the remains of my list with my toe. "It's time I start living beyond those rules, don't you think?"

He nods.

A small sob escapes my lips. I don't know whether to laugh or cry, be depressed or relieved. I lean down and scoop the scraps of paper into my hands. Toby opens the lid of my trashcan, and I toss them in. For a moment, I stare at the remains in the bottom of the bin, and then, running purely on emotion, I gather Toby to my arms.

He's solid and warm and alive against my chest, and I squeeze him with the fervor of every missed opportunity. At first, he doesn't return my embrace, perhaps too stunned by this unlikely turn of events. But eventually, when I don't let go, he wraps his arms around my waist and holds me back., his body shuttering slightly as I fight to hold back my own tears.

"This doesn't mean we're giving up on good hygienic protocol," I tell him when we finally break apart. "We're still gonna keep our hands away from our faces and wash frequently, right?"

He clicks a finger pistol at me and winks. "You betcha."

CHAPTER 37
week seven

I nstead of taking public transportation, Dad insists on driving us to the showcase in the Prius. After circling the block twice looking for the entrance to the closest underground parking, we're still one of the first families to arrive. We greet Aarush, who's placing the last of our pieces around the room, and spot Grandma, already nestled in a corner with a cup of tea.

The coffeeshop is smaller than I expected, with an undersized counter in the back and walls lined with floor-to-ceiling bookshelves. The remaining space is crowded with about a dozen bistro tables currently displaying our pottery. I worry there won't be enough room for all the students and their families once everyone arrives.

I worry there won't be enough room for me.

Grandma notices us and bustles over as only an elderly woman carrying a hot cup of tea can. After hugs are distributed to everyone but me, she sets off around the room. "Which ones are yours?" she asks.

Every student has six creations, one for every week of class, meaning there are sixty pieces scattered throughout the room. I give the closest tables a once over and find Toby's four-compartment caddy first.

"Here's one," I say, lifting the container by its handle. "This is yours, Toby. For your drone pieces."

He takes it from my hand and peers into the compartments. "This is perfect. Thanks."

"You're welcome." I glance over my shoulder at the door. Each time it opens, I'm disappointed when it's just another classmate.

"Let me see if I can find another." Dad meanders around, Mom following by his side as he picks up a bowl from a neighboring table. "Is this one?"

"It's beautiful, but no."

He picks up a vase beside the pot. "This one?"

I laugh. "No, Dad. You're terrible at this."

Toby wanders across the room and lifts my candlesticks off the counter. "How about these?"

"You're right," I say. "But you sorta cheated because I told you about those when I made them. And since they're the only candlesticks here they must be mine."

He holds them side-by-side for the rest of the family to see. "They're nearly identical. Who are they for?"

I cut my eyes to Mom. "They're for you. I thought maybe you'd like to put them on the dining room table. I know you don't like clutter, but I tried to make them…"

She holds up a hand to silence me and takes them from Toby. "They're spectacular, Phoebe." She studies the intricate detailing. "It would be an honor to display these in our home."

"Really?" Something unexpected wells up inside of me. "Thanks."

A warm blast of air from outside wafts into the café, and

when I turn to check out the newest arrival, my heart leaps inside my chest.

Until the very next second when panic sets in.

"There she is! Our pottery girl." Zaq waves to me from across the room. Behind him are Neveah and Devyn.

And JP.

Of course, my parents aren't big fans of the Neon Wingnuts' band members, so I knew better than to invite my new friends. It wasn't worth the battle, and besides, I didn't think JP and the others would want to spend a perfectly good evening looking at a bunch of amateur pottery with my family.

But somehow, they found out about the showcase and decided to come. Now all I can do is brace myself for Mom's reaction.

"Phoebe, why don't you introduce us to your friends?" Dad says, preempting Mom.

Introductions are made with nods and hellos. Devyn thanks Mom for allowing me to go to group therapy with her, and JP mentions something about visiting Walter in the hospital.

"You know Phoebe's boss?" Mom asks.

"Yeah," JP says. "He's the one who told me about the showcase tonight. Said he probably wouldn't be able to make it, and that I should come to support Phoebe in his place."

Something like approval crosses Mom's face. She likes Walter, and despite what she thinks of his ad hoc therapy methods, she trusts him. So maybe his endorsement will help her have a little more faith in my choice of friends. I chance a glance at JP and hope my expression conveys the gratitude I feel—not only for coming to see my pottery but for opening a dialogue with my mom as well.

Any contentment I feel is fleeting, though, with the confirmation that Walter won't be coming after all. He told me he'd try, but between recovering from the heart attack and his anxiety, I knew better than to hold out too much hope.

"Anyway, we better have something to report back," JP says, scanning the room. "So, show us your stuff, Phoebe."

I'm leading everyone around the room, explaining how I created my third project of the summer—a mug for my dad with 'Trust Me, I'm An Accountant' written across the front—when Aarush calls for everyone's attention from the back of the shop.

"Friends and families, welcome to the Keechad Pottery Studio Summer Showcase!" His announcement is followed by well-mannered applause from everyone but Zaq who whistles loudly between his teeth.

"Thank you for that fabulous reception," Aarush replies. "And thank you all for braving the evening commute to be with us here tonight." He goes on, gushing about what a privilege it was to work with such an inspired group of young artisans all summer. "I know you're all as impressed as I am with their work on display here tonight. And so, although I know it's a little out of character for a showing, I'd like to invite each of the students to share their best piece with us. Once they've finished, everyone please stick around and grab something to eat and drink. And students, don't forget to grab a box for your pieces at the end of the night."

As my classmates' take turns around the room, describing their favorite techniques or lessons, I steady myself against a nearby table, picturing myself doing the same. Visualization is a technique Roz taught me freshman year—a way of envisioning what you want into reality. I see myself presenting one of my pieces, and I do not pass out or have a panic attack.

When my turn arrives, I remain frozen for a moment, my feet cemented in place. Beside my dad, JP gives me a wink of encouragement, forcing me into action. I slip past my family, their smiles broad and full of pride, and start toward the candlesticks. But when the café door opens behind me and I see who's arrived, I make a slight detour, reconsidering which piece to share.

The flowerpot in my hand is far from my best work. It's not intricately detailed or even particularly well-formed. In fact, it's not unlike many of the hundreds of pots for sale at the weekend craft fairs Grandma used to drag me to as a child. It is, if I'm being honest, largely uninspiring.

And yet...

I gaze out into the sea of faces, overwhelmed by the number of people crowded into such a small venue. Some of them are classmates. Most of them are strangers. But a few of them are not.

My family—Mom, Dad, Grandma, and Toby.

My new friends—Zaq, Neveah, Devyn, and JP.

And all the way near the entrance, standing just inside the door, my best friend, Walter.

"I made this flowerpot for a friend of mine who accidentally broke his awhile back."

"Very thoughtful," Aarush says. "And what's that you've embossed there on the side?"

I lock eyes with Walter. I don't need a degree in psychotherapy to see he's having a rough day, struggling to be out in the world. Just like me, there's no 'fixing' him. No one-size-fits-all solution for eliminating our mental health issues. The two of us are never going to be completely free from them—they are as integrated into the fabric of who we are as the color of our eyes and the longings of our hearts. Despite them though, he's here, anxiety be damned.

"It says Dust Jackets. Come for the Books. Stay for the Friendship."

"How lovely," Aarush says. "I'm sure your friend will love it."

"I hope he will."

After a polite round-of-applause, I return to my spot beside JP and listen while the rest of my classmates share their pieces. Once they finish, I make a beeline for Walter.

"You came!" I say.

He smiles weakly, resting against Beverly for support. "Didn't have a choice. You braved a germ-infested hospital for me."

I reach out for his arm and his eyes widen at my touch. "Going there wasn't easy for me, and I know being here isn't easy for you either. But it means a lot to me."

"I had to physically drag him, Phoebe," Beverly says, giving Walter a playful jab in the ribs. "You wouldn't believe how he carried on."

My fingers are still pressed against Walter's arm. Beneath curls of hair, his skin feels rougher than I expect. "Oh, I can believe. We're both pretty stubborn when we wanna be."

He glances at my hand. "Pretty brave, too."

Beside me, Toby, JP, and the others arrive to welcome Walter and Beverly. Everyone shakes hands—much to my chagrin—and after the introductions are complete, Dad buys drinks and pastries for everyone in celebration of my achievements.

Around us, my classmates are celebrating their accomplishments as well—the successful completion of our course. My accomplishment, however, isn't so much about the pottery as it is having other people in my life to celebrate with. Like me, the pieces on the tables around us have all been transformed. The searing heat of the kiln has hardened them from greenware into stoneware, but even though they're stronger than they were before, it doesn't mean they're unbreakable. It just means they've been irrevocably changed and will never be the same again.

CHAPTER 38

week seven

By nine o'clock, the crowd has thinned. Walter left fifteen minutes ago with the flowerpot and Grandma took the fluted vase, so JP grabs a cardboard box from the floor to pack up Dad's mug, Mom's candlesticks, and Toby's parts container. After placing the pottery carefully inside, he crumples sections of newspaper to wedge between each piece and closes the lid.

"I think these are yours," he says to my mom, handing her the box.

She thanks him as Dad and Toby wander over. "It was really nice of you and your friends to support Phoebe here tonight."

"We wouldn't have missed it," JP tells her with a dimpled smile. "The four of us are headed to a small indie theater around the corner to catch a movie after this. Zaq and the girls already left to get tickets, but I can have them grab an extra if you wanna come with us, Phoebe?"

My breath hitches. He knows I'm grounded, and I can't believe he's being so bold.

I also can't believe how disappointed I'll be if my parents

don't let me go.

Mom clears her throat and shifts the box in her arms. "Phoebe's grounded—"

"But I think we could make an exception for tonight," Dad interrupts. "Don't you?"

"Really?" Mom and I say in unison.

"Yeah, I mean, it's a special occasion. And as long as she wants to go and promises to come straight home after the movie."

I nod enthusiastically.

"I'll make sure she gets home safe," JP assures him.

After a brief sidebar between my parents, Mom relents, my family heads out, and JP and I find ourselves alone together for the first time all night.

"Did we get all your pieces?" JP asks with one final glance around the room.

I shake my head. "Nope. Six weeks, six projects. My last one's over there, but it doesn't need a box. And also, it's for you."

His eyebrows knit together in confusion. "I thought the tip jar was my gift."

"You get two."

"Payment for being part of your therapy, right?" He winks, then takes off across the room. At the table, he picks up my last piece, running his fingers across the vent holes. "Is it a whistle?"

"More like a flute. It's called an ocarina," I tell him. "The earliest designs can be traced back to South and Central America over 12,000 years ago. I thought maybe you'd like to learn how to play it; a connection to your Ecuadorian heritage and all."

Without a word, he raises the mouthpiece to his lips and

blows. I lacked the courage to test the flute myself as I was creating it, so I'm relieved when the sound it produces is sweet and melodious. JP tries several different finger combinations, and in less than two minutes he's worked out a tune.

"I love it," he says finally.

"You do?"

"Of course." He slips the piece into his pocket. "I'm pretty psyched about the girl who made it, too."

"You are?"

"I am."

His words feel like an invitation, and I take a step forward holding out my hand.

He eyes it. "Are you sure?"

I nod, although I'll never be completely sure.

He reaches for me, and without stopping to overthink all the potential ramifications of what I'm about to do, I press my palm to his and intertwine our fingers.

My eyes close, blocking out every distraction—remaining stragglers, clanging dishes, and the rumble of traffic outside. All that's left is the two of us, his heartbeat pulsing against mine.

Everything about the reality of his hand is so much better than clay.

"You okay?" he says after a moment.

I open my eyes. He's smiling at me.

"Petrified," I say, acutely aware of his warmth, and the way his fingers fill the spaces between mine. Part of me wants to pull away.

But the other part never wants to let go.

acknowledgements

We authors put pieces of ourselves inside our books—especially the bits we like best—and when it comes to main characters, Phoebe is no exception. But as much as Phoebe embodies a handful of my more endearing qualities, she also represents many of my darkest fears and the parts of myself I usually keep hidden from the world. When I started writing *Phoebe Unfired*, I didn't know whether readers would care about a germaphobic girl struggling to make connections in summer of her sixteenth year, but I'm hopeful her story will resonate with anyone who's discovered that sometimes the only way around is through.

Thank you, first and foremost, to the best agent in the world, Ann Rose, and everyone at Prospect Literary Agency. Thank you for believing in me. For believing in Phoebe. For believing in small stakes and the power of quiet stories. I don't know where our path together will ultimately take us, but if the destination is anything like the journey, I know it's gonna be amazing.

To the Rosebuds, for being my soft place to land when it's all too much. For celebrating victories big and small and commiserating over rejections in the only nerdy way we know how—watching *Clue* together via Zoom. Thank you for being the best "siblings" I never knew I needed. It's an honor to count such amazing authors as my friends.

A huge shout out to Jenny Lane, my AMM mentor. You

chose Phoebe from a pile of wayward manuscripts and helped shape her from the rough ball of clay she was into the gleaming, glazed pottery she is today. Your friendship means the world to me, and I'm so grateful the universe saw fit to bring us together.

At the very beginning of it all, when Phoebe was nothing but an idea and a few messy chapters, Gracie Hunter wandered into my life, looking for a critique partner. Gracie, there would be no Phoebe without you. Your perseverance and honesty pushed me forward in those early months, and I will never be able to repay you for all the hours you spent bringing Phoebe to life.

And finally, thank you to my family. Thank you for giving me grace when I'm having a bad mental health day. For knowing my triggers and avoiding them when you can. For giving me space when I need it and staying close when I don't. Thank you for honoring my choices and never pushing me toward one treatment over another. Your love is my constant—a reminder that no matter what, I am perfect in all of my brokenness just the way I am.

CPSIA information can be obtained
at www.ICGtesting.com
Printed in the USA
LVHW031244041121
702393LV00007B/123/J